With the Band

L.A. WITT

Copyright © 2016 L.A. Witt
All rights reserved.

ISBN-13: 978-1535427371
ISBN-10: 153542737X

Copyright Information

This is a work of fiction. Names, characters, places, and incidents are either the product of the author's imagination or are used fictitiously. Any resemblance to actual persons living or dead, business establishments, events, or locales is entirely coincidental.

Second edition
First edition published in 2012 by Loose Id, LLC.
Copyright © 2011, 2015 L.A. Witt
(Un)Faded lyrics copyright Lia Wolff; used with permission.

Cover Art by Garrett Leigh

All rights reserved. No part of this book may be reproduced or transmitted in any form or by any means, electronic or mechanical, including photocopying, recording, or by any information storage and retrieval system without the written permission of the publisher, and where permitted by law. Reviewers may quote brief passages in a review. To request permission and all other inquiries, contact L.A. Witt at gallagherwitt@gmail.com

ISBN-13: 978-1535427371
ISBN-10: 153542737X

L.A. WITT

CHAPTER ONE

"*Next right,*" the bored, monotone voice of the GPS unit said.

I took the next right as ordered, and the county road ended. My tires thumped over the lip of the asphalt and crunched onto gravel. Judging by the cornfields, cow pastures, and farmhouses, one would have thought I was on my way out to audition for a country band instead of Schadenfreude, my brother and sister's hard-rock band.

A nervous knot coiled in my gut. I couldn't believe I was really doing this. My siblings had persuaded me to come back up to Seattle after the band and their male lead singer parted ways. They were hurting for a replacement, but it hadn't taken much arm-twisting to convince me. In the last six months, my love life had fallen apart and taken my own band with it, right when we were on the verge of being successful too. That and I was sick and tired of Los Angeles. Move back home, start over, and possibly join Schadenfreude? Yeah, that hadn't taken much thought. Even if I didn't end up in their band, it was good to be back.

The GPS chimed in again: "*This area has not been mapped. Route guidance will now end.*"

"You're so helpful." I turned off the GPS. Fortunately Todd had given me written directions from this point on, knowing it was far enough out in the sticks that modern technology still couldn't find it. I picked up the printed e-mail and continued dodging potholes down the bumpy dirt road.

I was only a mile or two out now. Almost there. I took a deep breath, trying to calm my nerves. *God, I hope I don't blow this.*

It was an incredible opportunity, and it didn't hurt that this would give me the chance to see Andre Koehler again. I hadn't seen him or his brother, Bastian, since they were in high school with Todd nearly a decade ago. Back then I'd secretly had a crush on Andre, and just for old time's sake, it would be fun to see him again. Not that anyone else needed to know about that. My sister was the only one in the band who knew, and Todd probably would've killed me if he knew the thoughts I'd entertained about one of his best friends. But what they didn't know wouldn't hurt me, and Andre was straight anyway. Engaged, last I heard.

That didn't mean I couldn't look. I just wouldn't touch, and I'd hope to hell I was what they wanted for the band. They were desperate, but from what my siblings had said, Andre and Bastian were more than a little picky about singers. A few had already auditioned, none warranting so much as a callback. They were getting down to the wire, though, especially for their next gig; as it was, this would be the only chance I had to rehearse with them because the gig was tomorrow night.

Even that wasn't a guarantee. If I wasn't what they were looking for or they didn't think I was ready for tomorrow's show, they still had Elena, my sister, singing lead for half the set. If they absolutely had to, they could do a gig or two without a male lead, and they'd sooner shorten their set than compromise their sound. That alone was enough to convince me I wanted to be a part of this band.

Up ahead, a mailbox shaped like a John Deere tractor came into view. According to Todd's directions, that was the driveway.

Here goes nothing.

I turned left at the tractor mailbox. Drumming the steering wheel with my thumbs, I followed the long driveway to a modest farmhouse with an immense detached garage. Todd's car was parked in front of the garage, along with my sister's VW Beetle and another car. I pulled in beside the Beetle and got out. Even if Todd's directions hadn't specifically said to go to the garage instead of the house, I'd have had no trouble figuring it out: The music coming from inside rattled my teeth even from out here.

I put in a pair of earplugs at my brother's recommendation and walked into the garage.

Inside, Elena looked up from banging the drums—which she occasionally played in between singing—and stopped. She grabbed one of the hi-hats to silence it. Flipping her electric blue hair out of her face, she smiled. "Hey! You found the place without too much trouble, I see."

I laughed. "Yeah, somehow managed to comprehend Todd's directions."

"Oh fuck you." Todd eyed me as he adjusted his guitar's amp. He gestured at a woman fussing with some sound equipment. "Rochelle, this my little brother, Aaron. Aaron, Rochelle." He gave me a pointed look. "And she's Andre's other half, so hands off."

"I'll keep that in mind." I chuckled, exchanging a knowing glance with my sister before I shook Rochelle's hand.

"She's Andre's girl," Todd said, "but we really only hang out with her because her grandparents let us use this place to rehearse."

Rochelle laughed. "Fuck you, McClure. You seem to be forgetting who writes half your music. Anyway, nice to meet you, Aaron. It's good to see not all the males in the family got the short end of the genetics stick." She and Todd threw each other good-natured glares.

Behind me, the door opened. Todd gestured past me. "Aaron, you remember Andre, don't you?"

"Of course I do." Bracing myself, I turned around, and my tongue stuck to the roof of my mouth. *Oh dear God, Andre, time has been kind to you, hasn't it?*

The Andre I'd known back then had certainly grown up. His dark hair was now bleached blond and pulled back into a messy ponytail. He was broad-shouldered and must have spent hours at the gym each day maintaining the physique that was currently wrapped in tight jeans and a tighter black T-shirt. By the looks of it, his arms were as well acquainted with dumbbells as they were with tattoo needles.

"Aaron! How are you, kid?" Andre extended his hand. Time had tempered his thick German accent, but it was still there, adding a slight edge to his words.

I cleared my throat. "Good, good. Just, you know, getting settled in."

He gave me a firm handshake and that familiar smile that likely earned him as many fans as his music did. A shiver ran up my spine. *Jesus Christ. Want.*

"Well," he said, "it's good to have you back in the neighborhood."

"Where's Bastian?" Elena asked. "Didn't he come with you?"

Andre gestured flippantly at the door through which he'd come. "He's outside. He was on his damned phone when we got here. Arguing with Bitchy McPsychopath again."

With a cough of startled laughter, I said, "With *who*?"

"Denise." Rochelle rolled her eyes and clicked her tongue. "Fucking crazy woman."

"Girlfriend, I take it?"

"Ex-fiancée, actually," Elena said. "Thank God he didn't actually marry her."

"Talk about a dodged bullet," Todd muttered. "Only thing I can think of that would be worse than breaking up with a woman like that is divorcing her."

"And the crazy beast is holding up rehearsal *again*," Andre muttered. He went back to the door, leaned out, and shouted something in German. The response was terse and also German.

Andre shot something back in the same language. Then in English, "Get in here and say hello to Aaron."

From outside the door, approaching footsteps crunched on the gravel and a familiar, accented voice growled a few curse words. Then, "Can't a man finish a phone call without—" He appeared in the doorway and halted in both speech and step when he saw me. His breath caught.

So did mine.

All the way here tonight, I'd thought I wouldn't be able to get Andre out of my head. Now that Bastian was here, I couldn't think at all.

In high school, he had been a scrawny kid with unruly dark hair and a gaunt face that probably didn't need to be shaved more than once a month. That kid and the man standing in front of me now were worlds apart. His cheekbones rose prominently above a stubbled jaw that made my fingertips tingle at the mere thought of touching. Both sides of his head were shaved, with the top left long and flipped to one side in a fringe that fell into a perfect curve that drew my attention straight to the gold ring in his left eyebrow.

That and his vivid blue eyes. Oh my God. Had they always been *that* blue?

His shoulders weren't as broad as Andre's, but they certainly weren't lacking. Judging by the way his T-shirt pulled snug across his abs, he wasn't lacking *anywhere*, at least not above the belt.

He hadn't worn his teens well, but he wore twenty-nine-almost-thirty like a fucking dream.

I suddenly realized I was staring. Then Bastian's cheeks colored. He cleared his throat and looked away, setting his case on one of the tables at the side of the room. I doubted more than a few seconds had passed, but it may as well have been ages, and it still wasn't enough time to drink in the sight of him.

"You remember Aaron, don't you?" Andre said.

Bastian snarled something in German, flicking his eyes toward his brother. To me, he said, "Good to see you, kid." His accent was less pronounced than his brother's, but it was there. He extended his hand. "So you're here to bail us out?"

I shrugged with one shoulder and shook his hand. "I certainly hope so."

"Guess we'll see, won't we?" He gave me a quick, tentative smile—*Is that shyness on your face, Bastian?*—before turning his attention to his bass, leaving me with my heart in my throat and my hand tingling from his touch.

I surreptitiously watched him shrug his jacket off his shoulders, and hoped to God no one heard my breath falter when that jacket fell away and revealed the toned, tattooed arms beneath the tight T-shirt. He turned around and pulled his bass out of the case, and I had to force myself to look away from his back and shoulders, or the way his belt sat just right above his narrow hips.

I'd never given Bastian a second thought when we were teenagers, but the grown-up Bastian was the very epitome of sexy. *Andre who?*

"Okay, Aaron." Elena pulled drawing my focus away from Bastian. "Let's show 'em what you've got."

Andre, Rochelle, and Bastian sat back to watch while Todd and Elena played backup for me. I'd done okay singing solo in front of people without the company of percussion or a guitar in the past, but tonight, even with their backup, my nerves almost got the best of me a few times. It wasn't that I was nervous about my singing ability. I knew I was good, and I didn't pretend to think otherwise.

I also knew the songs well enough to hold my own. I'd rehearsed with Todd and Elena while they were in LA to help me move, and we'd probably kept a few people awake practicing in the seedy motels along I-5 on the trip from Cali to Seattle. So I knew the songs inside and out, but what I hadn't anticipated was Bastian.

His arrival—or rather, my reaction to his presence—had thrown me completely off balance.

Every time I met his eyes, my pulse jumped. When he leaned back in his chair, lacing his fingers behind his head and crossing his boots at the ankles, the grooves of his abs showed through his shirt and I forgot the chorus to *Heaven's Demon*. I fucking nailed *Terra Firma*, one of the more difficult songs in the set, until he leaned on an armrest and absently ran his fingertip along his lower lip, and I completely bombed the second verse.

By the end of the half dozen songs my siblings had suggested we play, I was sweating like I'd just performed an entire set under hot stage lights. Aside from the nerve-induced fuckups, it was a good audition. Not one of my best, but judging by the nods the brothers exchanged, it was good enough. And fortunately I'd avoided getting a hard-on while I was in front of them. Nerves were good for something, at least. I made a mental note not to wear such tight jeans around the band for a while, though. Not until I was used to being around Bastian.

Todd clapped my shoulder. "Nice job."

I smiled. "Thanks."

"So," Todd said to the Koehler brothers. "What do you think?"

Andre looked at me and nodded slowly. "I think you'll be a great fit for the band, Aaron."

"Agreed," Bastian said. "Though a lot will depend on how you do onstage tomorrow night."

"Right, I know," I said. "Rehearsals are nothing compared to the real thing."

"We need to cut *Terra Firma* from tomorrow's set, though," Bastian said. "Don't get me wrong, Aaron, you're good, but I'd rather hold off on that one until we've rehearsed it more."

I nodded. "Fair enough." Pride wanted me to argue that I did, in fact, have that song down, but I bit my tongue. That would only lead to questions about why I couldn't get it right tonight.

"What about *Heaven's Demon*?" Elena asked me. "You didn't have that much trouble on the chorus when we practiced before, but…" Her eyebrows lifted.

"I think I'll be okay. It was just…nerves."

Andre thumbed his chin. "Will that be an issue onstage?"

I shook my head. "I don't get stage fright. Auditions fuck me all up, but I'm good onstage."

"Good to know." Bastian smiled, doing crazy things to my blood pressure in the process. The chair creaked when he pushed himself to his feet. I had to force myself not to take a step back to counter the one he took toward me, and his eyes were so intense I was sure he could see right through me to all the impure thoughts I had about him.

If he did, he didn't say anything. He just extended his hand and grinned. "Assuming all goes well tomorrow night, welcome to Schadenfreude."

CHAPTER TWO

After my audition, we jumped right into a rehearsal.

I'd lived out of state since just after high school, and aside from demo recordings and a few shitty videos my brother and sister had e-mailed me, I hadn't heard them perform. I'd certainly never *seen* them perform, and even in a rehearsal, they were incredible. I'd read dozens of reviews of the band, and every one of them said Schadenfreude had to be heard live to truly be appreciated. Truer words were never spoken.

When I sat back to watch them practice Elena's songs, they blew me away. Her voice was powerful and rock solid. Some female leads screeched and screamed or lived by the philosophy of *why sing one note when a dozen will do?* Not Elena. My sister powered through every verse and chorus with a pure, strong sound, and she made every long note her bitch.

Andre beat the hell out of the drums, and between my brother's screaming guitar and Bastian's bass line, they produced a powerful, clean sound, even with the mediocre acoustics of the garage. They were loud, they were definitely hard rock, and they didn't compromise at all when it came to the music itself. They complemented each other perfectly.

Some bands had an energy about them, that X factor no one could quite explain or quantify, and Schadenfreude had it in spades. Right then and there, I thanked about a dozen higher powers for the chance to stand in front of this band.

Even if their bassist *did* make my brain short-circuit simply by existing.

When the rehearsal was over, Rochelle pulled a few bottles of water out of an ice chest and passed them around. We all sat back for a few minutes and cooled off.

"Okay, I have to admit," Bastian said, "I thought you guys were crazy when you suggested performing so soon after having Aaron join, but..." He shrugged with one shoulder. "You were right. I think we can do this." He looked at me as he took another drink, and it wasn't just his compliment that made my cheeks burn.

Leaning against the garage door, Todd gestured with his water bottle. "See, guys? I told you he was a decent singer."

"A decent singer?" I picked up my jacket off the back of a chair. "Whatever."

"He obviously has the McClure ego," Rochelle muttered, shooting me a grin.

Andre laughed. To me he said, "You sure you can handle going onstage with us this soon?"

"Hell yeah," I said.

"Well, before you go onstage with us," Todd said, tossing his empty bottle into a trash can, "you get to go drinking with us."

Andre stood, capping his own water bottle. "Usual place?"

"Works for me," Todd said.

"I could definitely go for a beer." Bastian stood and pulled his bass strap over his head.

"Bastian's buying for everyone this time, right?" Elena asked.

Bastian chuckled, laying his instrument in its case. "Dream on, woman." He looked at me, opening his mouth to speak, but then Andre barked something at him in German. Bastian snarled a few words back over his shoulder. When he looked at me again, he threw me an apologetic smile but said nothing.

Obviously some things hadn't changed. Bastian and Andre were extremely close, always had been, but no one on God's green earth could fight like the Koehler brothers.

I chuckled. "How the hell do the two of you work together?"

Bastian cocked his head. "What do you mean?"

"You sound ready to kill each other half the time."

He laughed. "Anything in German sounds that way. I could tell you I liked your shoes and it would sound like I was insulting your family."

"I'd hate to hear what it sounds like when you *are* insulting my family."

"I wouldn't insult your family." He glanced over his shoulder, then looked at me with a mischievous expression. "Well, except your brother maybe."

"Hey, you'd better do that in English so I can join in."

Bastian laughed. Then he added, "My ex-fiancée hated it when I spoke German around her."

I cocked my head. "Why's that?"

Latching his case, he looked up. "She said it always sounded like I was saying something either insulting or crude."

"Were you?"

He gave me a sheepish grin. "Sometimes."

A shiver ran up my spine. I'd never thought a German accent or the German language were particularly sexy, but I suddenly wondered what it would be like to hear him talk dirty to me in his native tongue. Or in English, for that matter. Clearing my throat, I turned away, hoping my cheeks hadn't turned as red as I thought they had.

Mercifully Todd got my attention before I had a chance to attempt to speak.

"You know your way around Monroe?" he asked.

I shook my head. "Not really. Not anymore."

He nodded and gestured toward the parked cars outside. "Okay, well, just follow me out of here. It's pretty easy to find."

Andre eyed me, then looked at Todd. "You sure Aaron's even old enough to drink?"

"He is, but just barely," Todd said.

I laughed. "Kiss my ass, both of you."

"Okay, boys." Elena reached for the door. "Everyone ready to go?"

"There's beer waiting," Todd said. "I'm always ready for that."

Our caravan of cars kicked up dust on the dirt road on the way back to civilization. Once we were finally on the blacktop, we continued a few more miles until, one by one, we turned into a parking lot in front of a strip mall.

The bar itself was a sports pub at the end of the strip. Neon lights, pool tables, flat-screen TVs, the works. And of course, beer.

We commandeered a corner booth. The band must have been regulars, because it was mere seconds before a waitress appeared with two pitchers and several empty glasses.

"Thank you, gorgeous," Todd said to the waitress.

She rolled her eyes. "Oh, can it and drink your beer, McClure."

I laughed behind my glass. Yep, they were regulars.

"So how was LA?" Andre asked me after a while. "Is it true what they say about the women down there?"

Can't say I really noticed. "Oh, you know. Some of it's true, some of it's not." My eyes darted toward Bastian. Over the rim of his drink, he met my eyes and held my gaze for a split second before looking away.

"Come on now." Todd elbowed me. "The girls are supposed to be hot as hell in southern California. Way hotter than the ones up here."

"You want me to tell Lillian you said that?" I eyed him.

He glared at me. "Do it, and you'll be sleeping in a cardboard box."

I chuckled. "I'll just go stay with Elena."

"The hell you will," my sister said. "He kicks you out of his house, you're on your own."

"There's always Mom and Dad," I said with a shrug.

Elena shuddered. "I think I'd take the cardboard box."

"Hmm, good point," I said. "Hell, I think I'd rather go back to California than live with them."

Andre picked up his beer. "Speaking of which, I'm curious. What happened in California, anyway? I thought you had a pretty good thing going with your band."

"No shit," Bastian said. "From everything Todd and Elena told us, we figured it was only a matter of time before we were begging to open for you on your first headline tour."

"Things just"—I played with the label on my beer bottle—"didn't pan out the way we would have liked."

"Probably didn't help that a couple of band members were dating." Todd shot me a pointed look.

I chewed the inside of my cheek. "Yeah, probably not."

A grin tugged at Bastian's lips. "I'm guessing you were involved in that?"

"I had a…thing going. With the drummer." Or so I led people to believe. The drummer of my old band was female. It was my relationship with the guitarist that had fucked things up.

"Banging the drummer?" Bastian chuckled. "Appropriate, I suppose."

I forced a laugh. "You could say that. Then when the band started having problems, we started having problems, which made shit with the band worse, which…" I shook my head. "You get the idea."

Andre grinned. "Just as well the only woman in this band is your sister, then."

And it's just as well your brother is straight.

"Yep, definitely one advantage to this band," Todd said. "We're related, and they're…well, Koehlers."

Bastian eyed him. "What's that supposed to mean?"

Elena set her glass down. "It means I wouldn't touch either of you with someone else's pussy."

"Whatever." Andre gestured dismissively. "You know you'd hit this."

"With a car, maybe," she muttered.

After the laughter and mock offense died down, Todd said, "Well, I for one am glad it's not something this band has to worry about."

"No shit," Andre said. "No offense, kid, but dating within a band is just a bad idea."

"So I discovered," I said dryly.

"Isn't that what happened with Nailbomb?" Elena asked. "I could have sworn there were rumors they fell apart because—"

"They fell apart because they were *all* fucking each other." Todd wrinkled his nose. The hint of disgust in his voice set my teeth on edge. And I might have been imagining it, but I swore Bastian rolled his eyes before he took a drink.

"Well, I can't totally blame them." Elena shrugged. "I'd have done every last man in that band too, so I can see why they—"

"Damn it, El," Todd said. "I do not want to hear these things from you."

"What?" She shot him an innocent look. "It's no different than you going on about the girls in Cat Herders."

"Yes, it is." He gestured with his beer. "Because that doesn't involve my little sister."

She rolled her eyes. "Oh shut up."

"Either way," Todd said. "Bandmates fucking bandmates is just a bad idea. Period. Look what it did to Nailbomb, not to mention Perestroika."

"Oh man, Perestroika." Rochelle shook her head. "That was a fucking disaster and a half."

"What happened with them?" I asked.

"Lead singer was married to the keyboardist," Todd said. "At least until he went and knocked up the drummer."

"Didn't someone also bust him with the guitarist?" Andre asked.

"No, he was boning the guitarist from some other band," Elena said. "Plus a couple of roadies, if I recall."

"So it wasn't a relationship between bandmates." I raised an eyebrow. "It was people fucking around on each other."

Todd shrugged. "Which wouldn't have been an issue if they hadn't been involved with each other in the first place."

I bit my tongue. It was a moot point where this band was concerned. The damage to my band was done, and there was no sense arguing about it. I looked at Andre. "So what was the deal with your lead singer? Todd said you guys canned him, but I thought things were going pretty well with him."

Andre scowled. "No, Derek was probably the one thing that was really holding us back."

"Why's that?"

"He wanted to be a singer in front of a bunch of backup musicians," Bastian said. "We're a *band*. A group. So his ego was a huge problem."

"That," Elena said, "and he sucked." Rochelle and the guys nodded, murmuring in agreement.

"No kidding," Andre said. "I think every other review we got mentioned we were great...except for Derek."

Elena put her beer down. "Awesome performance...except for Derek."

"Blowing the crowd away, raising the roof, completely badass," Bastian said. "Except for Derek."

I laughed. "Wow, I didn't realize he was that bad."

"He was." Todd drained his beer and set the glass back on the table. "And now we have you, so we'd better not get any more reviews like that."

"No pressure or anything," Andre said.

I snorted. "Please. You won't get any reviews like that with me around here."

"Cocky bastard," Elena muttered.

"Not cocky." Bastian grinned, lifting his beer. "Confident. Exactly what we need." He winked, and my spine almost melted. Jesus, what was wrong with me? I'd never had a physical reaction to every damned thing someone did. At this rate, the man could probably sneeze and make me pass out.

"Call it cocky or confident," Andre said, "but you'd damn well better be able to put your money where your mouth is at the show tomorrow, McClure."

I raised my beer. "I fully intend to."

"Good, then maybe Schadenfreude can—" Bastian stopped in midsentence, glancing down as he pulled his cell phone out of his pocket. He rolled his eyes. "Fuck, *really*?" He let the phone clatter onto the table. "You'll never guess who's texting me."

"Wait, wait, don't tell me." Todd put his fingers to his temples and shut his eyes, cocking his head and pursing his lips. "I'm going to say…" He took a breath, then opened his eyes. "Denise?"

Bastian nodded, muttering something in German as he picked up the phone and read the text message.

"So what does she want now?" Rochelle asked. "Asking your opinion about what you should name your kids?"

He glared at her. "Very funny." He furrowed his brow at the message. "Eh, nothing important." He put the phone facedown on the table.

"Of course it's not important," Andre said. "It's from her."

They threw a few snide—I assumed—comments back and forth in German. Andre started to say something to the rest of us, but Bastian cut him off with something that probably would have been venomous even in English.

Whatever he said, Andre didn't argue. They quickly veered the conversation away from Bastian's ex, and the mood at the table lightened once again.

After an hour or two, once we'd had a few beers, then chased them with sodas so we could still drive, Todd looked at his watch. "I'd better get going. Lillian will have my hide if I stay out much later." To me he said, "You going to be able to find your way home?"

I nodded. "Now that I'm back in civilization and my GPS will work."

Rochelle looked at Andre. "I suppose we should get out of here too. I have to be in to work early tomorrow."

Andre drained his beer. "Yeah, me too." He handed her his car keys and pulled out a twenty to cover their part of the tab. Then he turned to me. "Good to have you in the band." He clapped my shoulder. "Don't fuck up tomorrow, all right?"

"I'll try not to."

"No trying." He wagged a finger at me. "Do it or don't, man."

"Yes, thank you, Yoda," I muttered into my glass.

He laughed. "See you tomorrow, kid. Good night, everyone. See you backstage." After some fist bumps and trash talk with siblings, Andre put his arm around Rochelle and they left.

Bastian watched the door close behind them, then turned around again. "I'll let them go ahead. At least then if Denise is waiting for me at the apartment, they can chase her off before I get home." I couldn't decide if he was kidding or not.

"Jesus." Elena rolled her eyes. "You really need to talk to that woman."

"Believe me, I have. On many occasions."

"Have you gotten to the part about 'we're through, leave me alone, you crazy whore'?"

He laughed. "Well, I haven't worded it *quite* like that." Sighing, he played with the label on his beer bottle. "She'll get the message eventually."

"Bastian, she's practically stalking you," Elena said. "That's not someone who's going to get the message anytime soon."

"Good point," he muttered.

"Honestly, she worries me. She keeps coming to gigs, she's calling and messaging you day and night, and you just said she shows up at your apartment."

"Yeah, but what's she going to do? Okay, she's crazy, but I don't think she'd do anything besides cry and tell me she's going to kill herself if I don't take her back."

"She's actually said that?" I asked.

Bastian nodded, rolling his eyes. "All the fucking time."

"Think she'd actually do it?"

"Doubt it." He sipped his beer. "She's all talk."

"Pity you didn't figure that out a couple of years ago," Elena growled.

"Tell me about it." Bastian sighed. "At least the security guys at most of our regular gigs know her and know not to let her backstage anymore."

"Well, there's three new guys at the House of Anarchy," Elena said. "You might want to give them a heads-up."

"Great."

"I'm not kidding, Bastian. She creeps me out. She's been all talk up to this point, but I wouldn't put it past her to do something to fuck with you once she realizes you really are done with her."

"Like what?"

"I don't know." She shrugged. "The inside of my skull isn't a padded room like hers, so I have no idea how she thinks. I'm not going to lie, though. She makes me nervous."

"Look, she's irritating, but she's harmless," he said. "There's nothing to worry about."

"I hope not."

Bastian didn't press the issue any further.

Elena drained her drink and pushed the empty glass away. "Guess we should get out of here eventually."

"Yeah, probably." Bastian looked at his phone, apparently just checking the time since no hostility or annoyance appeared on his face when the screen lit up. "Shit, it's almost midnight. How did that happen?"

"Time flies when you're having fun," I said.

"So it does." He sipped his drink, rolling it around in his mouth for a second. When he swallowed, I couldn't help but follow the ripple down the front of his throat with my eyes.

Then I met his eyes, and the flicker of a grin on his lips said nothing if not *I saw that.*

I quickly dropped my gaze.

"Okay, baby bro," Elena said. "Your drinks are on me tonight, but only because you're bailing my band out."

"Well, hell, if I'd known there would be free drinks, I'd have moved up here months ago."

"Don't get used to it." She rummaged through her purse for her wallet. "And that's also why I didn't tell you until afterward. Knowing you, you'd have ordered the most expensive thing they had."

I put a hand to my chest. "Elena, I had no idea you thought so low of me."

"You are related to Todd, you know," Bastian said, grinning.

"See?" Elena said. "Now shut up and be grateful. Let's go."

After Elena and Bastian paid the tabs, we migrated toward the parking lot. Elena stopped at the bar's door.

"I'll be out in a minute, Aaron," she said. "Don't leave yet. I need to give you the directions and everything for tomorrow."

"We're playing the House of Anarchy, aren't we?" I asked. "I know how to get there."

"Yeah, but you'll be parking in the employee lot, and you need one of the tags for your rearview." She gestured toward the back of the bar. "I just need to use the restroom, and I'll meet you outside."

She took off for the restroom, and suddenly I was alone with Bastian. We glanced at each other, but I quickly shifted my gaze to the parking lot ahead of me. I wondered if he did the same thing. Didn't know, because I was afraid to look.

We walked outside in silence. There was a good arm's length between us, but it would have taken a space the size of the entire parking lot to bring my blood pressure down.

I stopped behind my car. So did Bastian. So did my heart.

We both shifted our weight, exchanging uneasy glances in awkward silence. It would have been a hell of a lot easier to calm myself down if he didn't seem equally nervous around me. Wishful thinking? Maybe. All I knew was his body language said things I really, really didn't need to hear if I had any hope of working with him.

Finally he said, "Sorry to hear things didn't go well for you in LA."

I shrugged. "Hopefully they'll work out better up here."

"Oh, after what I heard tonight, I think it will." His lips curled into a grin and the streetlight glinted off his eyebrow ring when he narrowed his eyes. "Might want to stay away from the drummer this time, though."

I laughed. "You think?"

"Yeah, might be a good idea."

"I'll keep that in mind."

Our eyes met briefly, just long enough for me to be certain it happened. Then we both quickly shifted our gazes away.

Keys jingled, startling me back to life, and I looked up as he spun his key ring around his finger and caught them in his hand.

"I guess I'll see you tomorrow night," he said. "You sure you're ready for this after one rehearsal?"

"I'll be fine."

"Good." He smiled. "See you then."

We bumped fists, and I thanked God Bastian hadn't opted for another handshake. I wasn't sure my nerves could deal with that.

"See you tomorrow," he said.

"Yep, have a good one."

"You too." He turned to go. Tapping into some deep reserve of self-control, I forced myself to look the other way, telling myself I was watching the bar door for Elena. I *was*, but I *wanted* to steal one last look at Bastian's ass in those jeans and his shoulders in that jacket.

What the fuck? I'd had crushes and infatuations before. I'd been in love, and I'd been in lust before. This mind-scrambling, stomach-tingling something that Bastian did to me? That was new. The only one who had ever come close to giving me this kind of reaction was Jason, my ex. The guitarist with whom I'd brought my last band down in flames. And there was that raging crush I'd had on another band's lead singer, but even that combined with what I'd had with Jason couldn't hold a candle to this.

Maybe I was just attracted to musicians. No one quite understood an artist's passion like another artist, but damn if such a pairing wasn't disastrous sometimes. Mixing sexual and creative passion could work about as well as mixing beer and liquor. Sometimes it was fine, but when it wasn't? Miserable.

An engine rumbled to life behind me, and without thinking about it, I looked over my shoulder just in time to catch a glimpse of Bastian's profile as he pulled out of the parking space. I shivered.

Then his truck was gone, leaving me in the mostly deserted parking lot with only the sound of my sister's approaching footsteps, and I could finally exhale. Musician or not, I was definitely attracted to Bastian.

Oh well. I couldn't touch, but I could look. I could sure as hell look.

CHAPTER THREE

The first band was onstage, halfway through their set. Schadenfreude was up next, and my stomach was in knots. I didn't get stage fright as a general rule, but going up with a band after rehearsing once? I was the first to admit to being a little nervous.

From across the room, sitting cross-legged on a table, Rochelle shot me a grin. "You sure you're ready for this?" At least she didn't call me "kid." Then again, she was only a year older than me.

I took a breath. "Ready as I'll ever be."

"You're braver than I am. I'd have to practice with these guys for *months* before I ever performed with them."

"I've known them my whole life though," I said. "If I'm not over my embarrassment associating with them by now—"

"Hey!" Todd said.

Rochelle laughed. "Well, I can see who inherited the smart-ass genes in your family."

"At least I got the good looks," Todd muttered.

"That's debatable." She gave me a conspicuous down-up look, then winked. My face burned, and she laughed, so I guessed my cheeks were red. Then she cocked her head. "You know, now that I think about it, I've been to almost every Schadenfreude show in the last six years, and I've never met you until recently. Haven't you been to any of their shows? Ever?"

And hotter still my cheeks burned. "I, um…"

"Yeah, yeah, yeah," Todd said. "Way to be a supportive sibling. Eight years of Schadenfreude and he hasn't come to a damned show."

"Hey, it's not like you ever came to any of my band's shows either," I said.

"No, but you came up here to visit plenty of times."

"Well, if you guys had played over Christmas or Thanksgiving once in a while, I'd have gone to a show."

"Hmm, maybe it's a good thing he didn't come to any, Todd." Elena looked in the mirror and fussed with her hair, which was now styled as wildly as it was colored. "If he came to our shows before, then he just might be too embarrassed to get onstage with us tonight."

"She's got a point, Todd," Rochelle said.

Todd clicked his tongue. "Oh come on, we're not that bad."

I smirked. "Well, you aren't that bad now that you have me."

"Oh Jesus." Rochelle rolled her eyes. "You boys are obviously brothers. You're exactly alike."

"Hey, fuck you," Todd said.

"Elena, please tell me you're adopted," Rochelle said.

"Duh." Elena kept messing with her bright blue hair. "I got the hair color from my real parents."

"Whatever," Todd said. "You just don't want to be guilty by association. But sorry, you're related to him. Nothing we can do about that."

"I was more worried about being related to you," she said.

They exchanged glares. Then she laughed, shook her head, and shifted her attention back to fixing her hair.

"So," I said, "does this place allow stage diving?"

"Aaron McClure, we've been through this." Elena spun around and glared at me. "No. Stage. Diving."

I showed my palms. "What? Why not?"

"Because I don't want to have to explain to Mom and Dad why you're all busted up."

I shrugged. "I'll just say you and Todd beat me up."

"Just stay on the stage, would you?" She shot me her infamous half-pleading, half-threatening, "please don't force me to kill you" look.

I rolled my eyes and released a melodramatic sigh. "Fine, I'll stay on the stage."

Todd looked at me and raised an eyebrow. He probably knew as well as I did I had every intention of jumping off that stage, but he wisely kept his mouth shut.

Rochelle glanced at the door. "Where the hell are Andre and Bastian? You guys are on in like fifteen minutes."

"Probably doing what the Brothers Grimm do best," Elena said. "Getting into trouble."

"Isn't that the truth," Rochelle muttered.

"Do they know you call them that?" I asked.

"What? The Brothers Grimm?" Elena laughed. "Oh hell yeah. They know, and they hate it."

"You're such a good friend, Elena."

"Come on, they've called me worse."

"Oh? Like what?"

"Like their friend."

I snorted. "You're such a bitch."

"Hey, they make fun of me in German." She shrugged. "So I call them the Brothers Grimm. It balances out."

"Harmony in Schadenfreude." I laughed. "Beautiful."

The ready room door opened. I probably should have given myself a second to take a breath, steel myself, and at least *try* to prepare before I looked, but I turned without thinking about it.

Sweet Jesus.

Tight black T-shirt. Low-slung jeans. A studded belt that was just flashy enough to say *please direct your attention down here*, as if I needed any encouragement.

He'd been running late tonight, which probably explained the extra dusting of five o'clock shadow on his jaw. He hadn't had time to shave, most likely. Not that it mattered. Clean shaven or scruffy, he looked damn good.

He looked right at me and grinned. "Ready?"

Oh, you'd better believe—

I coughed. "For the show? Hell yeah. I'm ready."

"Good. Because we're on in five."

* * * * *

"Great fucking show, kid." Todd clapped my shoulder on the way offstage.

"Thanks." I was still out of breath, my heart racing from that rush of adrenaline that, no matter how many times I'd performed, never got old.

Also still breathless, Andre elbowed me when he walked past. "I think we'll keep you, McClure. What do you think, Bastian?"

"Fuck yes." Bastian gestured back toward the stage. "I think the fans would skin us alive if we said we weren't bringing him back."

Todd pulled his guitar strap over his head. "Damn right, I think—"

"Aaron. Michael. McClure." At the sound of my sister's voice, I turned around. Elena folded her arms across her chest and glared at me but failed miserably at keeping the grin at bay. "What did I tell you?"

I blinked, feigning innocence. "To throw myself off the stage and into the crowd at every available opportunity?"

"Yep, that's what I heard," Todd said.

"Sounds about right to me," Andre said.

"Oh shut up, both of you." She rolled her eyes, then smiled at me. "Looks like you're a keeper."

I grinned. "Even if I stage dive?"

She eyed me. "Yes, but you know what? If you do it again and you get hurt, don't come to me for sympathy."

"I wouldn't come to you for sympathy anyway, you coldhearted bitch." I ducked just in time to get out of the path of a flying towel.

"So," Andre said, "who's up for some drinking, partying, and general misbehavior?"

"I'm in," Todd said. "Aaron? We're celebrating our new lead singer, so you'd damn well better be there."

"Hell yeah." I gestured at my sweaty T-shirt. "After I grab a shower and change into something a little more presentable." A club with showers for performers. You had to love that.

"Good call," Todd said. "Bastian, what about you?"

"Oh, I think I could throw back a beer or two."

"You sure, old man?" Rochelle asked. "It's a bit late for—"

"Shut up," he growled. They exchanged playful glares, then laughed.

"Okay, I'm going to go see if I can find a booth." Andre headed out of the room but paused in the doorway. Eyes fixed on something outside the room, he said, "Hey, Bastian, you've got a package coming."

Bastian looked up from putting his bass away. "That's not funny, Andre."

I furrowed my brow, wondering what they were talking about.

Andre said something in German.

Bastian groaned, closing his eyes and letting his head fall forward. A string of what I could only assume was German profanity rolled off his lips.

"Sorry," Andre said. "Your shipment of crazy has arrived."

"Don't sign for it," Bastian muttered.

"Too late." Andre stepped away from the door and leaned against the wall, looking at his watch. "Delivery of psycho in three...two..."

As if on cue, a brunette sauntered into the room in a skirt that was way, way too short and a shirt that covered less cleavage than it showed.

"Hey, you." Her voice was so cheery it made me cringe. She threw her arms around Bastian and kissed him on the cheek.

"Hi, Denise," he growled. I could practically hear his teeth grinding from where I stood.

She rolled her eyes. "Jesus, don't sound so happy to see me."

If looks could kill, she'd have dropped dead right then and there. And for that matter, Bastian would have too. Good God, I could see why these two hadn't lasted.

"How exactly did you get back here?" he asked through his teeth.

"Oh come on. Security here knows me."

"Exactly my point," he muttered.

She cocked her head to one side. "Bastian, for God's—"

"Denise, now's not the time, okay?"

"The time for what?" She narrowed her eyes. "I just wanted to talk, but you're—"

"Why don't we take this someplace else?" he said, his voice low.

"Fine," she snapped.

He rolled his eyes. Then he closed his case and, without a word, followed her out of the room.

Everyone who remained, myself included, released our breath.

"What the hell was that all about?" I knew from the conversation last night that she was crazy, but they struck me as two people on the verge of splitting, not a couple whose relationship was already cold in the grave.

"Denise is…" Elena shook her head and clicked her tongue. "I don't even know how to describe her."

"Denise is what we call a 'slow learner,'" Todd said.

"Well, we knew that when she started dating Bastian," Andre said, snickering.

Elena laughed. "Oh come on. Be nice."

Todd shrugged. "Hey, if she's going to date the kind of human flotsam and jetsam I call friends, then…" He put his hands up and shrugged again.

"Hey, watch it, McClure," Andre said. "That's my brother you're talking about."

"I rest my case." Andre raised his fist like he was going to throw a punch.

Todd puffed out his chest. "Come on, come on, I can take it."

Andre shook his fist. "You want some of this?"

"Bring it."

They kept their fists up for a moment, eyeing each other like they were really going to get into a boxing match. Then they both laughed and headed out of the room, talking shit the whole way until their voices faded into the rest of the noise in the hallway.

"Well, I see some things haven't changed in the last few years," I said to Elena.

"Nope." She laughed as she pulled her blue hair back into a ponytail. "I think Bastian's the only one of the three of them who's grown up at all."

Oh, he's definitely grown up. I cleared my throat. "So, Denise? She just keeps showing up like that?"

"Unfortunately." Elena sighed. "He ended things weeks ago, but she just refuses to let him go. I'm not sure what she thinks she'll gain by pissing him off at every opportunity, but…" She trailed off and shaking her head. "I know he says she's harmless, but the woman worries me."

"What could she do? Annoy him to death?"

She laughed dryly. "You never know. I just, I don't know. I have visions of her crashing the stage or fucking with some equipment or something." She exhaled. "The thing is Denise knows the band means the world to him, and I wouldn't put it past her to try to pull something."

"Lovely."

"Yeah. Anyway, go grab a shower so we can go be social."

About twenty minutes after Elena and I joined Rochelle, Todd, and Andre at a booth, Bastian reappeared. His jaw was set, his shoulders were tight, and he looked ready to deck the first person who looked at him sideways.

That may have been closer to the truth than not. Though our bandmates rarely missed an opportunity to antagonize anyone within a five-mile radius, everyone left him well enough alone. No one asked and he didn't say, but Denise was nowhere in sight.

With some beer and bantering, Bastian relaxed. Before long, his ex-fiancée's intrusion was all but forgotten and he laughed and joked like the rest of us.

One thing that surprised me was how familiar the crowd at this club was with the band. They played here regularly, and it quickly became apparent that people knew Schadenfreude was friendly and social. Though some were shy about it, the occasional fan approached and asked various band members to dance. Some were wary of asking Andre because his arm was around Rochelle, but the odd brave soul worked up the courage and was rewarded with Rochelle encouraging him to go dance with the girl.

A cute blonde came up and stammered her way through inviting Bastian out to the crowded floor. His cheeks got a little red, and his shy, boyish smile did crazy things to my pulse. He opened his mouth to speak, eyebrows arched over apologetic eyes, hesitation written all over his expression. Then he glanced past her, and the reluctance vanished. He set his drink down, pushed himself up, and made an "after you" gesture to the starstruck girl. Just before the crowd closed around them, she slid an arm around his waist.

Oh you lucky, lucky woman. I went for my beer.

Rochelle and Elena both stared out at the floor, mouths agape and eyes wide.

Then Elena shook her head and looked at Rochelle, gesturing at Bastian. "Did—" She paused. "Did that just happen?"

"I think it did." Rochelle blinked a few times. "I...I'm..."

Elena looked around. "Keep an eye out. The other three horsemen will be here any second."

"What's so unusual about that?" I asked.

"That?" Rochelle gestured at Bastian. "Bastian Koehler does not dance. Ever. With anyone. He just...doesn't."

Elena furrowed her brow. "Maybe he's just enjoying the single life."

"That," Todd said over his beer, "or he sensed incoming crazy and took the nearest exit."

Elena sat up. "Incoming crazy? Where? I didn't—"

As if on cue, Denise dropped onto the bench beside me. Her eye makeup was smeared a little, complementing the extra redness in her eyes. Her shoulders were thrust back in a show of indignation, which had the side effect of nearly making her fall out of her blouse.

Rochelle raised her drink. "And suddenly the world makes sense again."

"What's that supposed to mean?" Denise asked.

"Nothing at all." Rochelle batted her eyes and offered a sarcastic smile before sipping her beer.

Denise glared at her, then turned toward me and offered a flirty grin. "So you're the new singer?"

I forced a smile. "Yeah. Name's Aaron."

"Great show," she said.

"Oh. Uh, thanks." I wanted to draw as far from her as possible. It wasn't in my nature to be rude, especially to someone I'd just met, but I'd already seen a demonstration of how volatile she could be. I didn't particularly want to find myself on the receiving end of it.

She turned to the remaining band members at the table and gestured at me. "You guys should definitely keep him. That was the best show I've seen in a long time."

"Really?" Todd said. "You know, we all thought he sucked, but now that he has your endorsement, maybe we'll keep him around." He rolled his eyes and picked up his drink.

Denise huffed. "Jesus, Todd, I—"

"Oh my God!" Rochelle squeaked. She gestured out at the dance floor. "Look at him *go*."

We all turned to watch Bastian and the lucky blonde, and my body temperature ratcheted up a few more degrees. The girl must have had double-jointed hips or something, judging by the way she moved. Good God, she could twist, turn, swivel…and Bastian had no trouble keeping up with her. He was behind her, hands on her waist, and they moved together perfectly. When her hips made a figure eight, snapped to one side, then went back the other way, his stayed right with hers. In fact, I couldn't tell whose movement guided whose.

"God*damn*," Elena said.

"Uh-huh," Rochelle said.

"Does your man know you drool over his brother?" Todd asked.

"Quiet, McClure. I'm ogling Bastian."

Denise released a sharp breath. "That son of a bitch."

"You know, he *is* single," Rochelle said. I didn't have to look to know the two were exchanging icy glares. That would have required looking away from Bastian, so I just let the fluctuating air temperature fill me in on what I couldn't see.

"He's single, and he's an asshole," Denise muttered.

"Listen, honey," Elena said, her voice gentle, "maybe you just need to give him some space, you know?"

"He's had plenty of space."

"Obviously not if he's still giving you the cold shoulder."

Denise clicked her tongue. "He's being a dick."

"Then let him go," Elena said. "You don't need that." When I glanced at her, her lips thinned into a straight line, and I swore I heard the unspoken *he sure as hell doesn't need your crap*.

"She's got a point, Denise," Rochelle said. "Besides, men can smell desperation a mile away. Right, McClure brothers?"

"Yep," Todd said.

"Damn right," I said, and Bastian chose just that moment to let his eyes flick toward us. I shivered, wondering if he picked up on the double dose of desperation coming from this table.

"I'm *not* desperate," Denise said.

"Yes, you are," Rochelle said as flippantly as she could. "*Anyway*, I still can't believe Bastian's actually dancing."

"And God in heaven, the man can *move*," Elena said.

Todd put his hands over her eyes. "You don't need to be watching that."

"Oh fuck off." She shrugged him away and kept watching Bastian, practically drooling on the table right alongside Rochelle. And me.

"Fuck this, I'm out of here." Denise rose. "I'll see you guys at the next show."

"Don't threaten us like that, Denise," Todd said.

"Fuck you." Denise shot every one of us a glare, then shoved her way into the crowd and disappeared.

Aside from a few glances in her direction, no one at the table acknowledged her exit. We were all too busy watching Bastian.

"Wow," Rochelle said, "I really didn't think that man could dance."

"Well, he obviously can," Elena said. "My God."

"No shit." Rochelle blinked a few times. "Fuck, look at those hips."

I took a long swallow of beer. Oh, I was looking, all right. At those hips, those shoulders, those hands. I wasn't jealous in the slightest. Quite the contrary: Every time his hips swayed with the blonde's or his hands slid up her sides, my self-control ebbed just a little bit more. When his lips brushed her neck, I bit my lip at the same time she bit hers.

"Christ on a cracker," Elena said. "I had no—"

"Okay, would you two stop salivating all over him?" Todd said. "It's giving me the creeps."

"Yeah, and you're probably getting wood watching him," Rochelle said.

Elena and I both snorted with laughter.

"I hate you all," Todd muttered. "Anyway, I think I'm about ready to call it a night. Aaron, you mind helping me take some gear down to the car?"

I drained my drink. "Not a problem." As much as I wanted to watch Bastian—*fuck, how the hell does he move like that without dislocating something?*—I jumped at the chance to get out of there before I went out of my mind.

Without so much as another glance toward that gorgeous bassist, I followed my brother out of the main part of the club and into the maze of hallways that made up the backstage area. He navigated it effortlessly, like he knew the whole place by heart. He probably did. A few dozen more performances here and I probably would too. I had eventually worked out how to navigate the streets and highways of Los Angeles. I could figure out the House of Anarchy.

Since we had three gigs in a row at this club, which the band often did, we didn't take all our gear home. Amps and various other pieces of band-owned sound equipment were locked up in a room backstage. Andre's drum set went in there, but Todd and Bastian both took their instruments home since they were more portable.

I helped Todd carry everything in, then went back to the ready room to get my jacket and keys so I could head home. Head home, get some sleep, and try not to think about hips and hands and *him*.

"So did my crazy ex eventually leave you alone?"

That lightly accented voice sent a shiver up my spine, which I masked by shrugging my jacket into place before I turned around.

Bastian leaned against the door frame, a wry grin pulling at his lips. I didn't look at his shoulders. Or his hips. Or his arms. I didn't. I did *not*.

"Yeah," I said. "Eventually."

He chuckled. "Good. I figured she would. Eventually." He pushed himself off the door frame and picked up his own jacket. Leather creaked when he put it on.

"She always hang around after shows?"

He shrugged and reached for his bass. As he put the case's strap over his shoulder, he said, "I had a little chat with security, though. They'll have the bouncers keep an eye out for her from now on. New guys just didn't recognize her, but I doubt it'll be an issue anymore."

"Good."

He sighed and rolled his eyes. "She might still be here tonight, though. I haven't seen her since she left the table, but knowing her, she's probably hanging around waiting for me somewhere."

"Doesn't have anything better to do?"

"Apparently not." He looked around the room, then checked his pockets, probably making sure he had his wallet, keys, and phone. Evidently satisfied he had everything he needed, he said, "You heading out?"

I nodded. "Yeah. Todd and I just finished putting everything away for tomorrow."

"Cool. I'm taking the long way out, just in case Her Highness is around. You're welcome to come with me."

"Probably should. Don't know my way around here yet anyway."

He laughed quietly. "It's easy to get lost here if you don't know your way. Come on." I followed him out of the room and down the hall, but instead of going straight, he went left. Without noticing, let alone heeding, a sign that read AUTHORIZED PERSONNEL, Bastian pushed a door open and gestured for me to follow him.

"Do we count as authorized personnel?" I asked, following him down a barely lit stairwell.

"Of course we do." He adjusted his bass on his shoulder. "We're Schadenfreude. This place is packed three nights a week because of us."

I chuckled. "And people call *me* cocky."

Bastian laughed. "Nothing wrong with a little cockiness." As if for emphasis, he continued past another such sign without a hint of hesitation. We went down one more stairwell, then continued along a few winding hallways. Dark, deserted, no one around except for him. Oh God, the things we could do in a place like this.

I shook my head, trying to focus on the simple task of following him and not mentally dragging him into one of the many rooms we passed. I'd been in a perpetual state of *want* all evening. Being alone with him like this wasn't helping.

I cleared my throat. "Did Indiana Jones plan this place out or something? I swear it's like a damned labyrinth."

"Yeah, no shit. It's a converted schoolhouse or something. Shitloads of rooms all over the place and hallways going everywhere."

"You ever get lost in here?"

He threw a grin over his shoulder. "Only when I want to."

I hoped he didn't notice when I stumbled over my own feet. If he did, he didn't say.

Moments later, we rounded a corner and I recognized the big steel door through which I'd come when I'd arrived at the club. Though the route we'd taken was hardly a shortcut, it did let us bypass some of the more crowded hallways and places where crazies might lurk.

Bastian pushed the door open, and we stepped out into the cool night air. A few people milled around in the alley with cigarettes and conversations, but Denise wasn't among them, so we continued across the alley and past the concrete wall dividing the alley from the employee and performer parking lot.

Among the cars and streetlights, Bastian slowed his pace, and without thinking about it, I did the same.

He stopped. I stopped.

For a moment, neither of us spoke. My heart pounded. Every time he looked at me, I was sure he'd see right through me. Christ, wouldn't *that* make things awkward? I'd had a straight guy catch wind of a crush before, and it took a while before we could be comfortable in the same room. I certainly hadn't had to get onstage with him. Or rehearse with him. Or—

Fuck, Aaron, get it together. Like, yesterday.

Bastian took a breath as if he was about to say something, then must have decided against it. He released his breath and put his fist out. "Great show tonight, kid. Do it again tomorrow night."

I bumped his fist. "Will do." Normally I thought that gesture was lame, but I was admittedly glad the band had adopted it as their customary greeting. At least that kept the physical contact to a minimum, which in turn kept me *just* this side of making an ass of myself.

"Anyway, have a good night," he said.

"You too. See you tomorrow."

"See you tomorrow." He smiled, then turned to go. I let myself watch him for just a few seconds, thankful his jacket and bass obscured the hips that had mesmerized me on the dance floor. I took a deep breath and headed for my own car with dozens of delicious images in my brain.

Great show tonight? Likewise, Bastian. Likewise.

CHAPTER FOUR

One thing I hadn't grown accustomed to since moving back from California was the constant flow of people through the house. I'd spent two years in a cramped studio apartment by myself, and now I shared a four-bedroom house with four other people and a cat. Aside from the cat, everyone who lived here was social as hell, and this place seemed to be the default hangout.

Todd and Lillian shared the master bedroom on the second floor. Across the hall from them, his roommate Lane had one room with his girlfriend, Jennifer. The other bedroom had been converted into Lane's office, and I had taken the remaining room downstairs. I didn't exactly have the ground floor to myself, though. Everyone made frequent use of the rec room and laundry room, plus going to and from the garage via the hallway past my door.

With everyone's varying work schedules, not to mention friends and bandmates coming and going, there was nearly always someone around. I rarely even had to use my house key unless I went in through the side door, because the place was almost never empty when I came home. Tonight was no exception.

I got home from the show around two thirty, and the driveway was clogged with cars. Every light on the second floor was on, and the TV flickered from the living room window.

"Great." I pulled up and parked on the curb.

On the way into the house, I looked at the gathered vehicles. What I didn't see was Bastian's truck. Andre's Mustang and Rochelle's car were also mercifully absent.

I went up the steps to the front door that led into the split-level. I could have easily gone around to the side door of the garage and slipped in undetected through the downstairs hallway. Or I could have gone in through the front and just headed down to the ground level.

All the booze in the house was upstairs, though, and I needed a cold one like nobody's business. So when I let myself in, I went up instead of down.

When I cleared the top step, Lane looked up. "Hey, hey, hey, here's the new star of Schadenfreude."

"The star?" Todd glanced over his shoulder, shook his head, and went back to his video game. "Don't encourage him, Lane. He won't be able to get his head through the door."

"He wouldn't be a lead singer without an ego," Lane said.

"Exactly why you don't need to encourage him."

"Hey, fuck you both." I laughed. "Besides, I can't have too much of an ego if I'm willing to appear on the same stage as these assholes."

Lane laughed. "Oh *snap*."

"Damn, dude," Todd said. "I put you up in my house, give you a spot in my band, and this is the thanks I get?"

"You gave me a spot?" I snorted. "This from the man who practically begged me to move back up here so I could bail his band out?"

He gestured dismissively. "Details."

Lane laughed again. To his girlfriend, he said, "You know, we could save some money by cutting off the cable now. These guys are entertainment enough."

"Yeah," Jennifer said. "And I give it a week before you'd be crying for your Food Network cooking shows."

"Cooking shows." Todd chuckled. "Such a manly man, Lane."

"Fuck you," Lane muttered. To me he said, "Grab a beer, have a seat, chill awhile."

"Don't mind if I do." I went into the kitchen to get a beer. I was exhausted but far too wound up to try to sleep. Drink in hand, I returned to the living room and sat on one end of the couch.

Todd and Lane traded off playing some video game or another. I watched, but my mind kept wandering back to the House of Anarchy.

At least now I knew I could get through a show on the same stage as Bastian. Then again, that was before I'd seen the way he moved on the dance floor. Fucking hell. His ex-fiancée may have been insane, but I could see why she didn't want to let him go. If he moved his hips like that in bed, no one in their right mind—or, well, even if they *weren't* in their right mind—would want to give him up.

I took a deep breath and slowly let it out through my nose, hoping no one else in the room noticed. Hopefully this crush would pass. It would dissipate as I got used to being around him, and sooner or later, another gorgeous man would come along and drive me to distraction.

My beer did nothing to settle my nerves. It made me a little more tired, but I just couldn't relax. There were too many people in this house and one too many on my mind.

"Well, I think I'm going to call it a night." I pushed myself up off the sofa.

"Need us to turn the volume down?" Lillian asked.

I shook my head. "My ears are still ringing from the show. I'm lucky I can hear the TV at all."

"Pity Todd doesn't have that problem."

"What?" Todd shouted.

"Oh shut up, you." Lillian threw a pillow at him.

I laughed and went downstairs. In my bedroom, I leaned against the door and closed my eyes. My ears were ringing, that much was true, but I certainly didn't have a problem hearing anything. The acoustics in this house were awful, and the sounds of chatter and video games made it loud and clear down to my room.

I doubted it would keep me awake, though. My thoughts would do a fine job of that on their own. Sighing, I rubbed my eyes. Maybe a shower would help. I'd grabbed one at the club earlier, but I figured another wouldn't hurt.

I went across the hall to the bathroom and got in the shower.

With no one else around to see my physical reaction, I didn't even try not to think about him. Not getting hard was simply not an option when I was alone with Bastian on my mind, so I didn't fight it. I braced myself with one hand against the wall, and with the other stroked my cock faster, faster, faster.

Closing my eyes, I let every image of him run through my mind in slow motion.

Watching him perform, watching him dance, watching him breathe. His quiet charisma offstage, his powerful energy on. Mischievous grin, shy laugh, those *eyes*. Jesus.

When Elena had belted out the climactic final verse of one of her songs tonight, I'd watched from backstage as Bastian put his foot up on his amp and threw himself into a powerful riff. His shoulders had tensed, and his forearms rippled with every note he sent thrumming through my consciousness. His brow furrowed here, his eyes closed there. Sometimes his lips pulled into a grimace. He lived and breathed the music just like we all did, but he made it so fucking sexy.

In my mind, I watched his body move in slow motion. Every twist of his hips, every thrust. The way his hair, stringy and wet with sweat, flew when he threw his head back. Oh God, I wondered if he did that when he came. If his hips moved like that, if his eyes shut tight like that, if when it was over he ran his hand through his sweaty hair while he caught his breath like that...

I'd never seen a man who could move the way he did. His hips twisted, thrust, and snapped, melting all the women in the crowd and making me wonder if he did that while he fucked. Christ, of course he did. Hips like that were *made* for sex. Just thinking of the way he moved them in that figure-eight pattern, fuck, I was on the edge. Right on the edge.

I closed my eyes, gritting my teeth as thoughts of him drove me out of my damned mind. Even this close to the edge, my orgasm caught me by surprise because I hadn't expected it to be so fucking *intense*. My knees buckled, my hand faltered, and I almost released a throaty roar before I remembered I wasn't alone in the house. I clenched my jaw and held my breath, struggling to stay silent while I came.

The strongest tremors quieted. I slowly released my breath. The hot water on my skin soothed the goose bumps along my back and neck.

Looking at Bastian now in my mind's eye, seeing him as the man and musician that he had become in the last ten years, I wondered how I'd ever overlooked him. Of course, I'd been just a kid back then, and to a degree, so had he. But now? He certainly wasn't the gangly kid I remembered from over a decade ago. He'd grown up, and I wanted him. Was he as passionate in bed as he was onstage? Did he personify sex the way he personified music? I'd been with plenty of musicians. Some were duds in bed because they poured all their passion and energy into their music, leaving little for a lover.

I couldn't imagine Bastian being like that. I just couldn't. Whatever had kept him off my radar in the past, I was damned certain of one thing now: Bastian Koehler was pure sex. Walking, talking, breathing, liquid *sex*.

I had to have him.

Then I remembered the terse exchange between Bastian and Denise. In spite of the hostility between them, her presence was a reminder of yet another reason he was out of my reach.

I rested my forehead against the cool tile and sighed, enjoying the last few tingling aftershocks of the orgasm he didn't know he'd given me.

Damn you, Bastian, why do you have to be straight?

CHAPTER FIVE

By the time we were finished with sound check, my entire body tingled with the echoes of Bastian's bass, and if I didn't get away from him for a little while, I was going to go out of my ever-loving mind. Under the guise of needing some air and something out of my car, I slipped outside during the opening act.

The House of Anarchy's rear parking lot was separated from the club by a graffiti-covered concrete wall and a narrow alley. A few employees—a bartender, a couple of security guys, and the kid who worked the coat check—hung out there, smoking right beside the steel door to the club. They obviously didn't give a shit about the laws requiring them to stay twenty-five feet away from the entrance, and I didn't care either as I walked past them, across the alley, and beyond the concrete wall.

The parking lot was deserted. Only employees and performers parked here, and they were all either inside the club or smoking behind it. All except a certain lead singer who couldn't get a certain bassist out of his head and thus needed to spend a few minutes pacing between the rows of cars.

I spun my car keys on my finger just to give my hands something to do. Naturally, every time they jingled against my palm, I remembered Bastian playing with his keys the same way in the bar's parking lot the other night. The keys to his truck. *That* truck. The one just three or four cars away from me, its unassuming black profile reminding me he was here. As if I'd forgotten.

"Fuck," I muttered, running my other hand through my hair. I had to get him out of my head. I wasn't likely to get him out of my system anytime soon, but this had to stop. It was a crush, nothing more, and by virtue of Bastian being both heterosexual and a bandmate, it couldn't be anything more.

"Get over it, idiot." I exhaled hard and rubbed my temples, thankful the concrete wall kept the smokers from seeing me talking to myself and pacing

Beyond that wall, the sound of the opening act spilled into the alley. A second later, the steel door shut with a heavy thud, cutting off the music. I took a deep breath. Their set was relatively short, so I needed to get back inside sooner or later. Maybe another twenty minutes or so. Plenty of time for some air, but not nearly enough to clear my jumbled, Bastian-saturated mind.

It didn't help that we'd been damn near tripping over each other all evening. Wherever I was, he was. Wherever he was, I was. Maybe it was just because we both had to be in the same places at the same times. Unloading equipment, setting it up, sound check, securing gear backstage. That was all it was.

The club's door opened, and the opening act's music once again flooded the alley. If I recognized the song from last night, they were about two-thirds of the way through their performance. Which meant it was almost time for us. With another heavy thud of the steel door, the sound cut off, leaving me to my pounding heart.

I was reading too much into things. Of course we'd run into each other constantly. Every bandmate was under the feet of every other bandmate all afternoon and evening. Elena and I had even made a joke out of the fact that we kept crashing into each other. She'd almost knocked me off the stage twice before we'd even started sound check. I was just more aware of Bastian because…he was Bastian. And he was there. And he'd worn those tight goddamned jeans and that leather jacket and—

I took a deep breath and slowly let it out through my nose.

He was here, and I would deal with it. Like everyone else in the band, I was a professional. I could deal with it, I would deal with it, and I would *not* let myself get carried away wondering if there was some hidden meaning in those loaded glances Bastian shot my way every once in a while. Because they weren't loaded glances, there was no hidden meaning, and even if there was, Bastian was a bandmate. I'd already found out the hard way what could happen when one mixed pleasure with this kind of business.

I needed to get it together and get over it. Schadenfreude had a crowd to wow and a roof to raise, and it was almost showtime.

I can do this.

I took another breath, set my shoulders back, and started toward the club, spinning my key ring around my finger and refusing to acknowledge where else I'd recently heard that jingle.

When I came around the wall and stepped into the alley, I stopped dead and nearly dropped my car keys.

The employees were gone, their discarded cigarette butts still smoldering on the damp pavement, but I wasn't alone.

Leaning beside the door, his hips cocked slightly, one knee bent with a booted foot flat on the wall, was Bastian. Our eyes met, and my heart jumped into my throat. His gaze was electric with intensity, and there was no surprise in his expression. No startled reaction to my presence. He hadn't come out here for any other reason, I was sure. He knew I'd be here.

For a moment, we stared at each other in silence. Gears seemed to be turning in his head as if he weighed some unspoken options, contemplated some unsaid risks and benefits. He narrowed his eyes slightly, like he could read me whether or not I wanted to be read.

I approached slowly, warily, not sure if I wanted him to think I was coming closer to him or just moving toward the door. I stopped with a few feet between us and watched him silently, trying to read him like he read me. He didn't know. Did he? And even if he did, he wasn't. Was he?

Whatever the case, he didn't move. He didn't speak. He didn't look away from me. I *couldn't* look away from him.

I dropped my keys into my coat pocket, surprised the muffled jingle didn't echo in the alleyway. Nearby, car engines purred and rumbled down the side streets. From inside the club came the bass line's thumping pulse and the drum's pounding heartbeat. Here between us, there was nothing but silence. Taut, unnerving silence.

When I could no longer stand it, I broke that silence. "Shouldn't you, um..." I shifted my weight. "Shouldn't you be getting ready to go onstage?"

Bastian shrugged, his leather jacket squeaking softly in protest. "Probably." He gestured at the closed door. "But like I said last night, this club is notoriously confusing to navigate if you don't know your way around." His accent drew my attention right to his mouth and the way it moved, the way his lips and tongue curled around every syllable. "I wanted to make sure you found your way back without any trouble."

"Oh." I cleared my throat. "Um, thanks."

"Anytime."

Neither of us moved. He didn't speak. I couldn't breathe.

A few long, quiet seconds ticked by before I found my breath and the ability to speak. "Well, I guess we should go inside."

"Yeah. We should." His jacket creaked when, without taking his eyes off me, he pushed himself off the wall with his foot and took a step closer to me. "We definitely *should* go back inside."

I resisted the urge to back away or move closer. I gestured past him toward the door. "Um, after you?"

Bastian took another step. "You might have to wait a few minutes then, because I was planning on staying out here a little longer."

I gulped. "Oh? How much longer?"

Another step. "Don't know." His eyes met mine. "I hadn't thought quite that far ahead yet."

"How far—" I moistened my lips. "How far ahead had you thought?"

"I'd gotten about this far." One more step, and we were unnervingly close together. "Beyond that?" He shrugged. "Anyone's guess."

My eyes were locked on his. I swallowed hard. It was a pointless action, since my mouth had gone completely dry.

Bastian inclined his head slightly. "Am I making you nervous?"

I nodded. "Yeah. A little."

"You don't have to stay." He glanced over his shoulder at the door, then looked back at me, eyebrows raised. "The band's waiting for us anyway if you want to go back in."

My feet wouldn't have moved if I'd tried to make them.

"Actually, I want to." I muffled a cough. "To stay, I mean. Out here." *Wow, really articulate tonight, aren't we?*

"Do you?" He wasn't quite as paralyzed as I was, and he shortened the distance between us by another half step. "Why is that?"

I couldn't decide whether to focus on his eyes or his lips. Neither did me a damned bit of good as far as getting my wits about me. The former were intense, the latter just barely curling into a grin that was as subtle as it was devilish, and he stood too close for me to look anywhere but right at him.

His eyebrow ring caught the low light when he tilted his head to one side, eyes still waiting for the answer to his question.

"I'm, um…" I paused. "Curious. To see…what happens."

The grin broadened into a smile. "Guess that gives us something in common."

A world away inside the club, the music changed. The percussion pounded out a rapid-fire tempo now, one that kept perfect time with my pulse.

Bastian turned his head a little, eyes losing focus for a second. "They're wrapping up their set," he murmured. "Only a couple more songs." His eyes flicked toward me. "Doesn't leave us much time."

"Much time for"—I gulped—"for what?"

His left shoulder rose in a nearly imperceptible shrug, one so subtle it didn't even warrant a squeak from his jacket, and I doubt I'd have noticed it had I not been so fucking in tune to every move he made. He lowered his voice. "Not much time to see if we have anything else in common."

He'd spoken so quietly that before I knew what I was doing, I'd leaned in to hear him better. Only after I'd done so did I realize I'd narrowed that sliver of air between us by the minutest mile.

"I think we might have a little common ground," he whispered, keeping me near with nothing more than the softness of his voice. "Don't you?"

"It's a…" Oh God, he licked his lips. Oh my fucking God. "It's a possibility, yes."

"Just a possibility?" He leaned toward me, and I mirrored him. *Fuck*, I could feel him breathing now. He watched my mouth as he whispered, "Seems like more than a possibility to me. But I—" He stopped abruptly when I bit my lip, and a shiver ran through him. Our eyes met again. He took a breath. "I could be wrong."

"Depends on what you're thinking, I guess."

"I'd be willing to bet…" He trailed off. My lips held his attention, and he moistened his again. Leather creaked as he brought his hand up and laid it on the side of my neck, and my pulse outpaced the distant percussion.

Our eyes met. His fingertips pressed into the back of my neck, and he tilted his head slightly, leaning in *just* a little closer. "I was going to say I'd be willing to bet we're thinking along the same lines."

"You might be right." I put my hand on his waist—*I'm touching him, I'm touching him, I'm fucking touching him*—and snaked my arm around him under his leather jacket.

"I think I *am* right." His fingers drifted into my hair.

"Only one way to find out." My lips almost touched his, the heat of his breath and skin warming the tiny pocket of cool night air remaining between us.

He said something. English, German, I couldn't tell. None of it made it to my brain because a heartbeat after the air between our mouths vibrated with his voice, he kissed me.

Oh. God. *Yes.*

The kiss happened in slow, slow motion, both of us drawing and releasing long, deep breaths as our lips moved together. My heart pounded with nerves and desperation and lust, lust, "I want you now" lust, but his body and mine moved like we had all the time in the world to just stand there and breathe each other.

I ran my fingers up the back of his neck, then let them hiss across the shaved side of his head before they met the soft, cool fringe of longer hair on top. Everything I touched was distinctly Bastian, and I still couldn't comprehend I was kissing *him*.

His jaw moved, he tilted his head a little more, and his lips coaxed mine apart. When his tongue met mine, something else slid past. Something solid, foreign, like a tiny pearl, and a second later, I realized it was a piercing. Nothing more than a smooth, round stud, but like his accent when he spoke, it was just enough to draw every last bit of my attention to his mouth.

His kiss was intense, overwhelming, and he explored my mouth just like I did his. Every time the stud brushed my lip or my tongue—and he did it deliberately, of that I had no doubt—I shivered, wondering what it would feel like on my cock. Holy fucking hell, I wanted him. I needed him. Like I'd never been with anyone before, I was desperate to touch and taste more of him. Never in my life had I wanted a man like I wanted Bastian Koehler right then.

When he broke the kiss, we were both breathless, our foreheads touching and his hands trembling on my neck. I couldn't look him in the eyes, so I closed mine, but even the heat of his skin and the nearness of his body were too much.

"I've been wanting to do that"—he paused, taking a breath—"since the night you auditioned."

"Oh, you're not the only one, believe me," I whispered.

He released a sharp sigh against my lips. "We can't…" He growled something in his native tongue. Then, "We shouldn't be doing this."

I swallowed, something sinking in my gut. I didn't want to let go, no matter how much I knew we needed to.

"We shouldn't, but—" He cut himself off with another deep, desperate kiss. I moaned softly into his mouth, my knees shaking when he pressed his hips against mine.

We held on to each other, stumbled back, then forward again. I struggled to find some semblance of balance while he threw my entire world off-kilter, and right about the time my knees almost failed me, Bastian shoved me up against the wall. His erection pressed against mine through our clothes, and I couldn't help releasing a low groan.

His jacket creaked. We both took and released ragged hisses of breath. Jeans scuffed across concrete like fingers scuffed across stubble, and oh God, I was kissing Bastian. Bastian, who kissed like his life depended on it, who smelled like leather, and who fucking tasted like sex.

Inside the club, on the outskirts of my senses, the percussion died away. The roar of the crowd engulfed what was left of the fading music, and a moment later, the emcee's voice boomed over the crowd.

We looked at the closed door, then back at each other.

"I think that's our cue." He swept the tip of his tongue across his lower lip. "They'll be calling us onstage in a few minutes."

I gritted my teeth and released a frustrated breath. "Damn it."

"No shit." He combed his fingers through my hair and kissed me again. "But we'll finish this."

Oh, you're damn right we will. I swallowed. "When?"

"Don't know. Soon. But we don't have time to work it out now." He kissed me once more, then let me go, and every place we'd made contact was suddenly ice-cold with the absence of him. He gestured at the door. "Go ahead of me. If we come back up together—"

"I know." With one last kiss and a parting glance, I hurried back inside. On my way down the hall to where the rest of the band waited to go onstage, I tried to think of anything but Bastian. I tried to focus on the music, the performance, the floor, the Mariners, *something*.

But all I could think of was Bastian.

CHAPTER SIX

We made it through the show. God only knows how, but we made it. It probably didn't hurt that Bastian was behind me the whole time, so I didn't have the sight of him to distract me. Even still, his presence was more than enough. When I was offstage during Elena's songs, it took a lot of slow, deep breaths, cold water, and thoughts about the unsexiest things I could think of to keep me from returning to the stage with a hard-on.

We finally wrapped up the set without any outward signs that I knew what Bastian Koehler's kiss tasted like. My bandmates and I congratulated each other on a great show, and no one seemed to notice Bastian and me avoiding each other's eyes.

As soon as we were finished clearing out our gear, I took advantage of the showers kindly provided to us by the House of Anarchy. I was sweaty as hell from the show, but I also just needed a little distance from Bastian and a few minutes to collect my thoughts.

I fully expected my rational side to chime in at this point and remind me of all the reasons we shouldn't do this. Everything stayed silent on the rational front, though, and all I heard over the rushing water were the three words that still sizzled across my nerve endings:

"We'll finish this."

God, I hoped so. My lips still tingled from his kiss the way my ears rang from the show. Right or wrong, good idea or bad, I needed to finish what we'd started, if only to get him out of my system so I could focus on the band and the music.

I turned off the water. *Speak now or forever hold your peace, rational side.*

Not a peep.

Once I'd changed into clean clothes, I went back to where I'd left the band. Everyone milled around, discussing plans for the rest of the evening and what we needed to work on at the next rehearsal. Everyone except Bastian, that is.

I looked around, then casually said, "Where's Bastian?"

Rochelle glanced up. "You just missed him. He went to take some gear back to the farm. Did you need something?"

"Oh, no, I was—" I paused, swallowing hard. "I needed to ask him about something, but it can wait." He'd left? That was...odd. I glanced at the time on my phone, also surreptitiously checking to see if he'd texted me, which he hadn't. "I'd better get out of here myself."

"We're all heading over to Andre and Bastian's place in a bit," Elena said. "You want to go?"

"I, ah, no, I think I'm just going to call it a night." I pulled my keys out of my pocket, spun them once, and shivered when they jingled against my palm. I cleared my throat. "I'll catch up with Bastian at rehearsal tomorrow. It was nothing important."

"Okay, well, we'll see you at rehearsal. Great show, kiddo."

"Thanks." We exchanged a quick hug before I headed downstairs.

When I pushed the heavy steel door open and stepped out into the alley, I hadn't even realized I'd expected to see Bastian standing there until I *didn't* see him. The alley was vacant except for a few employees and their cigarettes, and in the parking lot, the unassuming profile of Bastian's black pickup was gone.

I got into my car and pulled out of the parking lot but hesitated before turning onto the main road. I could go to the farm and try to catch up with him there, or I could go home and hope for the best next time we saw each other. Had he had second thoughts? Had his rational mind kicked in while mine sat back in lust-induced silence? Was I supposed to read between the lines and follow him or take it as a hint that everything in the alley had been a mistake? Follow him or give him space?

"We shouldn't be doing this."

Wasn't that the truth. I'd already had one band wind up as part of the smoldering wreckage of a relationship.

Should I do this?

Absently I moistened my lips, my breath catching at the memory of his piercing sliding over my lips and tongue. No one on God's green earth kissed like Bastian. With the way his mouth moved when he kissed or spoke, and with the presence of that tiny, smooth stud in his tongue, I could only imagine what else his mouth was capable of.

Before I could think about it any further, I turned, got on the freeway, aimed my car toward the east, and put the gas pedal to the floor.

Thirty-five minutes and a few million second thoughts later, the John Deere tractor mailbox sent my pulse into overdrive.

Chewing my lip, I turned down the long driveway. There was only one vehicle parked in front of the barn, and that was Bastian's pickup. The tailgate was down, the bed empty. A few more minutes and I probably would have missed him, but he was here.

One last onslaught of hesitation flooded my mind, but I ignored it and put the car in park. I hadn't come all the way out here to turn around and run in the opposite direction. The scales would tip in favor of either *we shouldn't be doing this* or *we'll finish this*. One or the other. Now or never.

I killed the engine.

Got out of the car.

Walked up to the garage.

And, hoping I wasn't making *too* many mistakes by doing this, pushed the door open.

Bastian knelt beside some equipment, his back to me, but as soon as the door opened, he turned, and when he did, he sucked in a breath.

Rising slowly, he whispered, "Aaron."

We stared at each other, the sound of my name hanging in the air that crackled around and between us. If he hadn't been surprised to see me in the alley earlier, he certainly was now. He swallowed hard. So did I.

And just like earlier, I was the one to finally break the disconcerting silence.

"You…" I paused, not wanting to sound put out or accusing. "You took off so quickly…"

"Yeah. I know. I'm sorry." He scratched the back of his neck and looked at the floor between us. "I'm…" He shook his head. "I guess I just needed to get out. Away."

"From me?"

He chewed his lip. "I guess, yeah. Not you. Just…" He closed his eyes, pinching the bridge of his nose for a second. "I don't mean it like that, Aaron. This whole thing just…caught me…"

"Off guard?"

Bastian nodded.

"Except you were the one waiting for me in the alley."

"I know." He kept his eyes down and absently ran the tip of his tongue across his lower lip. "I mean, this whole thing. With… Ever since I saw you here the night you auditioned…" He looked at me through his lashes. "Listen, I meant what I said earlier, that I hadn't thought any further than that moment. And now…" He shook his head. "Fuck, I know this is a bad idea."

"Maybe it is," I said.

"Look, no one in the band knows," he said, barely whispering. "About me. Not even my brother. *Especially* not my brother. I want to keep it that way."

"My brother doesn't know about me either. Elena does, but no one else."

"And with both of us being in the band, that just makes things even more complicated." He chewed his lip. "And I keep wondering if it was stupid for us to be out there in the open like that. What if someone had come out of the club? Or the parking lot?"

I nodded. "I know. Believe me, I know."

"I mean, it's one thing if the band found out. Andre and Todd wouldn't like it if they knew, but they'd get over it. Eventually." He folded his arms across his chest and shifted his weight. "Now, the public? Record execs? That could go either way."

I nodded. "Yeah, I know what you mean." Seattle was about as progressive as anywhere in the country when it came to accepting homosexuality, but Schadenfreude wanted to be more than a regional band. The fact was record agents may have been willing to sign openly gay pop bands, but hard rock or heavy metal? Not so much. Sure, there were some, but they were the exception, not the rule.

What I wondered, though, was who he was trying to convince: me or himself.

I moistened my lips. "So what do we do?"

"I don't know." Bastian blew out a breath and ran a hand through his hair, absently finger-combing the fringe out of his face. "The only thing I know right now is that no matter how much we shouldn't do this, that doesn't change a goddamned thing."

"What do you mean?"

Looking up through his lashes again, he met my eyes. "I was waiting for you in the alley because I wanted to know if I was imagining things. Now I know." He dropped his gaze. "And I still want you so fucking badly."

I shivered. "So should I stay or go?"

"If I had an ounce of sense, I'd say you should go." He gave a quiet laugh. "But it's a hell of a lot easier to convince myself this is a bad idea when you're not here."

Mirroring what he'd done in the alley, I moved closer, and just like mine must have earlier, his posture stiffened and his breathing quickened with every inch of ground I gained. When I stopped less than an arm's length from him, he swallowed hard.

I chewed the inside of my cheek. "Am I making you nervous?"

His eyes flicked up to meet mine. When I put my hand on his waist, he closed his eyes and released a ragged breath.

"Still think this a bad idea?" I asked.

"I know it's a bad idea." His hand came to rest on my hip. "The band..." The other hand found its way to my neck. "This could blow up in our faces so easily."

I put my free hand on his arm, letting it drift slowly up to his shoulder. "Someone could find out."

"Wouldn't take much." He slid his hand from my hip to my lower back.

"We're alone now. No one's going to see or hear us here." I moistened my lips. "Which means if we get started, there's no reason to stop."

His eyes met mine. "Oh, there's every reason to stop." The hand on the small of my back pressed in, drawing me toward him. "But that doesn't mean we will."

I pulled him closer. "But we should."

"Yeah, we probably should." His lips neared mine.

Oh my God, the heat of his body turned me on. "We definitely should."

"In that case..." One hand still on the back of my neck, he tilted his head and leaned in even closer. "Speak now or—"

I kissed him.

There was no slow and gentle this time. We went straight to breathless, desperate, and *fucking hell, I need you so damned bad.* Just as we had in the alley, we stumbled back, struggling to stay upright and get closer to each other at the same time.

I was vaguely aware that we were moving. Not just fighting gravity, but following a more deliberate path now. His body guided mine a step at a time across some undefined expanse of space, but his kiss occupied most of my senses.

My back hit the wall.

A shiver ran up my spine when he dipped his head and kissed beneath my jaw, then down the side of my neck. He flicked his tongue across the hollow of my throat, making me gasp. In a low voice, he said, "I've been wondering about that since you showed up for your audition." His accent was thicker now, his voice dropping to a growl.

"Wondering about what?"

The tip of his tongue made a warm circle just above my collarbone, the stud clicking against his teeth. "What your skin tastes like." He kissed me again, and breathless and desperate didn't even begin to describe it. Everything that had happened in the alley was a platonic peck on the cheek compared to the way we wound each other up now.

His hand slid over the front of my jeans, and I broke the kiss with a sharp release of breath.

"Oh fuck," I murmured.

"We shouldn't be doing this," he whispered, squeezing my cock through my jeans anyway, "but Aaron, I just...I want you so fucking bad right now." He didn't wait for a response before he kissed me. His lips went to my neck while his hands fumbled with my belt buckle and zipper.

Against my throat, Bastian said something in German. His voice was hoarse and guttural, the words sounding like a primal growl. Sharp, hot breaths against my neck punctuated each harsh syllable. Whatever it was he'd said, he could have said it in perfect English and I doubted I would have understood it. My mind couldn't process words, not with the heat of his body so close to mine. He kissed me again, and my back arched off the wall when his fingertips slipped past my jeans and boxers and teased my cock.

Fuck, I wanted him. Needed him. Craved him.

I sucked in a breath through my nose but didn't break the kiss. Couldn't break the kiss. His mouth felt and tasted too damned good. Even when he slowly, gently stroked my cock, even when a shudder ran down my spine and almost knocked my knees out from under me, I just couldn't stop kissing him.

It was only when his touch, his perfect rhythm, drove me almost out of my mind that I finally broke away from his lips and released a soft groan. "Oh God," I breathed as he kissed my neck.

He flicked his tongue across my earlobe. "You're almost there, aren't you?" His chin brushed my neck. "You're right on the edge. I know you are; Christ, I know you are." He stroked faster, and I could barely breathe, barely think, barely suppress the cry that was just seconds away. I was desperate for release but also wanted this to go on and on and on because what he did just felt so fucking good. *Fuck, let me come. Please let me come. No, no, I don't want this to be over, not—God, Bastian, let me come.*

I pulled in a breath and started to release it in the form of a throaty groan, but he cut me off with another kiss. Though there was no one around to hear us, his mouth muffled my voice, reducing it to little more than a whimper.

Just when I was on the edge, just when I was about to completely let go, I sucked in a breath, but the air I inhaled was cool, completely devoid of Bastian's mouth or body heat. Confusion had just nanoseconds to set in, wondering why I couldn't taste him anymore, wondering where he was, before the answer came in the form of his lips around my cock.

"Oh fuck…"

I knew I wouldn't last, not when I was this turned on, but time slowed down. The scales balanced between my earlier impatience and this slow-motion savoring of every fucking second as his lips and hand tightened and released in tandem while his tongue ran along the underside of my cock.

The tip of his tongue swirled around the head of my cock, making my entire body seize. He let his piercing glide across my skin, the gentle touch of the smooth, solid stud knocking the air out of my lungs as if he were slamming his cock into me.

I kept my eyes screwed shut, knowing the second I looked at him, the second I drank in the sight of him so hungrily sucking my cock, I'd lose it.

But I couldn't resist, and just when I looked down, he looked up, and time thrust itself back into motion with an orgasm so intensely violent I couldn't even exhale, let alone cry out.

He stood and kissed me, the taste of my own semen on his tongue making my head spin. I tangled my fingers in his hair, and I breathed him, tasted him, couldn't get enough of him.

It was all over so quickly, with just minutes passing since I'd arrived at the farm, but I was as breathless and spent as if we'd been at it for hours. My hands shook. So did Bastian's as they combed through my hair. We kissed gently, lazily, and I had no doubt we were nowhere near finished tonight.

Especially when he reminded me with a brush of his hips over mine that he was still rock hard.

I reached for his belt buckle, but he caught my wrist.

"Not here," he said.

"What? Why not?"

"Because I don't have any condoms or lube with me."

I shivered. *Oh hell yes.*

Our eyes met. No doubts, no questions. He was fucking me tonight.

"Listen," he whispered. "The rest of the band is probably at my place."

I nodded. "I know. They said they were headed that way. My housemates are probably home, but if we keep it quiet…" I raised my eyebrows.

He grinned. "I'll try my level best." When he kissed me again, the subtlest hint of semen meeting my tongue, I wondered if I stood a chance in hell of being quiet if I had him naked in my bed, in me. Oh God, I wanted him in me.

I broke the kiss, touching my forehead to his and breathing hard against his lips. "My place?"

"Yeah. I'll stop on the way and get"—he paused, licking his lips—"everything. And I'll meet you there. Your place."

I nodded again. "Before we go, though…"

His eyebrows lifted. "Hmm?"

"Just one more kiss."

CHAPTER SEVEN

If I learned one thing about Bastian that night, it was that there was no such thing as just one more kiss. Or more specifically, there was no such thing as just one more *short* kiss. By the time we finally pulled ourselves off each other and made it into the driver's seats of our respective vehicles, a good ten minutes had passed since *"just one more kiss."* A *really* good ten minutes.

Bastian's headlights stayed in my rearview most of the way before he turned off, presumably stopping to get condoms and lube as he'd said he would. I gripped the steering wheel, forcing myself to take slow, deep breaths to keep my anticipation under control. Patience. Patience. We'd be in the same bed soon.

I turned down my street, and my heart nearly stopped.

Oh shit. Lights were on. Cars were in the driveway. Andre's sleek black Mustang. Elena's VW Beetle. Lane's car. Todd and Lillian's cars were probably in the garage. Everyone was here. What the fuck? They were supposed to be at Bastian and Andre's.

No matter. They were here. Whatever the reason, it had to be dealt with. I parked on the curb in my usual spot. Still belted in, I turned off the engine and quickly texted Bastian: *The band's at my place.*

Even after the "message sent" confirmation came up, I stared at the phone. My heart pounded. Another opportunity for him to have second thoughts. And maybe he'd had some anyway. He'd even said it was easier to convince himself this was a bad idea when I wasn't with him, and I wasn't with him now, except maybe as a lingering taste on his tongue.

While I waited for his reply, I went inside and upstairs to where everyone hung out in front of the television. I leaned casually in the threshold between the hallway and living room. The band—with two exceptions, of course—cheered and hollered over some car-racing game along with our housemate and everyone's respective significant others.

"I thought you guys were going to Andre's," I said.

Elena shrugged. "We were, but the guys wanted to play Xbox tonight instead."

"They don't have an Xbox?" I said. My phone beeped, and I pulled it out of my pocket.

"We did, until your brother fucking fried it," Andre muttered.

"That's such crap, and you know it," Todd said.

"I don't know, Todd," I said, surreptitiously pulling up the message, certain Bastian was bailing. "Sounds like something you would do." Whatever he said in response was lost on me because the words on my cell phone's screen sent my pulse soaring: *Then I guess we'll just have to be quiet. Be there in five.*

"You want to play?" she asked.

I shook my head. "Nah, I think I'm going to call it a night."

"We're not going to keep you up, are we?"

"I don't think that'll be a problem."

Lillian looked at me. "Ears ringing again?"

I laughed. "Yeah, par for the course when I've got these guys playing all that noise right behind me."

"Oh whatever," Todd said.

"Yeah, no shit." Andre glanced up from his game. "We have to listen to you caterwauling up there, so—"

"Yeah, fuck you," I said. "All right, all, have fun. I'm going to bed."

On my way down the stairs, I overheard Todd say, "Has Bastian gotten back to you yet?"

"Nope," Andre said. "Went home and went to sleep, knowing him."

"Yeah, probably off to get his beauty sleep," Rochelle said.

Todd laughed. "Well, I suppose at his age, you never can get too much of that."

"Poor old man," Rochelle said, snickering. "Can't stay up late with the kids anymore."

Elena snorted with laughter. "Oh, Jesus, he's not that much older than any one of you."

I just chuckled to myself before I rounded the corner at the bottom of the stairs and could no longer make out their bantering.

I went outside and waited for him by the garage, watching the shadows in the backyard. The laughter and trash talk that came through the upstairs windows made my heart pound, so certain was I that someone would come out onto the back deck at any moment. Even if they did, it was on the second floor, so they might not see us, but I hoped they stayed inside. Hoped Lane or Rochelle could wait to have a cigarette. Hoped no one needed a breath of fresh air. Hoped—

Grass rustled, and a second later, Bastian materialized from the darkness. His gaze darted up toward the deck and the faint light that illuminated him from above. He was just slightly out of breath, making me wonder if he'd sprinted over from wherever he'd parked the truck.

Without a word, I gestured for him to follow me into the garage. We slipped from the garage into the hallway, then into my bedroom, and I carefully closed the door as if anything more than the stealthiest click would alert everyone upstairs that my room contained not one but two people.

I leaned against the closed door.

Our eyes locked. For the space of a few heartbeats, the only sound in this room was the soft, rhythmic squeaking of his jacket while he caught his breath. From just beyond the walls came the murmur of all the people who couldn't know about this. In the back of my mind and the thundering of my heart were all the reasons we couldn't do this.

But in the tense, silent air between us existed all the reasons we *had* to do this.

Never taking his eyes off me, Bastian unzipped his jacket, the slow creak of the zipper reverberating up my spine. With one shrug, he shook it off his shoulders, and he broke eye contact just long enough to watch himself toss the jacket onto the floor with a muffled thud and the faint jingle of car keys.

I pushed myself off the door. With a series of similar, if less steady, motions, I took off my own jacket and let it fall to my feet, my eyes never leaving his.

I swallowed hard.

Bastian swept the tip of his tongue across his lower lip.

The distance between us evaporated. Hands on hips, arms around waists, breath on skin, Jesus Christ, yes, his lips on my neck. I bit back a moan when his stubbled chin brushed just above my collar.

"Still think we shouldn't do this?" I whispered.

"Mm-hmm." He raised his head. "But we're going to." He kissed me, picking up right where we'd left off with that breathless desperation from earlier. My mind went completely blank, and I didn't care. His kiss was amazing beyond words, and that was all I needed to know.

And...bed. The bed. That was where we needed to be.

I nudged him with my hip—*holy fuck, he's hard*—and we took a step. The next step wasn't so steady, both of us stumbling. I thought we might have this kissing and moving thing down, but we tripped over each other's feet and Bastian's jacket. We both grunted in surprise when we went down, tumbling onto his back with me on top. We paused for a startled second, staring at each other. Then we both shrugged and went right back to kissing passionately. Neither of us made any move to get up.

A shirt came off. Another. Frantic, trembling hands fought with belt buckles. Shoes thumped against nearby furniture. Jeans and boxers slid over hips. My heart raced when skin met skin, faster still when his thick, erect cock brushed my own. Bastian rolled me onto my back, and I pulled him down to me, kissing him hungrily and wrapping my arms around him.

The bed was less than a foot away, but this would have to do. Just getting from the farm to here was enough of a wait. I needed him right here, right now.

"Fuck me," I begged, my voice trembling. "God, please, Bastian, please..."

"You'd better believe I'm going to fuck you," he growled. "That's exactly why I'm here." He leaned away to grab his jacket. He fumbled around in one of the pockets. Then he was over me again, condom and a small bottle of lube in hand.

He sat up and tore the wrapper with his teeth. I had to close my eyes as he put the condom on; just the sight of his cock, of his hands on his cock, of him putting a condom on so he could fuck me was too damned much. When the lube bottle clicked, I bit my lip.

Then he was moving. Changing position. One hand came down on the floor beside me. His hips brushed my inner thighs. He guided his cock to me, and the slick coolness of the lube against my skin made my head light.

"Aaron," he whispered. "Look at me."

I opened my eyes, blinking into focus.

He leaned down and kissed me lightly. "I've been wanting to do this since the other night."

Eyes never leaving mine, he pushed into me slowly. His lips parted. So did mine. We both released long, ragged breaths, but neither made a sound until a low growl emerged from the back of his throat. His shoulders quivered—restraint? Holding himself up?—as he slid deeper, and I almost released a groan. I hadn't realized *just* how much I'd craved his cock until now, when he was deep inside me.

And there he stopped. He furrowed his brow and sucked in a breath. Then he leaned down to kiss my neck, and we both gasped when he withdrew slowly.

"Oh God, you feel good," I whispered.

"You feel fucking incredible." His lips touched my skin as he spoke. "Tell me how you want it. Fast, slow, whatever you—"

A door closed overhead, startling us both. Feet thumped across the ceiling, voices vibrating through the floor.

In spite of the intrusion, of the oblivious murmur of bandmates and housemates minding their own business, Bastian didn't miss a beat. He didn't pick up speed, continuing to take long, smooth strokes, but he didn't stop.

"Tell me," he whispered. "I want to know—"

"Bastian, they're—"

"Shh." He kissed the underside of my jaw and pushed into me so deliciously slow. "No one can see us. No one can hear us." His voice was low, soft, and still I prayed the doors and walls kept the words from leaving our private little world. "No one can hear, and I can't stop until I come inside you."

I shivered. "Jesus…"

"Tell me," he said. "However you want it, Aaron, I want to—" A gasp interrupted his speech, and a tremor rippled through him. "Do you want—"

"Just like this. Just the way you're doing it."

"Like this?" he whispered, pushing as deep as he could before withdrawing slowly. I nodded, suppressing a groan. He bent and pressed his lips to my collarbone, and just as a low growl vibrated against my skin, he buried his face against my neck. I couldn't tell if he did it to stifle his voice or just to kiss me, but either way, the sound was muted and the touch of his lips gave me goose bumps.

I bit my own lip, trying to keep quiet, but he felt so good, so damned good, so unbelievably good, I was rapidly approaching the point of not caring. I thought nothing could ever feel more incredible than the mind-blowing orgasm he'd given me earlier, but with each stroke he took inside me now, I knew I was wrong, that that had been only the beginning, that he was fucking me straight into a level of ecstasy I couldn't yet begin to fathom.

There was sex.

There was hot sex.

And there was sex with Bastian. On my bedroom floor, impossibly silent, too desperate to move except when moving meant getting closer and deeper, sex with Bastian fucking Koehler. To hell with all the reasons this wasn't a good idea.

"Oh God," he groaned, his voice barely audible. "Oh God, I'm—" His body tensed, trembled, his fingers twitching on my shoulders. I grabbed onto the bed frame, thankful it didn't make a sound as I used it for leverage to rock my hips in time with his thrusts. The carpet burned my back and shoulders, especially my lower back, but I didn't care, not when another low moan emerged from the back of Bastian's throat, just loud enough for me—no one else in the world—to hear.

Throwing his head back, he moaned, "Oh God, oh God, oh God..." His voice caught. He sucked in a breath, and momentary panic swept through me, worried he'd forget himself and let out a roar, but when he slammed himself deep inside me, he just released a sharp huff of breath through his nose, held my hips to his and shuddered once, twice, again.

Eventually the shaking tapered off and his breath came back. Then he pulled out slowly and raised his head to kiss me gently.

"I don't know how the fuck I'm supposed to stay quiet when I'm fucking you," he murmured.

"Hell if I know." I ran my fingers through his sweat-dampened hair. "But I—*oh God.*" He stroked my cock and leaned down to kiss me again. I closed my eyes and tried to remember how to breathe.

"Like that?" he whispered.

I swallowed hard. "You really want everyone to hear this, don't you?"

"Absolutely not," he said. "Trying to stay quiet isn't easy, but it just makes things that much hotter." He didn't give me a chance to reply before he kissed me. Faster and faster he stroked my cock until his kiss was the only thing standing between us and a cry that would have drawn the whole neighborhood's attention.

But then his hand slowed. Slower still. Almost stopped.

"What I really want," he whispered, pausing to kiss me again, "is for you to fuck me."

God, whatever I did to deserve this, I am so not worthy.

We both sat up to take care of condoms—his off, mine on—and change positions. I reached for the lube, but he beat me to it.

"Here," he said with a grin as he poured some into his palm. "Why don't I give you a hand with that?" Before I could respond, he stroked the lube onto my cock, drawing a low groan from my lips.

"Fuck," I breathed. "Let me…let…" Judging by the way he squeezed, released, squeezed, released, he knew exactly what he was doing, the teasing bastard.

"Hmm," he murmured, kissing me lightly, "not quite enough lube yet." He put on a little more, and there was next to no friction at all with his tighter-looser-tighter strokes. Much more of that and—

I caught his wrist. "Get on your knees. *Now.*"

He grinned again. "Just promise me one thing."

"Hmm?"

His voice dropped to a growl, and like never before, his accent made my mouth water. "You'll fuck me good and hard."

"Only one way to find out." My voice was surprisingly steady. "Turn around."

He licked his lips, then did as I asked. Once he was on his hands and knees, I guided myself to him.

Then, through the delirium of *want, want, want*, I remembered he'd recently broken up with someone. With a woman. After several years.

"Bastian, how long has it been?" I asked, pushing against him but only giving him a little. "Since you've done this?"

Over his shoulder, he murmured, "Too damned long."

I chewed my lip. "Should I go slow, then?"

He shook his head, whispering something that sounded like, "No, I'm fine."

Caution prevailed, though. I gave him a little. Withdrew. A little more.

Bastian shivered. "Fuck me, Aaron," he said over his shoulder, his voice just soft enough for discretion but still with an undercurrent of undeniable need.

"I am," I teased, sliding a fraction of an inch deeper. "I'm just—"

Without warning, Bastian slammed back against me, and in a heartbeat, my vision went white and I was all the way inside him. I gripped his hips, holding him to me and hoping anyone upstairs interpreted my startled grunt as a cough or something equally benign.

Bastian moaned softly, letting his head fall forward. "Fuck…"

"You okay?" I asked.

He nodded.

"You sure?"

Another nod. "God*damn* it, you feel good."

Relief rushed through me. Though he was the one who'd made the move, I was sure I'd hurt him. Holding his hips to steady us both, I pulled out slowly. After a few slow, easy strokes, I picked up speed, fucking him hard and fast, all the while disbelieving I was inside him, fucking him, fucking *Bastian*. This had to be a dream. It had to be.

Oh well, if it was, it was a damned good one, and I'd enjoy the hell out of it.

With every thrust propelling me closer to a powerful orgasm and nothing to keep me quiet, I screwed my eyes shut and held his hip with one hand while I brought my other hand up and dug my teeth into my second knuckle, praying for both restraint and release.

Distant laughter faintly registered in my senses, emphasizing that people were dangerously close by, reminding me that we were a careless moan away from discovery. In that instant, I realized Bastian was right, and the secrecy, the need to stay absolutely and impossibly silent, sent a shudder of pure lust straight up my spine, and I came with a breathless whimper.

I slumped over him, resting my head between his shoulders. My knees burned from the carpet beneath them, just as my back stung from earlier. A little pain, a hell of a lot of pleasure. Seemed like a fair trade to me. And at least that meant I hadn't been dreaming. This was real. Bastian and I had really had sex on my bedroom floor, and it was amazing.

When I stopped shaking enough to hold myself up, I pulled out and got rid of the condom. Then we finally made it into my bed. For the longest time, we didn't move or speak. I rested my head on his shoulder, he stroked my hair, and we caught our breath.

After a while he turned on his side, and I faced him.

He kissed my neck. "*That* was hot."

"It was." I trailed my fingertips up and down his arm. "And it was definitely not what I expected tonight."

He chuckled. "I didn't either. But I have to admit, I was hoping."

"Oh really?"

"Of course." He kissed beneath my jaw. "I've been wanting you since the other night and haven't been able to do a damned thing to take the edge off."

"So I'm not the only one."

"Absolutely not." He kissed my neck again.

"I hoped this would happen," I said, "but didn't think there was a snowball's chance in hell. Especially since I could have sworn you were straight."

He laughed, trailing his fingers down the side of my neck. "One of my deep, dark, dirty secrets, Aaron. I'm actually a rampant, relentless, insatiable"—he leaned down to kiss just below my ear—"bisexual."

I shivered at the touch of his lips. "I never would have guessed."

"I've gotten pretty good at keeping it quiet."

"Speaking of keeping things quiet." I looked up at the ceiling. Everyone still carried on, oblivious to us.

Bastian sighed. "We will definitely have to keep this quiet." He looked at me. "Assuming we…keep doing this."

"Think we should?"

"Of course not." He kissed me. "But I want to."

"So we just keep sneaking around, fucking whenever we can, and hope no one finds out?"

"Got any better ideas?"

"Nope."

He trailed his fingertips up the center of my chest. "It'll be easier once one of us moves out of our brother's places, but this will have to do for now."

I put my arms around him. "Then I guess we'll just have to make do with it, won't we?"

He pulled me closer, and just before our lips met, he whispered, "I think we'll manage."

L.A. WITT

CHAPTER EIGHT

Schadenfreude was notorious for back-to-back-to-back gigs, and last night had been the second in a three-show stretch. Less than twenty-four hours after we'd finally broken the tension in the alley, I returned to the scene of the crime. Walking across the alley from the parking lot, I shivered, trying not to think about everything that had happened here last night. There would be time to think of all that later.

In my bed. In his arms. I shivered again. *Breathe, Aaron.*

Forcing myself to think about the music and all of that other professional crap, I went inside and joined the band backstage. Bastian hadn't yet arrived, but a new face caught my eye. Todd called me over and gestured at the stranger.

"Rob, this is my brother, Aaron," Todd said.

"I've been hearing great things about you," the new guy said. "Rob Stillman. I'm Schadenfreude's manager." He gave me a firm handshake. "And judging by what I heard about last night, I'm wondering what your brother was thinking keeping you a secret from us."

"Last night?" I gulped. *The concert, idiot.* "I mean, um, what did you hear?"

"Well, unfortunately I couldn't be at the last couple of shows myself," he said. "But some rather important people were. And they liked what they heard."

"Check out this review." Todd held up a piece of paper, then read from it. "'With a new lead singer at the helm, local band Schadenfreude is better than ever, and I predict they'll be a force to be reckoned with now. Singing must be in those McClure genes, because newcomer Aaron McClure is easily sister Elena's equal. The tone quality of a classically trained musician, the kind of full, powerful sound that could as easily be found in an opera house as a stadium packed with thousands of rock fans. The only question is, where have the McClures been hiding this talent, and are there more siblings we don't yet know about? Five out of five stars.'"

"Here's another one." Elena approached, holding another piece of paper. "'This band has always been strong as a whole, and now that they've parted ways with the lackluster lead singer who's held them back for the last several years, Schadenfreude is unstoppable. They've found the missing piece. Four and a half stars.'"

Rob clapped my shoulder. "You're a hit, kid."

"Thanks." I smiled.

Rob and Todd went on about some details for the next show, but my mind was elsewhere. The knot in my stomach was wound tighter than it had been before last night's show, and it had nothing to do with the music.

Just a couple of hours to go before I could touch Bastian again. All we had to do was make it through this performance and get back to my place. Or his. Or a backseat somewhere. I didn't care.

At the same time, I wondered if a few hours and a little bit of distance had given Bastian a chance to think about this rationally. Everything last night had happened in the heat of the moment. Not a lot of thinking, just a hell of a lot of doing. It was easy to forget all the reasons this could be a bad idea or complicate things because it was impossible to think about anything but each other.

But the morning sun often had a funny way of bringing uncomfortable truths to light. For all I knew, Bastian had done some thinking and realized this wasn't such a good idea.

It wasn't a good idea. That much I knew from experience, but hell if I could help myself.

My entire body still ached from everything he'd done to me last night. When I'd looked in the mirror this morning, it hadn't surprised me in the least to see a few bruises here and there. Everything about this, from his hungry kiss to the desperate, insatiable way he'd fucked me, was perfect. Everything.

Everything except the very fact we'd slept together, that is. There were so many reasons why this could blow up in our faces, but it was just too damned right to be wrong.

Voices from down the hall raised the hairs on the back of my neck. I swallowed hard, steeling myself against his presence. Part of me worried he'd call it off. Part of me worried I'd burst into flames as soon as we were in the same room.

Footsteps approached. The murmur of voices became more distinct, became a conversation in German, and as that conversation came through the door, no longer separated from me by walls or distance, I turned around.

Our eyes instantly met from across the room. My knees almost buckled. His expression spoke loud and clear. If his eyes were to be believed, the last thing on his mind was calling tonight off.

Breathe, Aaron, breathe.

For a moment, I was afraid everyone else in the room felt the electricity in the air as acutely as I did, but no one seemed to notice. Rob and Todd continued their conversation. Rochelle and Elena were preoccupied with some sound equipment. Andre kept talking to Bastian in German.

No one felt it, but I could think of nothing else.

"All right, now that everyone's here," Rob said. "I've got an announcement."

"Elena's having your kid?" Bastian said, ducking when Todd tried to cuff him upside the head.

"Aaron *is* your kid?" Andre said.

"Yeah, yeah, something like that." Rob rolled his eyes and flipped the brothers off. "Anyway, in more professional news, we're going to the Midstate Amphitheater for the Battle of the Bands in August. Win this one, and you're in for three performances at the End of Summer Rock-out."

"Fuck, yes!" Bastian said. The other guys high-fived.

Elena leaned toward me. "We've been trying to get into that Battle for three years. It's competitive as fuck just to get in."

"Think we have a chance at winning?" I asked.

She grinned. "With you singing? Oh hell yeah."

"So no pressure?"

"Nope, none."

"This is big, guys. Really big," Rob said. "The Rock-out will be fucking crawling with scouts, and we've already got the attention of a few record agents. Win the Battle, get into the Rock-out, and this could be the gig that lands you a deal."

"Guess we shouldn't fuck it up, then?" Todd said.

"No, please don't fuck it up." Rob craned his neck slightly, looking past us. We all turned. One of the club employees leaned in the doorway.

"Sound check in five," he said.

"Well, that's your cue," Rob said. "Knock 'em dead, guys."

* * * * *

Sharing a stage with Bastian during sound check was torture, and the performance itself turned out to be the most agonizing exercise in self-control I had ever endured. It would have helped if I'd resisted stealing a glance at him every chance I had, but I didn't, and everything Bastian did, every subtle little nuance that no one else would have noticed, drove me crazy.

His hand sliding up the neck of the bass.

His nimble fingers turning the knobs on the amp and expertly manipulating strings.

The way his hips moved when he played. Just like they did on the dance floor. Just like they had last night when he'd fucked me with that silent, violent desperation.

The occasional glint of silver when he spoke or sang backup made my mouth water. I struggled to breathe just remembering the way the piercing brushed against my tongue when he kissed me. Or, my God, when he'd teased my cock with it.

Mercifully, when I sang, my back was turned to him. At least then my only reminder of him was each deep, thrumming beat of the bass line reverberating through my body.

A particularly powerful riff sent a shiver up my spine, and I stumbled over a lyric but recovered quickly. A beat later, one of his notes didn't quite ring true, like his finger had missed the string or hadn't struck it quite right. During another song, later in the set, it happened again. Somehow, knowing he was probably just as distracted did nothing to help me focus.

We made it through the show, though. On the way offstage afterward, we exchanged the briefest look, and I almost tripped over my own feet.

He caught my arm, laughing quietly. "Learning to walk, are we?"

I laughed. "Shut up."

We looked at each other again and kept walking.

While we all decompressed backstage, Andre put his arm around Rochelle's waist and said, "You guys are all staying for Rochelle's birthday, right?"

Shit. I'd forgotten all about that.

"*Another* birthday?" Todd said. "Damn, woman, don't they stop letting you have them after a while?"

"Shut up, McClure." Rochelle laughed. "You've had more than I have."

"She's got you there, Todd," Bastian said.

"Okay, okay," Todd said. "Hell yeah, we're all staying. Aren't we?" He shot the rest of us a look.

"I'm staying," I said. *Can't promise I won't drag Bastian downstairs for a few minutes, though.*

Bastian rolled his eyes and sighed melodramatically. "I guess I could be persuaded to stay for a little while."

"Would a threat of bodily harm be enough to persuade you?" Rochelle gestured menacingly with Andre's drumsticks.

Bastian laughed. "Like you could catch me."

"I can outrun you."

"I can run faster scared than you can angry."

"Pussy." Andre clicked his tongue. "You'd run away from a girl?"

Bastian put his hands up. "Hey, she's a mean girl. You'd run from her too."

"And don't you forget it." Rochelle shot him a playful glare.

"I won't, I won't." Bastian pretended to cringe. "Just don't hurt me. I'll stay, I swear." He gave me an apologetic shrug and a devilish look. *Just wait until we get out of here*, that look said.

I shivered. Wait until we get out of here, indeed.

After instruments were secured, we moved from the backstage area into the crowded club. Getting to the bar was a challenge as clubgoers occasionally stopped us for autographs and conversation. Though Schadenfreude wasn't a signed band, they'd been a wildly popular local band for some time and had attracted their fair share of fans. Groupies, even.

Eventually we made it past our adoring public to the bar to start the liquid portion of Rochelle's birthday celebration.

"What's the poison tonight, Chelle?" Andre asked over the music.

"Tequila all around," Rochelle said. "Assuming y'all are man enough to shoot Cuervo."

"Ugh, why is it always tequila with you?" Todd groaned. "I think I'm still hungover from your *last* birthday."

Rochelle elbowed him. "Because it's fun to watch you suffer."

"Tequila it is." Andre laughed. To the bartender, he said, "Six shots, Cuervo Gold."

"Make it five," Bastian said. "I'm driving home, better stick to something that won't rot my brain quite as much."

"Fine," Andre said. "Five shots of Cuervo Gold, one sippy cup of water for the wuss."

"Fuck you." Bastian laughed. He flipped Andre off and ordered himself a beer.

We slid into the VIP booth Andre had reserved earlier in the evening so we wouldn't have to scour the packed club for a place to sit. We laughed, drank, and carried on, a steady stream of fans wandering by the table for autographs and photos.

"Doesn't seem like as many people want pictures tonight," Todd shouted over the music.

Bastian laughed as he set his beer down. "Maybe if you'd take a shower and shave—" He grunted when Todd elbowed him in the ribs.

"He's got a point, Todd," Elena said, giggling from the safety of the other side of the table.

Todd scowled. "Chelle, she's too far away from me. Would you mind smacking her for me?"

Rochelle snorted. "I'm not doing your dirty work, McClure."

"Well, I could kick her," Todd said, his eyes narrowing while a laugh tugged at the corner of his mouth. "But I'd run the risk of kicking you instead."

"Then I would suggest you come up with a different strategy," Rochelle said. "Because if you kick me, you're going to be playing your guitar from a hospital bed for a while."

Todd started to speak, but a fan came up to the table just then, so he snapped his mouth shut. The fan, a girl in her early twenties from the looks of it, turned a bit red as the entire band looked her way.

"Hi, um," she said, glancing off to one side as if looking for reassurance from some unseen third party. Evidently finding the courage she needed, she looked back at the band. "I wanted to see if Aaron would, um... Do you want to dance?"

My eyes widened. I glanced at Bastian, hoping Todd thought I was looking his way.

"Well, that depends," Todd said, cocking his head and stroking his chin with his thumb and forefinger as if playing with a phantom beard. "What kind of dowry are you offering?"

The fan looked mortified, as if she wasn't sure whether or not to take Todd seriously.

"A dowry?" I rolled my eyes. "Shut up, Todd." To the girl, I said, "Sure, I'll—" I paused, glancing at Bastian again. His lips tightened into a grin, and he gave me an almost imperceptible nod. I nudged Rochelle. "Get out of the way."

Rochelle scoffed. "You know, a simple 'excuse me' would suffice."

"I know," I said. "But 'get out of the way' is more my style."

"Asshole," Rochelle muttered, laughing as she scooted out of the booth to let me out.

On the way to the dance floor, the fan slid her arm around my waist. "I hope this wasn't too forward," she said, leaning toward me so I could hear her over the music.

"Not at all." I smiled. "I didn't catch your name, though."

"Emily."

"Nice to meet you. I guess you already know my name, don't you?"

She blushed. "Yeah, I do." We exchanged smiles, and that seemed to relax her a little.

By the time we got to the dance floor, it was too loud to talk, so we didn't bother. Emily put her hands on my hips, and we danced to the beat of some earsplitting excuse for a cover of a song I recognized but couldn't name. The floor was crowded, so we moved closer together, close enough I could smell the perfume and alcohol on her. The latter was probably a little liquid courage to go along with the prodding from her friends, a group of girls who laughed and squealed as they watched us from the sidelines.

Apparently either the booze or the girls gave her some more courage, because she slid her hand down and squeezed my ass.

Startled, I looked at her, and her cheeks got a little darker.

"Sorry." She giggled.

I laughed. "It's okay."

She smiled, and we continued dancing. I glanced over her shoulder and met Bastian's eyes. He was watching us, lips parted and beer tilted as if he had been about to take a drink but forgot about the bottle in his hand. Bastian shifted in his seat. Nothing about his expression or body language suggested he was jealous or otherwise put off. *Why Bastian, if I didn't know any better, I might think this was turning you on.*

I let my hands run up Emily's sides, mimicking the way I'd held on to him when we'd fucked, and Bastian remembered his beer just in time to keep from dropping it. He swallowed hard, looking away and coughing into his fist.

Busted. A shiver ran up my spine.

I held his gaze from across the room. Judging by the ripple that went down the front of his throat and the way his tongue darted across his lower lip, he was imagining the same thing I was: that the hands on my body were his, not Emily's.

Bastian picked up his beer, taking a long swallow but not once shifting his eyes away from us. From *me*. When he put the bottle down, he held it in both hands as if trying to keep himself cool. The intensity of his gaze turned my knees to water.

Time to get the hell out of here before we burn the place down. I turned my attention back to Emily, and when the song was over, I politely bowed out of an offer for another dance or a drink. Emily kissed me on the cheek before she walked away to her screaming friends.

On my way back to the booth, I realized Bastian was gone. Before I had a chance to feel a pang of disappointment, I realized where he was: on his way to the dance floor.

With his arm around a leggy blonde in a halter top.

He met my eyes. When we passed each other in the dense crowd, he surreptitiously grabbed my ass. We glanced over our shoulders and he winked. I smiled and kept walking.

"She was cute." Rochelle got up to let me back into the booth. "Did you get her number?"

"Of course," I lied. I nodded toward Bastian. "So is it 'dance with Schadenfreude' night again?"

Rochelle laughed. "Not that I know of. Don't know what's gotten into him lately, though." She gestured at Bastian with her glass. "That man *never* dances. Especially not with a stranger."

Todd looked around. "Batshit von Crazy Pants isn't here, is she?"

Elena craned her neck. "I don't see her."

"Maybe he just wants to dance," Rochelle said with a shrug.

"Guess he's full of surprises, isn't he?" I met Bastian's eyes from across the room as his hands snaked around the blonde's waist and he kissed the side of her neck, raising the hairs on the back of mine. He said something to her, and I swore I felt the vibration of his voice against my skin. I squirmed in my seat. *Trust me, Chelle. He's not dancing with a stranger.*

He threw surreptitious glances in my direction, every fleeting look we exchanged flying under the radar of the rest of the band. Every second of eye contact sent ripples of electricity right to all the nerve endings that tingled at his phantom touch. He ran a finger up the center of her back, and it was all I could do not to give myself away with a violent, spine-straightening shiver.

Much more of that and I might have had to fuck him right there on the dance floor.

They turned to one side, and I caught sight of his cell phone peeking out of his pocket. I couldn't help grinning to myself. *Is that opportunity I hear knocking?*

I pulled my phone out of my pocket.

"You're not making a call in here, are you?" Todd shouted over the music.

"No, Einstein. I'm just replying to a text." I thumbed a message into my phone and sent it. Then I watched. *Please have your phone on vibrate. Please have your phone on vibrate.*

Bastian's phone lit up, and he glanced down. Then he looked at me. I grinned and put my phone down. He swallowed.

"You know," I said. "It's getting late, so I think I'm going to call it a night. I've got an early morning tomorrow."

"How are you getting home?" Elena asked, raising an eyebrow.

"I'm going to do a few more tequila shots and then drive home." I rolled my eyes. "Come on, sis, you know me better than that. I'm taking a cab."

She nodded with approval. "Okay then."

I wished Rochelle a happy birthday, then shouldered my way through the crowd. I hurried backstage, down the hall, and out into the alley. The alley and parking lot were both empty, thankfully, but I leaned against my own car just in case a bandmate came out. Alcohol in my system or not, I didn't want to explain to one of them why I was waiting near Bastian's car.

It was a warm night, but I shivered anyway. I tapped my foot rapidly on the pavement, just trying to release some of the tension. Then I paced. Then leaned on the car and tapped my foot. Paced. Leaned.

Come on, Bastian. Come on. I wasn't sure how long it had been since I'd sent the message, but guessed it was at least fifteen or twenty minutes. Knowing Bastian, he was trying to make a subtle escape, to keep the rest of the band from guessing we were leaving together.

The parking lot was mostly deserted but for a few employees on their way home or club-goers wandering down the alley to another watering hole. For the most part, it was silent. Every time the door opened or a new cadence of footsteps joined the mix, my heart quickened.

Taking a few deep breaths, I tried to calm myself, but every time I closed my eyes, I saw Bastian on the dance floor with the blonde. Moistening my lips, I shuddered, imagining his hands had been drifting up *my* sides. His hand had been on *my* stomach, pulling *me* up against what I was certain was a rock-hard cock. His lips had been against *my* neck. The thought made me shiver.

The door opened as it had dozens of times, letting the noise from inside spill out into the night before slamming closed and cutting off the sound. This time, the new footsteps were sharp. Hurried.

My eyes flew open, and I sucked in a breath when I met Bastian's eyes. It was all I could do not to meet him halfway, but I resisted. There were still people around, plus the possibility of a band member coming out of the club at an inopportune moment. It was enough of a risk just being spotted leaving together; I didn't dare do anything more than that here again.

"I left as quick as I could," he said as soon as he was within earshot. Closer now and quieter, he added, "Didn't want them to think we were leaving together."

"I know." I smiled.

"That and I was trying to reassure the girl I was dancing with that I really wasn't trying to get into her pants."

"Well, I can't blame her for thinking you were," I said.

He grinned. "Hey, she was dishing out as much as she was getting. I think she kind of freaked when I said we should move off the dance floor. Thought I was going to try to pick her up. Little did she know…" He winked. "My sights were set elsewhere."

The shivering turned into full-blown shaking, and I clenched my jaw to keep my teeth from chattering.

Unlocking the truck doors with the remote, he looked at me and cocked his head. "You okay? Cold?"

"Nope, I'm not cold." I hugged myself anyway.

"Then why are you shivering?" he asked as we both got into the truck.

Sliding into the passenger seat, I said, "Because I'm hot."

His lips parted, and it was his turn to shiver. I fastened my seat belt, then reached across and put my hand on his thigh. He jumped, almost dropping his keys.

"What's wrong?" I grinned. "Jumpy?"

He laughed and turned the key in the ignition. "You could say that."

"Good." I winked at him.

Neither of us spoke as he pulled out of the parking lot and headed down the street. Chewing his lip, he white-knuckled the steering wheel with both hands. *I know the feeling, Bastian.*

A green light turned yellow up ahead, and I wanted to scream with frustration. We were too far away to try to make it, so Bastian slowed down as the light changed to red. The car came to a gentle, maddening stop.

"Thank God," Bastian growled. "I thought they'd all stay green."

Puzzled, I looked at him and started to speak, but he pulled me close and kissed me. His hand went into my hair, and his tongue parted my lips, exploring my mouth quickly and desperately.

A horn honked, and Bastian broke away, slamming on the gas and waving an apology to the car behind us. My heart raced, and my mouth watered for more.

"Christ, that didn't help at all, did it?" Bastian whispered. He sounded breathless.

"What do you mean?"

"I mean now I'm even hornier than I was before the light changed." His hand slid over my thigh, making my pulse jump.

"That makes two of us." We exchanged a quick glance in the low light, and the smoldering look in his eyes took my breath away.

Bastian turned his attention back to the road, and I couldn't help noticing the whine of the engine when he pushed down just a little harder on the accelerator.

CHAPTER NINE

Just like he had last night, Bastian parked a few streets over in case anyone came home who might recognize his truck. Neither of us said a word on the short walk from the truck to my house.

The house was dark. The driveway was deserted.

I led him around to the side door of the garage. As I fumbled with my keys, he stood behind me and trailed his fingers down my sides. Pulling my hips against him, he kissed the back of my neck. I stiffened, taking in a sharp breath. It was impossible to say what distracted me more, his hard cock pressing against me or his lips on my neck, but suddenly the simple task of unlocking my door was like disarming a nuclear weapon.

His hand left my hip and grasped my elbow before sliding down my forearm to my hand.

"Here," he said, his breath whispering across my neck. "Let me." He covered my hand with his and closed his fingers around it. His other hand snaked around to my stomach and pulled me closer to him, kissing the side of my neck as he—we—turned the key.

After the door had clicked shut behind us, he made no move to let me go. He pushed me up against the door, kissing my neck and pressing his hips against mine. The familiar garage smells—motor oil, dust, God only knew what else—took a backseat to Bastian's leather jacket and his mouthwatering, masculine scent, and my head got lighter with every breath of him. He raised his head and kissed me, liquefying my spine and my knees with the slow, controlled way his lips and pierced tongue took command of my mouth.

I wanted to beg him to let me go long enough for us to get from here to my bedroom, but break this kiss? Not a chance. Speech would probably have been lost on me anyway. Just the fact that we were breathing the same intimate air again—even if it was stagnant, car-scented air—turned me on beyond reason.

One hand slid over the front of my jeans. Though his every move was slow and his every touch almost painfully gentle, his sharp, unsteady breaths belied his calm, controlled exterior. When his trembling fingers ran up the side of my neck, they gave away the hunger beneath the surface.

I held on to his jacket and forced myself to break the kiss long enough to whisper, "Bedroom. Now."

"Right." He took a breath. "Bedroom. We—" His mouth was against mine again, and that calm, controlled exterior fell apart a little at a time. More when I ran my fingers through his hair. Still more when I pushed us off the door and forced him back a step. After a second of hesitation, he took over and stepped back himself, pulling me with him. I had visions of us tumbling onto the concrete floor like we'd fallen onto the carpet of my bedroom the first time. I was all for lying wherever we fell, but I had my limits.

Calling on every ounce of restraint I still possessed, which wasn't much, I held the front of his jacket and separated us.

"Come on." I paused to lick my lips. *Oh, God, I can still taste him.* "Bedroom, before we end up fucking in here."

Bastian nodded, and we separated completely. Tripping over our own feet was marginally safer than tripping over each other's, and we made it through the dark garage, down the hall, and to my bedroom. The second we stepped into my room, he kicked the door shut and caught me by the arm, stopping both of us so suddenly we nearly tumbled to the floor again. He steadied us, turning me around and slamming me up against the door just as he had in the garage, but this time kissing me so hard it was painful.

I couldn't decide if I wanted to shove his jacket over his shoulders and out of the way or grab it and use it to pull him closer to me. Fortunately he made it a moot point, dropping his jacket with a single, sharp shrug. When he kicked it away from our feet, his hips moved slightly and his cock brushed against mine.

"Oh fuck," I whispered.

"Like that?" He put his hands on my hips and pulled me against his rock-hard erection.

"Yes, I fucking do," I said just before he kissed me again. We moved away from the door frame, inching toward the bed, and struggled to strip each other without breaking the hungry, breathless kiss.

I tugged at his shirt, and he pulled away just long enough to take it off. When he put his arms around me again, he slipped his hands beneath my shirt and pushed it up over my head. My shirt hadn't even hit the floor before Bastian's lips were on my neck, the coarse brush of his jaw making me shiver. His hands ran up and down my back as he kissed my neck, my collarbone, my shoulder, then my neck again. Inhaling deeply through his nose, it was his turn to shiver just before his hot breath warmed my skin.

Clothes were replaceable. Neither of us flinched when a seam ripped or a button snapped off. All that mattered was getting this damned fabric out of the way.

Even breathing was optional. It made perfect sense to forego air for Bastian's deep, passionate kisses. My head spun anyway, so it didn't matter if it was from lack of oxygen or from the way his mouth tasted. Besides, there was plenty of time to breathe whenever he stopped to kiss my neck, and holy fuck, he loved doing that.

He stepped back, tugging my belt to pull me with him, but then he paused.

"Wait," he whispered, looking down at me. "My God, Aaron, you're..." He ran his hands up my sides, staring at me, his lips parted as if in disbelief.

I realized this was the first time we'd slowed down enough to stop and look at each other, *really* look at each other, and just as I apparently mesmerized him, he mesmerized me. I trailed my fingertips up his ripped abs and across his broad chest, tracing the edges of his tattoos—a serpent coiled around his left upper arm, a pattern of abstract knot work around the other. I couldn't find the words to tell him how incredibly sexy he was, but when I met his eyes, words were unnecessary.

Still gripping my belt, he pulled me back to him, and we kissed like never before. I pushed him backward, and after a little stumbling and tripping, we fell into bed together. As much as I wanted to get the rest of his clothes off, both of our hands strayed from his belt and zipper, instead combing through each other's hair, tracing angles and contours. Touching. I didn't want anything between our bodies, but getting clothes out of the way meant taking my hands off him, and we couldn't stop touching each other.

His fingertips trailed down my back, leaving goose bumps in their wake. He broke the kiss with a gasp when I let my hand drift over his cock. He tried to kiss me again, but just before his tongue met mine, I squeezed him gently through the denim, and the shudder that ran through his body made him throw his head back with a throaty groan.

Finally he found my lips again, kissing me deeply.

I slid my hands under his jeans and boxers and pushed both of them over his hips. The warmth of his skin beneath my palms made me draw a sharp breath through my nose, but my lips never left his. Even as I gently stroked his cock, we didn't break the kiss this time. Wouldn't. *Couldn't.*

Arching my back beneath us, I pressed my body against his. I slid my free hand around to the back of his neck and pulled him closer, moaning into his kiss.

Somewhere in my mind, I was aware of the need to have him inside me, to feel him come, to seek my own release, but the need for an orgasm barely registered over the need to feel him. The need to *breathe* him.

He rolled onto his back and brought me with him. We separated long enough to get his jeans and boxers the rest of the way off. Before his clothes had even hit the floor, I was over him again, and he drew me into another kiss, as if he was desperate to taste my mouth again, like I'd been away for hours instead of mere seconds.

He started to put his arms around me, but I caught his wrists and gently pinned them beside his head. His gaze flicked toward my hand, then met my eyes.

"I've been waiting all damned night to fuck you," he whispered. "If I don't—" He sucked in a breath, screwing his eyes shut and growling when I held his wrists tighter. "Fucking hell, Aaron…"

I kissed him again, and his quiet, frustrated whimper made me that much harder. The only thing stronger than my need for his cock was his desperate need to give it to me, and though teasing him meant denying myself, that was a price I was willing to pay.

I bent and kissed his neck, deliberately letting my stubble graze his skin like his had mine, and his wrists twitched in my hands as he curled his fingers into tight fists.

"Let me fuck you," he pleaded. "Please. Please, I can't wait." A hot, ragged breath warmed the side of my neck.

I flicked my tongue just below his ear, grinning to myself when he whispered curses in both English and German. Trailing lingering kisses down his neck and the center of his chest, I watched his face. Every time his lips pulled into a grimace of frustration and arousal, every time he closed his eyes and exhaled, I had to resist the urge to grab a condom and beg him to fuck me like I knew he wanted to. The temptation was almost too much, but I loved taking it this slow when he was this wound up. It took everything I had to restrain myself, but it was worth it. *Well* worth it.

"Tease," he growled.

"Yeah, and?" I laughed. "What's your hurry?"

"Oh fuck," he breathed. "Aaron, I can't—" When I ran my tongue around his nipple, he gasped and his entire body jerked as if I'd shocked him.

"What?" I said. "You okay?"

"Oh my God, yes," he said. "I've just never…" He moistened his lips. "No one's ever done that."

"You're kidding." I did it again, making a slow circle with my tongue around his nipple.

"Holy—" He gasped. "That is absolutely…" He trailed off when I gently held his nipple between my teeth and teased it with my tongue. Groaning softly, his arched back sank to the bed when I moved to his other nipple.

He swore and trembled and struggled just to breathe, and I couldn't wait anymore. There was only so long I could resist him when he was like this. I had to have him right now.

I came up to kiss him, and as soon as I released his wrists, he threw his arms around me and hauled me down to him. Whatever control he'd tried to convey earlier, he abandoned. His kiss was made of violent desperation, as was the way his fingers gripped my hair, my shoulders, the back of my neck, anything they could grab on to. Oh fuck, he was amazing like this. If he was hot to begin with, there were no words to describe the way this man came alive in bed.

When our lips finally broke contact long enough for me to speak, it was my turn to beg. "Fuck me. Please." I half expected him to deny me just for a little turnabout, but he didn't.

"Thought you'd never ask." He kissed me and rolled me onto my back. Then he leaned away and grabbed a condom from the nightstand while I got out of the last of my clothes.

The sound of tearing foil made me tremble with anticipation. The lube bottle clicked open, then closed, and I almost lost my mind watching him. Hands that had been so rock steady on the strings of his bass now shook, barely able to manipulate the condom or the lube bottle. I couldn't decide which of us was more wound up.

Either way, there was only one way we were going to calm down anytime soon, and the minute Bastian had the condom and lube on, I got up on my knees. He knelt behind me, running his hand over my back and hips.

"This is all I've been able to think about all day," he whispered, pressing his cock against me. "All. Fucking. Day." He pushed a little harder. We both gasped when the head of his cock slid inside me. Christ, he felt good, and could only moan, closing my eyes as he slowly moved deeper. Sheets bunched between my fingers as my hands curled into loose fists and a shudder rippled up my spine.

"Like that?" He sounded breathless.

I nodded, that simple motion requiring every last bit of concentration I could muster. Breathing was almost too complicated; the only thing I could do was completely surrender to him and how incredible he felt.

His hands moved up my back and down my sides and then again, his touch as slow and gentle as the deep, spine-tingling strokes he took inside me. *God, don't tease me, Bastian,* I wanted to say. *Fuck me hard.* Unable to speak, I rocked back against him, hoping he'd get the message.

He did. He matched my faster rhythm. When I moved a little faster, so did he. When I slammed against him, he thrust back with equal force.

Then he took over. Fast. Deep. Oh God. I flinched when his fingers dug into my hips, pressing in enough to possibly leave bruises again, but I didn't pull away. With every thrust, every fast, hard thrust, my orgasm built. And built. And built.

His fingers dug in a little more, smarting just enough to bring me partway back to earth. The pain, mild though it was, jarred me, a ribbon of red cutting through the white-hot delirium of pleasure, but it quickly faded away and left me to the ecstasy Bastian gave me.

"Do you like that?" He sounded for all the world like he barely kept himself in control. "Tell me if it's..." His rhythm faltered, and his voice fell to a moan. "Talk to me, Aaron."

"Just..." I shivered. "Just like that." Still it built. Holy fucking hell, I was going to lose it. Completely lose it. Something in my mind reminded me to stay quiet, just in case someone was home and awake, but even that internal censor hung by a thread because the tension in me was so fucking close to breaking.

When it finally released, it did so slowly, like something deep inside me was not breaking, not exploding, but unraveling one thread at a time. And it didn't stop with me, I realized when Bastian exhaled sharply and shuddered against me.

"Oh God, Aaron, I'm—" Another shudder. "You feel so good... I can't...I can't..." He growled something in German, then slammed into me and held me to him while his cock twitched inside me.

For a moment, everything in the room was still and silent, both of us unmoving as if caught in a freeze-frame, each waiting for something—one of us, the universe, *something*—to give the word for life to resume.

His fingers loosened their grip on my hips. I released my breath. He withdrew slowly, and my arms trembled, threatening to buckle at any moment. He stepped away to get rid of the condom while I waited for the room to stop spinning around me.

When he came back, we collapsed onto my bed in each other's arms, lovers that probably shouldn't have been but were nonetheless.

I rested my head on his chest. He put his arm around me, his hand still trembling a little on my shoulder. My eyes were still wet from the tears my climax had triggered, something that had *never* happened to me before, and my body still ached for more. Not just more sex, more of *him*.

What are you doing to me, Bastian?

"So have you gotten enough of me yet tonight?" I asked, lifting my head and grinning at him.

Bastian returned the grin. "Not a chance."

"Good. Because I'm not done with you yet."

He brought me up to kiss him, whispering, "Bring it on."

Even while he kissed me, worry worked its way into the forefront of my mind, twisting my stomach until I couldn't ignore it.

This wasn't a one-night stand anymore. Not a reckless, impulsive decision to be made, regretted, and forgotten. Both times, we'd had the space of a car ride to come to our senses, and we'd done no such thing. We'd come here, we'd come together, and we'd…come.

And I wanted to do it again. Consequences be damned. Now that I'd had him twice, a third time wouldn't be enough.

Bastian looked at me, brow furrowed. "You okay?"

I exhaled. "Yeah, but…" I paused. "What exactly are we doing, anyway? Fucking, obviously, but…"

"I don't know. I'm just kind of playing it by ear." He ran his fingers through my hair. "All I know is this seems like the only thing that makes a damned bit of sense to do."

I shivered, not sure if it was from what he said or from the light touch of his fingertips trailing down the back of my neck. Somehow, in spite of his touch and his damned existence, I found my voice. "So what should we do?"

"What do you want to do?"

"What I *want* to do," I whispered, "is to keep doing exactly what we're doing, but—"

"Then that's what we'll do." His lips silenced any protest I thought to make. And maybe I had thought to protest. About something. To express some doubt or hesitation that crossed my mind. Whatever part of my mind that doubt had crossed, though, ceased to function when I parted my lips for the tip of his tongue.

Bastian was kissing me. How the fuck was a man supposed to think like this? Too much skin touching skin. Too much gentle, spine-tingling contact between his mouth and mine. Too much Bastian.

I held him tighter and didn't think anymore.

CHAPTER TEN

"Looks like that's all the heavy stuff." Bastian secured a tie-down over all the gear in the back of his truck. Another performance down, another stage of equipment cleared, another night of coasting under everyone else's radar while we exchanged glances.

"What's left?" I asked. "Just your bass and amp, right?"

"That and Todd's amp, but he should be on his way down with that right now."

"I'll head up and make sure we didn't leave anything else."

He nodded. "As soon as Todd comes out, I'll go in after you, and we can bring my amp and bass down."

"See you upstairs." We exchanged a quick look, the closest thing we dared to a kiss or a touch while the rest of the band was nearby. Then I headed back across the alley and into the club.

Tonight had been another insanely successful performance. We'd added a couple of new songs to the set. The fans had gone out of their minds, giving security a run for their money a few times. My sister wasn't happy that I'd gone stage diving into such a wild crowd, but those were the crowds that were the most fun.

For as much as I'd enjoyed performing with my last band, even with all the personal drama and bullshit, it had never been as fun as it was with Schadenfreude. They—*we*, damn it—were a high-energy band. The music Bastian and

Rochelle wrote was incredible, and every damned show was a rush.

On my way upstairs, Todd and I passed in the hall. His guitar case was on his back, and he carried his amp in one hand.

"That's the last of your gear, right?" I asked.

He nodded. "Yep. I'll dump the amp off on Bastian; then I'm out of here for the night. I'll see you at home."

"See you there." We bumped fists and continued in opposite directions.

When I stepped into the ready room backstage, Denise was there. Fortunately she was occupied with bending my sister's ear about something or another. Elena and I met eyes while I pulled a bottle of water out of the case, and hers screamed *help me*.

I offered an apologetic shrug and pulled my phone out of my pocket. I quickly sent a text to Bastian: *Denise is backstage*. Hopefully he'd get it before he walked back here and discovered her presence for himself. In the meantime, I leaned against a table and sipped my water, pretending to be interested in a nonexistent text message.

"He won't fucking listen to me," Denise whined.

With her back to Denise, Elena rolled her eyes, then turned to face her. "Maybe he's just trying to let go, hon. I don't think he's out to hurt you."

Denise huffed. "But I really, really need to talk to him." She dropped her gaze for a second, then added quietly, "I'm…late."

Elena's posture straightened. "Late? Like *late*?"

Denise nodded.

I was a little slower on the uptake and nearly choked on my drink when I realized what she meant. I quickly and quietly cleared my throat and did the best I could to regain some semblance of dignity without drawing attention to myself.

Elena shot me a glance, then shifted her weight and folded her arms across her chest. "Denise, tell me you're joking."

Denise shook her head.

"Shit." Elena ran a hand through her hair. "Have you taken a test?"

Denise bit her lip and shook her head again.

"Why the fuck not?" My sister made an exasperated gesture with both hands. "Jesus, that's the first thing you need to do. So you know one way or the other."

"No, I need to talk to Bastian about it."

Elena laughed uncomfortably. "I think you'd better have something a bit more concrete than 'a bit late' before you drop that bomb on him."

While they continued talking—Denise whining, my sister being the voice of reason—my phone beeped. I expected an acknowledgment from Bastian, but instead it was a "failed to send" message. Shit. My signal inside this club sucked, so I shouldn't have been surprised.

I set my empty water bottle down and slipped out of the room, hoping to catch Bastian. He needed to talk to her this time, but I at least wanted to make sure he had some warning before he was in her presence. I made it about ten feet from the door before he came around the corner.

"Denise is in there," I said.

He groaned. "You're fucking kidding me."

"Nope. Elena's trying to get rid of her, but..." I hesitated. "Bastian, I think you should talk to her."

He cocked his head. "Why?"

I chewed my lip. "Um, well, it sounds like... It might be..." I swallowed hard.

Bastian's brow furrowed. "Aaron, is there something I should know about?"

"Well, she's hinting rather strongly that she's pregnant."

He blinked. "Seriously?"

I nodded.

He stared at me incredulously for a moment. Then he laughed and shook his head. "Well, I feel for whatever idiot she trapped into that mess."

"Uh, I think she's implying *you're* that idiot."

He rolled his eyes. "Not a chance."

"Oh good, there you are." Elena's voice turned both our heads. "Bastian, you need to talk to your girl—"

He put his hand up. "My girlfriend? Don't think so."

"Yeah, well, she needs to talk to you."

"Tough shit. She and I are well past the point of talking." He looked at me. "Come on; let's get the rest of this shit out of here. Todd's waiting by the truck, and he wants to leave."

"I think you do need to talk to her, Bastian." She eyed him. "Would you *please* talk to her?"

"No. I've told her, and I'm telling you, I'm done with—"

"If nothing else so she'll stop whining to me?"

"Just do what I do," he said with a shrug. "Ignore her. Don't answer her calls. Leave the room."

Elena sighed. "Easier said than done."

He raised an eyebrow, the piercing glinting in the light. "And you wonder why it took me six years to do it?"

"Well, regardless, you need to talk to her." Elena shot him the same "don't argue with me" look she used on me. "Like, *now*."

Bastian put his hands up and shook his head. "Look, I'm trying to stay as far from her as I can right now. You said yourself she's bordering on creepy, stalkerish behavior, so—"

"Yes, well, that doesn't negate the fact that you might have certain…responsibilities." She raised an eyebrow, a silent demand for him to read between the lines.

He stood his ground. "No. Elena, listen, I understand you mean well here, but—"

"Bastian, thank God." Denise's voice made him cringe and curse under his breath. She caught up to us and put her hand on his arm. "We need to talk."

He glared at her. "No. We don't." He turned and started to walk away.

"I might be pregnant, Bastian."

He stopped in his tracks. For the most fleeting moment, Denise's pitiful expression shifted to a cunning mask of smugness. The spider who'd just felt the fly get tangled in her web.

Slowly Bastian turned around. He rested his weight on one foot, tilting his head to the side, every inch of his body language screaming annoyance and impatience. Not a flicker of panic or concern.

She folded her arms tightly across her chest.

I shifted my gaze back and forth between them, trying to read them both. She looked entirely too self-satisfied for a woman who was worried she was carrying her ex's baby. He looked irritated and not in the least bit worried like I'd expect from a startled possible father-to-be.

With her eyes narrowed and her lips pulled into a sneer, Denise said, "Now that I have your attention—"

"Actually no, not really." He hooked his thumbs in the pockets of his jeans and switched his weight to the other foot as if to emphasize just how unfazed he was by this conversation.

Her fists went to her sides, and her lips pulled back from her teeth. "You son of a bitch, you—"

"Yeah, yeah, yeah, I've heard it all before." He stepped toward her, and she stiffened when he put his hands on her shoulders. Looking her right in the eye, he said, "If you are, in fact, pregnant, why the hell are you telling me about it?"

Her jaw dropped. "Are you really that fucking stupid?"

He shrugged. "Apparently I am. Enlighten me."

She held up her left hand, waving the engagement ring back and forth right in his face. "It's *yours*, Bastian."

He didn't even flinch. "No, it isn't."

"What? How can you say that?" She stared at him, fury and confusion contorting her features. "We only broke up a month ago. This would have happened two or three months ago."

He released her shoulders and took a step back. "Which would confirm my suspicions that you were sleeping around."

She gasped. "What? You son of—"

"Save it, Denise." He let her go and turned to walk away. Over his shoulder, he said, "If you're pregnant, it's not my kid. End of story."

I chewed the inside of my cheek. Bastian wasn't the kind of asshole who'd turn his back on a pregnant ex, was he?

"Bastian fucking Koehler!" she shrieked. "You'd really leave me high and dry like this?" When he turned around, she put on the pitiful face again.

"What do you want from me?" he asked with a shrug. "We're not getting back together. No way in hell. If it's money you need, might I suggest going to the real father? Or perhaps pawning that ring you insist on wearing?"

She pulled in a hiss of breath. "You're an asshole." She stormed out.

He watched her go, then rolled his eyes and released a sharp breath. "Well, now that that's taken care of..."

"Bastian." Elena shot him a disapproving look. "Are you really—"

"This isn't up for discussion," he said sharply. "It's between Denise and me." He glanced in the direction his ex had gone. "Well, her and whoever else she's been fucking."

For a moment, I thought my sister was going to argue, but she just put her hands up and shook her head. "Fine. It's between you guys."

"Thank you." He gestured toward the ready room. "So, with that taken care of, I need to take all the gear back to the farm. I'm outta here."

"You need a hand?" I asked.

He hesitated, glancing at my sister, then shrugged. "If you don't mind going all the way out there, sure."

"Good," Elena said. "Put his lazy ass to work and make him earn his keep."

"Earn my keep?" I snorted. "I do that at the mic during every damned show."

"Yeah, well, time to pull your weight and do some heavy lifting." She looked at Bastian. "Don't let him slack off. Make him carry some of the heavy stuff."

Bastian just laughed. To me he said, "Come on, kid. Let's get this crap out of here."

I followed him down the hall. Glancing over my shoulder to make sure my sister was out of earshot, I said, "Kid? Really?"

He grinned. "Just keeping up appearances."

"Good idea, old man."

"Hey!" He laughed and elbowed me.

"What?" I put my hands up. "Just keeping up appearances."

"Uh-huh. Well, if I'm so old, maybe you should do all the heavy shit while I supervise."

"Or not."

"Then show some respect." He tried to glare at me, but we both laughed.

On the way down to the truck with Bastian's amp and bass, I couldn't shake the knot in my stomach after watching his conversation with Denise. Sure, she was a manipulative bitch from everything I'd seen, but he hadn't even flinched at the possibility of her being pregnant. I'd known guys who, short of being presented with a paternity test, would deny having ever touched a woman once she said she was pregnant. Bastian wasn't that type, was he?

Something about the whole conversation didn't add up. Or at least it added up in an unsettling way. Either Denise really was that crazy and manipulative, or Bastian had played more of a role in the dysfunctional part of their relationship than he'd let on.

Bastian slammed the tailgate. Then he turned to me, absently spinning his key ring on his finger. "Want to ride with me or follow me?"

"Might as well save gas and take one car."

His eyes flicked toward the club's door. Then he nodded. "Sounds good. This place is on my way home anyway, so I can bring you back to your car."

"Think anyone will wonder?" I asked. "I mean, if I'm going with you…"

"Relax." He smiled. "They'll just be glad I'm not dragging one of their asses back to the farm to give me a hand." He shrugged. "Your sister didn't bat an eye at you coming down here with me. No one raises an eyebrow when we're alone for a few minutes. I think we're in the clear as long as we keep laying low."

"Good," I said quietly. We exchanged quick smiles, mine with much less enthusiasm than his, then went around to get into the truck.

His relaxed demeanor didn't help settle the knot in my gut at all. It wasn't just because of his certainty that no one had caught on. He honestly didn't seem upset or concerned about *anything* just now. He was so unaffected it was like he didn't even remember the conversation with Denise. I wasn't sure how to feel about that.

"You're quiet all of a sudden." He glanced at me, then slid his hand over my thigh. "You okay?"

"Are you…" I swallowed, looking at him in the flicker of passing streetlights. "Are you absolutely sure she's not pregnant with your kid?"

He laughed softly and squeezed my leg. "Trust me, there's nothing to worry about with this one. She's pulled the pregnancy card a few times when I've left or threatened to leave, and has conveniently 'miscarried' every time I've come back to her."

I blinked. "Are you serious?"

He nodded, rolling his eyes. "That's the kind of manipulative shit I put up with for six years. She was hell-bent on trapping me in that relationship, and that was one of her favorite techniques, sick as it may be."

"Okay, so she's cried wolf a few times, but is there any possibility—"

"No." He shook his head. "Not a fucking chance."

"How do you know?"

"Quite simply? Because we haven't had sex in six months."

"Really?"

"Really. She cut me off because..." He paused, furrowing his brow. Then he shook his head again. "Fuck, I don't remember what I did, but she cut me off. Then she figured out I was thinking of leaving again, and she suddenly wanted it left, right, and center."

"But you didn't sleep with her?"

"No. Particularly not when she suggested foregoing condoms so we could 'be closer' to each other."

"Oh Jesus."

"Yeah. Kind of a mood killer when you suspect someone's trying to trick you into knocking her up so she can trap you."

"Does she really think you're that stupid?" I asked. "That you can't do a little simple math?"

"Probably," he muttered. "That and she made the mistake of drinking herself blind a few times when we were fighting, and she thinks we slept together those nights."

"Seriously?"

He rolled his eyes and nodded. "Kind of makes me wonder what else she thought of me, if she thinks I'd ever lay a hand on her when she was in that kind of state. Yeah, we slept together those nights. As in, she passed out and I slept next to her. But I didn't touch her."

"Good to know."

He squeezed my leg again, then put his hand back on the wheel. "Aaron, trust me, if I had ever gotten a woman pregnant, I'd have bent over backward to make sure she was taken care of. I wouldn't ditch her. Wouldn't even think of it." He glanced at me before returning his attention to the road ahead. "You didn't think I would, did you?"

"Well, I..." I chewed my lip.

"Come on, really?"

"I didn't think you would, no. Just, when someone comes in and throws that kind of accusation down, it's a bit..."

"Disconcerting?"

"Just a bit."

"Tell me about it."

"But no, to answer your question, I didn't think you were that type. I certainly hoped you weren't."

"Don't worry. I'm not." He paused. "Christ, can you imagine how she'd react if she knew who I was dating now?"

I laughed. "Does she know you're bi?"

"No, definitely not. No one knows except you and the other two guys I've dated."

"You've really kept it that quiet?"

He nodded.

"Think you'll come out eventually?"

"Maybe." Bastian sighed. "I don't know. The older I get, the more I hesitate to come out. It's like, if I was going to, I should have done it years ago. Back when everyone is supposed to figure this shit out."

"You did figure it out then, didn't you?"

He nodded. "Yeah, which is why I feel weird about telling my family I kept it from them all this time. Especially Andre."

"I know the feeling." I blew out a breath. "Elena knows, but Todd? I've never quite been able to tell him. I'm surprised he hasn't gotten suspicious, since he's never met any of my alleged 'girlfriends.'"

Bastian shot me a quick look. "I thought you *did* have some girlfriends."

"Nope. I've never dated a woman in my life."

"Really? Not even in high school?"

"No, I knew I was gay before I ever even thought to date anyone." *In fact, I knew pretty much from the moment a certain pair of German-accented brothers set foot in my house when I was twelve.*

He glanced at me. "You never questioned it?"

"Oh, I questioned it. I think everyone does. But once I realized I was into guys, that was pretty much it. What about you?"

He laughed. "I think I was the most confused bisexual on the planet," he said, chuckling. "I knew I was into guys, but I still wanted girls, and I couldn't figure out what the fuck I was supposed to call myself. Wasn't until my first boyfriend in college that I figured out what the hell bisexuality was." He paused. "Wait, so if you've never had a girlfriend, what really happened with your last band?"

"I wasn't dating the drummer. I was dating the guitarist."

"Ahh, now it makes sense. What happened with him, anyway?"

I sighed. "Like I said before, we couldn't separate our personal problems from the band, or our band problems from the relationship."

"What kind of band problems?"

"Clashing egos, mostly." I laughed bitterly. "Doesn't bode well for a band *or* a relationship, you know?"

"Oh no shit. Good times."

"That and the rest of the band really didn't like the fact that we were together."

"I can imagine." The side of his thumb beat a rapid cadence on the steering wheel. "I don't think Schadenfreude would be too happy about this, either. Never mind the part about accepting we're both queer, just the fact that two band members are sleeping together."

"That I believe."

Bastian sighed. "Hell, the band didn't even like Denise hanging around because our problems distracted me."

"What about Rochelle? I mean, she hangs around, but what about if she and Andre are having problems?"

"They agreed from the beginning that if they're fighting or something, she doesn't come to rehearsals or shows. And there've been a few periods like that, but for the most part, they get along, so…" He shrugged. "If they were ever to split, she's not a part of the band itself. Sure, we'd lose one of our songwriters and a pair of hands backstage, but we wouldn't be down a member."

I chewed my lip. "Whereas if something happens with us…"

"Exactly." He put his hand on my knee. "We're taking a pretty big risk by doing this. I won't pretend we're not."

I nodded. "I know." We both fell silent. Finally I said, "If we keep doing this, the band's bound to find out eventually."

Bastian chewed his lip. "Yeah, I know."

"Maybe we should tell them."

"What?" He looked at me, eyebrows raised. "Are you serious? Aaron, our brothers damn near shit themselves when your sister made eyes at the lead singer before Derek. If they found out we're…that we're doing a hell of a lot more than looking at each other…" He trailed off, shaking his head.

"Right, I understand. But as I said, they're bound to find out. I'd rather they heard it from us, on our terms, rather than someone finding out by accident." I was all too aware of the other option and prayed he didn't suggest it. While it may have been the safest choice, I couldn't stomach the idea of ending this to avoid conflict within the band.

He said nothing for a long moment. He took and released a deep breath, and when he ran his thumb back and forth along the side of my leg, I put my hand over his.

After a while, he said, "This would be a hell of a lot for them to digest."

"Maybe if we ease them into it."

He furrowed his brow, eyes darting toward me. "Ease them into it? What do you mean?"

"Start with one of us coming out. Let the dust settle for a while. Then the other."

Bastian shuddered, drumming his fingers on the steering wheel. "Fuck, I am *not* looking forward to that."

"I know. But if we're going to keep doing this, we'll have to go there eventually."

He nodded slowly. "I don't know how my family will take it. Well, my parents will probably be cool. But Andre..." He rested his elbow below the window and chewed his thumbnail. "Listen, it's up to you when you want to bring it up to your family. For now, as far as *this* is concerned, let's just see where things go. With us, I mean."

"Fair enough." A knot in my gut unwound. Secrecy sucked, and eventually telling the band and our families wouldn't be pleasant, but it was better than throwing in the towel on...whatever it was we were doing.

Up ahead, the John Deere mailbox came into view. Despite the road being completely deserted, Bastian put on his turn signal, probably out of habit. Neither of us spoke on the way down the long driveway, even after Bastian pulled in front of the garage and turned off the engine. We both got out, wordlessly going around to the back of the truck to unload it.

He reached for the handle on the tailgate, but I grabbed his wrist. He looked at my hand, then at me, his brow furrowing in the dim glow of the garage's single floodlight.

I put his hand on my waist. "I figured, since we have a few minutes alone…"

He laughed softly and slid his free hand around the side of my neck. "You know we've never been capable of a short kiss, right?"

"I wasn't after one. Now come here, you."

As they always did, this kiss went on and deepened and weakened my knees. Bastian's hand drifted up my back while the other combed through my hair. His jacket creaked, keeping time with every unhurried movement we made. When he touched my face, the backs of his fingers trailing lightly across my cheek, I shivered and pulled him closer.

By the time one of us—and I couldn't say who—broke that gentle kiss, my legs and breathing were as unsteady as if we'd been throwing each other around like two desperate, insatiably horny men. And I wondered when we'd started kissing like this instead of that anyway, because it was far too comfortable and familiar to have been the first time.

Bastian ran the tip of his thumb along my lower lip. "Have I mentioned lately how much I fucking love the way you kiss?"

"Hmm, no, don't think you have." I let my lips brush his when I added, "But you're more than welcome to do it as much as you want."

"Tell you?" He ran his fingers through my hair. "Or kiss you?"

I didn't answer. I just raised my chin and kissed him.

After a while, we separated again, looking at each other in the low light. He watched himself trace my jaw with the backs of his fingers. Then he glanced at the truck bed. "We should get all this stuff into the garage."

"We will." I slid my hand around the back of his neck. "But first…"

"Let me guess." Bastian grinned, pulling me closer. "Just one more kiss?"

CHAPTER ELEVEN

The House of Anarchy definitely lived up to its name. When the fans went crazy—and they nearly always did—it was all security could do to keep them from rushing the stage. The band fed off the crowd. The crowd fed off the band. It was a fucking madhouse, and I loved it. Every minute of it.

The last two songs in the set were Elena's, but I didn't leave the stage yet. During Todd's screaming guitar solo, I took a few steps back from the edge of the stage, and the crowd raised their hands, egging me on. Elena shot me a disapproving look. I just grinned. We both knew exactly what I was doing. I'd done it at every show thus far in spite of her pleas, warnings, and threats.

She rolled her eyes and continued with her song. I glanced at Bastian. He grinned and shook his head. One of the security guys gave me a dirty look.

Tough shit, guys. The fans love it.

With the crowd going insane and the air on fire with the chorus of "Serrated," I jumped off the stage and into the dozens of waiting hands. They passed me back toward the middle of the crowd, then off to one side, the lights and faces blurring around me as the fans tossed me around.

Crowd surfing wasn't for the faint of heart. The fans grabbed my clothes, my arms, my legs. I swore someone even tried to pick my pocket. Good thing I'd left my wallet and keys backstage. Still, it was fun. It was like moving over a ground made of hands. Grabbing, passing, touching hands.

Abruptly the crowd jolted to one side, then the other. The cheering and shouting below me took on an undercurrent of something else. Distress. Panic.

Time shifted into slow motion. The ground of hands lurched, disappeared on one side, and I knew a split second before I dropped that I was falling. Just enough time for a silent *oh shit* before someone under me collapsed.

Several people went down, myself included, and we landed in a tangle of limbs. The side of my ankle hit the floor in the same instant the crowd shifted, and something in my knee twisted in a direction it wasn't intended to twist.

I was vaguely aware that the bass line had faltered for a couple of beats, but most of my senses were focused on my knee. It didn't hurt yet, but it would. Adrenaline kept the pain at bay, and if I was lucky, maybe it would last long enough for me to get back to the stage. Or at least out of this shifting-jostling-shoving mob of limbs and shoulders. Every time I came down on my left foot, more panic surged through me, more *this is going to hurt*.

I looked toward the stage. Elena and I made eye contact, and the creases in her forehead asked if she needed to stop the show. The fans who'd fallen with me had gotten to their feet without getting trampled, so I gave her a quick thumbs-up. She nodded once and continued with the show.

Someone's foot landed on top of mine in the same instant the crowd pushed to the right. My body moved with the crowd. My foot stayed planted for just a heartbeat before the other foot's owner was probably shoved off balance as well.

What had twisted the wrong way twisted again, finding yet another direction it wasn't intended to go, and holy shit, *now* it hurt.

It hurt, and I was still in a sea of people. My heart pounded. I grabbed gulps of air when I could, fighting back the irrational certainty that I was drowning. Crowds didn't make me nervous until I had reason to get out of them, and now I needed to get the fuck out of this one.

There was only one way back to the stage without fucking myself up further, and that was back on top of the crowd. Whether I wanted to or not, that was where I was going, because a few fans hoisted me up and launched me onto the waiting hands of everyone else.

Every time someone grabbed or even jarred my leg, more excruciating pain shot through me. I couldn't tell which flickering, colored lights were from the show and which were pain induced. Gritting my teeth, I managed to get to the front. One of the security guys helped me back up onstage, and I got to my feet. Well, my foot. Clenching my jaw, I struggled to keep my weight off my left leg while we closed out the show.

When we were clear of the stage, Todd and Bastian materialized beside me. After they'd handed their guitars off to Rochelle and Elena, they each pulled one of my arms around their shoulders and put their own arms around my waist. With their help, I made it into the ready room backstage, and they eased me into a chair.

"You all right?" Bastian asked.

"How bad is it?" Todd furrowed his brow, looking down at the leg I'd favored.

"I'm fine," I said through my teeth. "Just need to put some ice on it, and it'll be fine."

Andre appeared. "You need someone to take a look at it? Maybe we should take him to the emergency room."

I shook my head and put my hand up. "No, no, it's not that bad."

"Come on," Todd said. "You need to elevate it. Bastian, you mind going and getting some ice from the bar?"

"On it." In a second, Bastian was gone. Todd pulled up another chair and helped me prop my leg up on it.

In no time flat, the room was flooded with club employees and security guards. One of the security guys chewed me out for stage diving. The club manager did the same. Then another security guy. I couldn't hear them over the relentless pain in my leg and the endorphins rushing through my system, so I just nodded, made a few bullshit promises not to jump off the stage again, and thanked God when Bastian walked in with a bag of ice.

"Here, this should help," he said.

"Thanks." I pressed the ice against my knee. The pressure hurt like hell, but after a minute or so, the cold helped. A little.

Once I'd convinced everyone and their mother that I didn't need an ambulance or a ride to the ER, the club employees left me to ice my leg in peace. Well, relative peace.

"Aaron McClure, you fucking idiot." Elena cuffed me upside the head.

"Hey, hey, no striking the wounded, bitch."

"There's nothing wounded about your head." Folding her arms across her chest, she glared at me. "Though after what happened out there, I have to wonder."

"Oh come on." I fidgeted, trying and failing to get comfortable. "I'm hardly the first person to ever stage dive."

"Most people can walk afterward, though," Todd said.

"Shut up," I said, chuckling.

Elena cocked her head, looking at my leg. "So how bad is it?"

"Hurts like a bitch." I shifted again, this time sucking in a hiss of breath when the movement hurt enough to blur my vision.

She sighed and rolled her eyes. "Well, that's what your dumb ass gets for crowd surfing."

"You gonna be okay?" Todd asked.

I nodded. "Yeah, just need to ice it for a few minutes and I'll be fine."

"All right," he said. "Well, we're going to go drink, dance, and have a good time while you sit here and think about what you've done."

I laughed, and he elbowed me playfully before he, Andre, and Rochelle left. Elena and Bastian stayed behind, though.

"You guys don't have to stay," I said. "I'll probably be fine in a few minutes."

"Then we'll wait a few minutes to make sure," Bastian said.

"That and we don't want to leave you unsupervised," Elena said. "You might jump off your chair and hurt yourself."

I flipped her the bird.

"Watch it, Junior, or I'll break your other leg."

"You would too."

"Damn right I would." She eyed my leg. "Is it getting any better with the ice?"

"Not really." I shifted a little, wincing. "Still hurts pretty bad."

She knelt beside me. "Roll your pant leg up."

"Why?"

"I want to see if it's swelling."

"Actually..." Bastian cocked his head. "I don't think you'll have much luck rolling it up." He gestured at my knee. "It's already swelling."

"Try moving a little," Elena said.

Gritting my teeth, I took my foot off the chair and tried to bend my knee. As soon as I moved it, fresh pain ripped through the joint. I put my foot back on the chair and took slow, deep breaths until my vision had cleared.

"I think you'd better go to the emergency room," Elena said. "I'm serious."

I exhaled. "I don't think it's that bad."

"Yes, it is."

"Even if it isn't," Bastian said, "she's right. You should go. If there's anything really wrong, it'd be better to get it checked now than later."

Elena pursed her lips. To Bastian, she said, "If I take him in, do you mind driving everyone else home?"

"I've only got room for one in the truck." He paused, glancing at me. "Maybe I should take him."

"You don't mind?"

His eyes flicked toward me, and I hoped to God my sister didn't see the way his lip curled ever so slightly. "Nope, don't mind. Besides, you played ambulance driver last time, so I think it's my turn anyway." He offered me his hand. I clasped his forearm, and he helped me to my feet. He kept a hand on my shoulder while I took a step. I winced, clenching my jaw, but took another step. I could do this. It wasn't that far. Just out the back of the ready room, down the hall, down—

"Oh fuck," I groaned. "The stairs."

Bastian thought for a moment, then pulled his keys out of his pocket. "I'll bring the truck around to the front. You'll have to get across the club, but it's level. Elena, can you help him that far?"

"Of course."

"Don't leave me with her," I said. "She'll shove me off the curb just for spite."

She put her arm around my waist, letting me put some of my weight on her. "Well, that'll teach you not to crowd surf, won't it?"

"Probably not."

Bastian chuckled. "I'll see you two out front."

With Elena's help, I made it out of the backstage area to the main part of the club. The more I tried to walk, the more I agreed with her and Bastian. Something wasn't right. I'd walked off my fair share of injuries, but not this one.

Getting through the crowd wasn't the most pleasant experience, but it could have been worse. Though this wasn't as dense as a midconcert mob, it was still a gauntlet of moving, dancing, occasionally shoving bodies. A few people recognized and tried to stop us for autographs. They quickly caught on that we had somewhere else we needed to be, though, and stood aside, watching us with wide eyes.

About halfway to the door, Todd stepped through the crowd. "Need a hand?"

"God, yes," Elena shouted over the music. "He's gained weight since he was a kid. You noticed that?"

Todd pulled my arm around his shoulders again and pretended to sag under my weight. "Goddamn, Aaron, she's—"

"Oh fuck you both."

"Don't make us drop you right here," Elena said.

Fortunately, for all our bantering and shit talking, I had no concern at all that my siblings would drop me. Elena might threaten to, if only to keep me from crowd surfing, but neither of them would actually do it.

A security guard held the front door open for us while a couple of bouncers kept clubgoers back enough to let us past. As promised, Bastian's truck was out in front of the club. He'd pulled up alongside the curb, as close as he could get to the front door, and stood beside the passenger door.

I got in, thankful he hadn't jacked his truck up like it was so trendy to do. As it was, it was high enough to be challenging.

"All set?" Todd asked, leaning on the open door while I buckled my seat belt.

"Think I'm good."

"Will you be okay for tomorrow night's show?"

I groaned. "Crap, I'd forgotten about that." Naturally if I was going to fuck myself up, I had to go and do it when we had three gigs in a row. During the first show, of course.

"We can always wheel you out in a wheelchair," Elena said.

"Yeah, you would too," I said. "I'm sure I'll be fine, but I guess we'll see what the doctor says. Thanks for the help."

"Anytime, bro." He put his fist out. "Get the good drugs."

"I'll see what I can do." I laughed and bumped his fist. He closed the door and headed back into the club with Elena.

Bastian slid into the driver's seat. "Doing okay?"

"I'll live."

For a while, neither of us spoke. Now that I was off my feet again, the pain was less intense, but it was still enough to cloud my vision.

The light up ahead turned yellow, and I held my breath, cringing in anticipation as Bastian slowed down, but the stop was smooth, gentle, and didn't jar my leg at all. I released my breath and relaxed against the seat.

He glanced at me. "Sorry, didn't mean to—"

"No, you're fine."

"Just checking," he said.

I closed my eyes and let my head fall back against the headrest. "So are you going to lecture me about crowd surfing too?"

Bastian laughed. "Hell, no."

"Thank God. I think everyone in the club did."

"Eh, only because you fell. Once you're up and walking again, no one will bat an eye except the occasional security guard with a stick up his ass."

I managed a quiet laugh. "And my sister."

"Well, yeah. But she's gotta be protective of her baby brother."

"Don't know why she's so freaked out about crowd surfing."

"I could grab your knee if you need a reminder."

I opened my eyes and glared at him. "Don't you dare."

He chuckled. "I won't, I won't."

"Ah well," I said. "Guess Elena was right about it anyway. I mean, I did manage to hurt myself."

"Oh please. It's not like she hasn't jumped off the stage a few times."

"Really? I figured she was afraid to stage dive."

Bastian laughed aloud. "Trust me, your sister is *not* afraid of stage diving."

"So she's just afraid of *me* stage diving?"

He shrugged. "She's protective. Honestly, I think she'd still do it if she wasn't afraid of what might happen to the fans."

"What do you mean?"

"Well, you know how the fans like to grab whatever they can get their hands on, right?"

I nodded. Crowd surfing definitely wasn't for anyone who didn't like being touched.

"Now imagine what would happen if she was out there, under the watchful eyes of her brothers and two guys who may as well be her brothers, and someone decided to put his hand where it didn't belong."

"Yeah, I see your point."

He grinned. "So she's probably just being protective of her little brother like we're all protective of her."

"Well, good." I rolled my eyes and gave a dramatic sigh. "Glad to know she's got the whole band behind her and I've got the *girl* keeping an eye on me."

Bastian laughed. "Not to worry." He glanced at me and winked. "I'm looking out for you too."

"That makes me feel so, so safe."

"Want to walk?"

"No, really, it makes me feel safe, Bastian. Really."

He braked just hard enough to emphatically slow down but still avoid jarring me too much.

I laughed and put my hand up. "Kidding, kidding! Please don't make me walk."

"Damn right you are." He accelerated again.

A few minutes later, he pulled up right in front of the emergency room.

"Well, you're on your own from here," he said. "See you tomorrow night."

I shot him a glare, and he laughed as he put the truck in park and killed the engine.

When I got out, I let my left foot touch the ground to provide some stability, letting it bear as little weight as humanly possible, and it was enough to turn my vision white for a second. I put a hand on the truck, and when Bastian appeared beside me, he gently held my arm until I'd caught my breath.

"You okay?" he asked.

"Yep. That's why we're at the emergency room."

He clicked his tongue. "Smart-ass," he muttered. "Come on, put your arm on my shoulder." He put his around my waist.

Instinctively I glanced around the parking lot. "Bastian, we're—"

"You're on your way into the emergency room," he said. "No one's going to think twice about it. I'm not telling you to grab my ass, just put your arm around my shoulders. Unless you want to put your weight on your knee?"

I put my arm around his shoulders.

It was late on a Friday night, which meant the waiting area was a handful of chairs shy of standing room only. A twisted knee wasn't exactly a priority over some of the other injuries and illnesses that came in with stretchers and flashing lights, so I figured we'd be waiting a while.

Against one wall, I found a couple of vacant chairs. Bastian had me prop my leg on the second. For a moment I just closed my eyes, basking in the sweet relief of having my weight off my knee. The pain was creeping back in, though, especially as the ice melted.

Once I was situated, Bastian said, "I'll go sign you in, and then I need to move the truck. Do you have an insurance card or anything?"

"Yeah, I do." Thank God my insurance hadn't yet lapsed from my day job in California. Might as well take advantage of it before it ran out. I pulled out my wallet and handed him the card and my ID. "I really appreciate this."

"Don't worry about it." He smiled. "You okay for a few minutes?"

"I'll survive."

"I'll be right back. Don't go anywhere."

Somehow I didn't think that would be a problem.

CHAPTER TWELVE

I'd spent my fair share of time in emergency rooms over the years. They were all different but all the same. Each had their own fan of outdated magazines on blandly colored tables. The air was heavy with that sterile, eye-watering smell of alcohol and latex or whatever nonlatex substitute they used these days. There was always some arrangement of fish making laps around a tank full of fake coral and a wobbling plastic scuba diver.

I always seemed to end up in one of two types of ERs. Sometimes they were efficient, with stretchers and wheelchairs taking corners on two wheels while they got people in and out so fast the automatic doors never even managed to close. Other times, they were crowded, clogged with the wounded, sick, and bored who were being subjected to some sadist's idea of quality television while the nurses at the triage station looked as bored as the fish in the tank. Funny how there was nothing more frantic than a nearly empty waiting room, and nothing more sluggish and inefficient than a packed one. My guess was that the latter occurred not because an excessive number of people had chosen that time to get sick or hurt, but the staff wasn't doing a hell of a lot to move them through unless they were on death's doorstep.

Tonight it was a slow, inefficient night, which meant patients weren't moving and the ice on my leg had long since turned to water.

I gritted my teeth and glared at the triage station. Bastian had gone up twice to try to get me another ice pack, but forty-five minutes after we'd arrived, none had materialized. I closed my eyes, taking a long, deep breath through my nose and telling myself for the hundredth time I could deal with it.

Bastian squeezed my shoulder. "How you holding up?"

I looked up at him—with a shortage of chairs, he'd opted to stand against the wall beside me while I propped my leg up on the only other available chair—and shrugged. "I'll live."

"That's not what I asked." He nodded toward my knee and the useless ice pack. "Is that helping anymore at all?"

"Not in the least," I growled.

He looked at the triage station, then back at me. "I'll be right back." He didn't wait for me to say anything before he pushed himself off the wall and left the waiting area. He caught the attention of a nurse strolling by with a cup of coffee. I couldn't hear the conversation from where I sat, but Bastian's body language said it all. At first he was almost apologetic, gesturing toward me, showing his palms, gesturing again. He was the very picture of patience and pleading.

She, on the other hand, sipped her coffee and glanced at her watch. Bastian tilted his head, and though I couldn't see his face, I had no doubt the shift in posture was accompanied by some expression of *that's bullshit, don't fuck with me*. He made another gesture toward me, and it was sharper this time. The nurse looked at him with no expression, and her next casual sip of coffee probably had his teeth grinding with irritation. I rolled my eyes. Most nurses were awesome, but I swore every emergency room had one like this.

Finally Bastian walked past her and went around to the other side of the triage station. He was out of my sight now. I chewed the inside of my cheek, watching the crowd of white coats and pastel scrubs for the bassist in black, wondering what he was up to.

Minutes later, he reappeared. Without a word, he leaned against the wall beside me again. Seconds later, a nurse appeared with a fresh ice pack in her hand.

"Here you are." She handed me the ice, then glanced warily at Bastian before looking at me again. "Just let me know if this one starts to melt, okay?"

"Will do."

With another sideways glance at Bastian, she went back to the triage station. As I pressed the ice against my knee—*ah, sweet relief*—I eyed him.

"What the hell did you do?" I asked. "Threaten them?"

He just grinned. "I have my ways. Now ice your knee."

I laughed, shook my head, and iced my knee.

Another forty-five minutes and three ice packs later, one of the nurses called my name. And thankfully they brought a wheelchair. Though I didn't particularly like being carted around, the idea of walking more than a few steps just then made my skin crawl.

The nurse took us into a room, and I hoisted myself onto the hard bed.

She stacked a few pillows on the bed along with a couple of ice packs, then held up a folded hospital gown. "Change into this. Then you'll need to keep your leg iced and elevated until the doctor comes in."

Once she was gone, Bastian grinned. "Do I need to leave so you can change?"

I laughed. "Yeah, God forbid you see anything."

He chuckled. "Actually..." He pulled his phone out. "Your sister's probably freaking out by now. I should go call her and let her know what's up."

"Sure you don't want to stay for the show?"

"I'll hold out for the private, full-contact show." He winked, then stepped out of the room.

About the time I'd gotten situated with the lovely hospital gown and my leg on top of the pillows with glorious, glorious ice against it, Bastian returned.

"What did Elena say?" I asked.

"She didn't answer. I left her a message." Then he shot me a mischievous grin and leaned over me. "And now that we have a minute or two alone..." He kissed me.

"You're not helping with the swelling, you know," I murmured.

"What does that have to do with your knee?" He trailed his fingertips down the side of my face, and my shiver had nothing to do with the ice piled on my leg. If there existed anything that could make me forget about the pain for a few seconds, it was his kiss, so I rested my hand on the back of his neck and kept him there, drawing it out for a long moment.

He raised his head, slowly running the tip of his tongue across his lower lip. "You know, with as slow as they've been all night, we could probably get away with a *lot* in here."

I blinked. "You're joking, right?"

He laughed and patted my shoulder. "Yes, I am."

"Oh, you fucking tease."

"I'll make it up to you, I promise." There was a chair by the door, so he pulled it up next to the bed and sat. He folded his arms on the bed beside me.

"How much do you want to bet we're going to be here awhile?" I asked, putting one hand behind my head and resting the other on top of his arm.

"Probably." He laced his fingers between mine. "In which case it's a good thing you're the one lying down, not me. I'd probably fall asleep."

"So it's true what the rest of the band says?" I laughed. "That you're getting too old to stay out late?"

"Uh-huh, that's it." He yawned. "Has nothing to do with being old. Has to do with being at work at seven in the morning all fucking week in between rehearsals and shows."

"Ouch, that's gotta be exhausting."

"Yeah, but it keeps the money coming in."

"What is it that you do, anyway?" I asked. "Since I never have time to ask when we're alone."

"Guess your mouth is usually busy, isn't it?" He laughed. "I'm an IT. I keep the company's network up and running in between telling morons to restart their computers."

"Sounds exciting."

He rolled his eyes. "Oh, it's thrilling. At least I'm not in management. I do enough babysitting with the band."

I laughed. "So this is babysitting?"

"That's not what I meant." He grinned. "No, I've actually kind of gotten used to being the adult in the band. Well, one of them. I keep an eye on Andre, your sister keeps an eye on Todd, and we both kept an eye on that dipshit who used to sing for us." He watched his thumb make gentle arcs across the back of my hand, then said, "Trust me, this isn't the first time I've taken a band member to the emergency room after a show. Since your sister and I are usually the only sober ones…" He trailed off and shrugged.

"Really?" I freed my hand just long enough to adjust the ice pack on my leg, then slipped it into his again. "You guys frequent customers here or something?"

"Oh, we've had our share of…incidents."

I raised an eyebrow. "Such as?"

"Let's see. Did Todd ever tell you where he got that scar on his forehead?"

"He said he got into a fight with a drunk fan."

Bastian laughed aloud. "Is that what he told you?"

"I assume that isn't what really happened?"

"Let's just say he had a little argument with the corner of a piece of sound equipment, and the equipment won."

"Are you serious?" I snickered. "So was the sound equipment drunk?"

"No, but Todd was."

I laughed. "For some reason, I'm not surprised."

"And there was the time some jackass threw a bottle at us during a show at…" He paused, furrowing his brow, then shook his head. "Some club that's not around anymore, thank God. Hit Derek in the arm."

"And he had to go to the ER for that?"

"No, he had to go to the ER after he thought he could beat the fuck out of the guy who'd thrown it."

"I take it he was mistaken?"

Bastian nodded, rolling his eyes. "The guy was twice his size and drunk off his ass. That and Derek was a pussy anyway."

"You guys had many problems with band members getting into fights?"

"Just with Derek. Fucker had a temper like you wouldn't believe. One more reason I'm glad his idiot ass isn't part of this band anymore. He was becoming a liability." Bastian scratched the back of his neck, then let his hand rest on top of mine again. "But enough about him. He's gone and good riddance."

"And hey, he made room for me when he left."

Drawing light circles on my wrist with his fingertips, he said, "Exactly."

For a while, we just shot the breeze, talking about the band, some upcoming gigs, things like that. At some point, he said, "So I have to know, where did you learn to sing like that? I mean, I'm assuming you didn't learn to sing yesterday."

"Maybe I did."

"Not with that voice you didn't." He winked.

"Could be genetics. You've heard Elena."

He grinned. "And she's had insane amounts of training. Natural talent only goes so far. Being as good as you are requires work, so spill it."

My cheeks burned. "How do you know I didn't sell my soul for it?"

Pausing, he furrowed his brow and pretended to be in deep thought. "Then I'd say the devil got fucked in that arrangement."

I laughed and rolled my eyes. "I suppose you got your silver tongue in a similar deal, then."

"Come on now, it's not *all* silver." The tip of his tongue darted across his lower lip, letting the stud catch the light.

I barely kept myself from shivering.

He slipped his fingers between mine and gently clasped my hand. "So," he said, looking more than a little smug as he raised his pierced eyebrow. "Where did you learn to sing?"

I shrugged. "My parents encouraged all of us to get involved in music somehow. Todd wanted to play guitar. Elena and I both wanted voice lessons."

"Did you ever pick up any instruments?"

"You mean you don't remember me subjecting everyone in the house to my earsplitting attempts at clarinet and trombone in school?"

Bastian snorted. "Please. Whenever I was at your place, I was busy going deaf listening to your brother's attempts at guitar."

I laughed. "He got the hang of it eventually, though."

"We all did." He smiled. "You heard how bad we were in the beginning, but we figured it out."

"Good point. It was actually kind of nice when Todd and Elena moved out and I didn't have to wear earplugs or headphones all the time."

He laughed. "Your poor parents."

"Yours too, right?"

"Well, true. But they may as well have worn earplugs anyway with as mouthy as Andre and I were."

"You?" I smirked. "Oh, I can't imagine that."

He just laughed.

"Okay, so what about you?" I ran my thumb back and forth along his wrist. "What made you start playing?"

He shrugged, and a hint of color in his cheeks emphasized the sheepish smile. "An act of rebellion gone wrong."

I raised an eyebrow. "How so?"

"My father was a musician," he said. "Always playing his guitar. Christ, I barely even remember the man without a guitar in his lap. I think it spent more time on his knee than Andre or I ever did." The sudden bitterness in his voice startled me, as did the momentary distant look in his eyes.

He shook his head again, evidently bringing himself back into the present, and looked at me. "Anyway, my mother married my stepdad when I was eleven. Dragged our asses halfway around the world to live with him here in the States. And I hated him. *Hated* the bastard." He was quiet for a second. "He hated loud music too. So I got hold of a bass—didn't really know the difference between that and a guitar at the time—and played the fuck out of it just to piss both of them off."

I blinked. "You seriously just did it to piss off your parents?"

A grin tugged at the corner of his mouth. "Sort of. I mean, Andre and I have always been musically inclined. But if it hadn't been for my stepdad and my mother, I wouldn't have spent every last waking hour playing it." He laughed softly. "Then I guess I started getting good at it, so my stepdad made me take lessons. And the rest, as they say, is history."

"Only you could make a career out of something you did just to fuck with someone."

"It wasn't the only thing I did to fuck with them." He snickered. "Andre and I were right bastards to our stepdad. Looking back, I wonder how he put up with half our shit."

"Oh God, what else did you do to the poor man?"

"We refused to speak English most of the time," he said. "We were both pretty fluent when we came to the States, but we'd even speak German to him and act like he was the idiot because he couldn't understand us."

I rolled my eyes. "Now that's just mean."

"I told you, we were bastards."

"Did your mother at least teach him some German so he knew what the hell you were saying?"

"No. She told me a few years ago that she never did because"—he paused, snorting with laughter—"she didn't want him to understand all the crap we were saying about him."

"Oh my God, you guys *were* mean."

"Well," he said, giving me an innocent look. "I never said I only used my tongue for good."

"I don't know, I kind of like it when you use it for evil."

He winked. "Duly noted."

"Especially when—*oh fuck.*" I screwed my eyes shut and sucked in a breath.

Bastian's chair creaked. "You all right?"

I put a hand up, hoping it came across as *give me a second*. Between the ice and sitting still, the pain in my leg had receded to a dull ache until, in a moment of lapsed judgment, I'd shifted around to get comfortable. Oops.

I took a few deep breaths and waited for the fire to die down. Slowly the pain faded, and I exhaled. "*Fuck*, that hurt."

"What did you do?"

"Moved."

"Dumb-ass."

"Fuck you."

"Not here, Aaron," he said, not even trying to hide the grin in his voice. "Someone might catch us."

I managed a quiet laugh. Finally I opened my eyes. "Remind me not to move again."

"Don't move again."

"Thank you, Koehler. Really."

He chuckled. Then he squeezed my hand gently. "How's the ice? Do you need me to get another pack?"

"They're getting a little warm." I looked at him. "You don't mind?"

"Of course not." He stood, then leaned down to kiss me. "I'll be right back."

It didn't take him long at all. He must have put the fear of God into the staff earlier. That or he'd found someone who didn't think it was an inconvenience to get some ice. Whatever the case, he was back in minutes.

"You're a godsend." I started to sit up and reach for the ice packs, but he held them up and gestured for me to lie back again.

"You just stay there," he said. "I've got this."

"Bastian, I can—"

"Stay."

I rolled my eyes and sighed. Then I reclined again and laced my fingers behind my head. Bastian carefully picked up the old ice packs and tossed them in the trash. Then he set a new one next to my knee. Oh God, I hadn't realized just how much the old ones had melted until the cold of the new set in.

When he put the second on the other side of my knee, I jumped.

"Ow, fuck!" I said through clenched teeth.

His hands flew up. "What? What did I do? Are you okay?"

I laughed and relaxed. "Just fucking with you."

He held the third ice pack right over my leg. "You know, if I were to drop this right now—"

"Bastian, don't you fucking dare."

He held it a little higher, raising both his eyebrow and one corner of his mouth.

"Bastian…"

He snickered. "That's what I thought." He put the last pack across my knee, adjusting it so it would stay in place. "This okay?"

I nodded. "Much better. Thank you."

"Anytime." He leaned over me, carefully resting his weight on the bed as he came down to kiss me. "You holding up okay?"

I ran my fingers through his hair. "Could be worse."

He trailed ice-cooled fingers down the side of my face. "Yeah, I could think of worse ways to spend the evening."

I smiled. "I could think of better ways too."

"True." He let his lips just barely brush mine. "But I guess this is what we get, so..." He shrugged with one shoulder, then kissed me again. I put an arm around him. Then the other. His tongue teased my lips apart, and I raised my head off the rock-hard pillow just to get a little closer to him.

When our lips separated, I exhaled. "Damn it, now I need to think of something other than how much I want to be in *my* bed instead of *this* bed."

He laughed and ran his thumb across my cheekbone. "In your bed with me, I hope."

"*Ooh* yeah." I couldn't resist and pulled him down for another long kiss.

Eventually he broke the kiss and sat beside the bed again. "I suppose you don't have to mention that particular swelling to the doctor."

"Yeah, no shit." I adjusted the hospital gown, but as expected, it didn't do a damned bit of good.

"Sorry," Bastian said with a grin that said he was anything but. He shifted in his chair.

"Well, at least I'm not wearing skintight jeans," I said, giving him a conspicuous glance.

He grinned. "And I'm not the one who will have the doctor's undivided attention when he comes in."

"Uh-huh." I closed my eyes and took a few deep breaths, then looked at him. "Okay, so, for the sake of distracting myself, what made you guys decide to call the band Schadenfreude, anyway?"

"It's more guttural. *Schadenfreude*. The *r* comes from the back of your throat."

"That's what I said." I repeated the band's name a couple of times, exaggerating every syllable.

"You've almost got it," he said.

I tried it a few more times.

Bastian laughed. "No, no, Schadenfreude."

"Schadenfreude." I tried it again, slowly. "Schadenfreude."

"You're almost there." His eyes twinkled with amusement.

"Damn me for not being a native German speaker."

"Actually you've got it." He winked. "I just like watching your mouth when you say it."

"Dirty bastard."

"Guilty as charged."

I laughed, but that resulted in just enough movement to ignite more pain in my leg. Grimacing, I said, "You're not helping at all, just so you know."

He batted his eyes. "Terribly sorry."

"No you're not."

"You're right." He squeezed my hand gently, and some of the humor left his expression. "You okay, though? Seriously?"

"I'll live."

"I certainly hope so." He chuckled. "Anyway, the band's name pretty much means our brothers and I were shit-faced when we named the band."

I raised an eyebrow.

He laughed. "Okay, okay, so it literally means 'finding pleasure or amusement in the misfortunes of others.' Something like that, anyway. Kind of like when people laugh at slapstick comedy. You know, a *Three Stooges* kind of thing."

"I suppose it's appropriate that the four of you would name your band after something like that."

He gave me a shy but mischievous smile. "Well, we really were drunk off our asses…" He trailed off, snickering for a moment. "We were all playing video games with Todd at our apartment, and Andre got up to, hell, I don't even remember what he was doing. Probably getting another beer. Anyway, he ended up falling. Took a pretty bad spill actually, but Todd and I couldn't stop laughing. We were that drunk, it was that funny, and…" He offered an apologetic shrug.

I laughed aloud. "That's just wrong."

"What can I say?" He grinned. "Some things never change." He ran a hand through his hair. "Anyway, he kept bitching about it the next day. Said his arm hurt. We kept laughing. The day after that, it still hurt, so he went to the doctor. Found out he'd fractured his wrist."

"Oh my God."

Bastian laughed. "When Andre showed up to rehearsal in a cast, Todd and I laughed so hard we cried. He said something about schadenfreude, and we all went, 'That's it!'" He shrugged. "He couldn't play for a few weeks, but we were just starting out then, so it wasn't like we had any gigs yet. Anyway, that's how the band got its name."

"You guys are awful." I paused. "Seems oddly appropriate after the way you and your brother fucked with your stepdad, though. I'm sure there was plenty of schadenfreude involved in that."

"I love watching you say that."

Well, I guess I'm not the only one who likes watching someone's mouth move. I cleared my throat, certain my cheeks had darkened at my own unspoken thought. Before he could comment on that, I said, "Your accent isn't as strong as it used to be."

He shrugged. "Time does that."

"Does your German ever get rusty?"

"Not with Andre and my mother around," he said. "If I spend too much time around them, my damned English starts getting rusty."

"Well, if I'd known I'd be around the two of you this much, I'd have taken a different language in high school."

He laughed. "But if you did, then you would be able to tell when I'm saying dirty things to you."

"Presumably if you're saying something dirty to me, you want me to know it's dirty, don't you?"

He inclined his head. "Good point."

I started to speak, but a knock at the door turned both our heads. Bastian casually pushed his chair back a few inches, safely into "we weren't touching" territory, and rested his hands in his lap just before the doctor stepped into the room.

"Mr. McClure?" the doctor asked, looking at me over my chart.

"That would be me."

"Dr. Paul Bradshaw." We shook hands. Then he looked at Bastian. "And you're…"

"Bastian. Just the sorry bastard who got roped into driving him down here."

I glared at him. Dr. Bradshaw laughed quietly.

"We're bandmates," I said.

"Ah, I see." The doctor looked at the stack of ice packs on my knee. "So according to the triage nurse, you twisted your knee. What were you doing at the time?"

"Being an idiot," Bastian muttered behind his hand.

I flipped him the bird. "Stage diving."

The doctor looked at me, then Bastian, then me again. "So, being an idiot, then."

Bastian snickered.

"Okay, fine, I was being an idiot." I shot Bastian a glare. "You would find this funny, wouldn't you?"

He shrugged. "What can I say? I like a little schadenfreude."

"Ass."

"Well," Dr. Bradshaw said. "You're certainly not the first person I've treated after stage diving and crowd surfing." He raised an eyebrow. "And you're definitely not in the worst shape."

"Guess that's a good thing," I said. "Could be a hell of a lot worse, right?"

"I'll be sure to mention that to your sister." Bastian tried to give me a disapproving look but then laughed.

Dr. Bradshaw set my chart aside. "Let's have a look and see what the damage is, shall we?" He poked and prodded my knee, tested the range of motion, then poked and prodded it some more in case it didn't hurt enough already. Bastian grimaced, alternately watching the good doctor's torture and giving me sympathetic glances.

After a few minutes of making sure my knee really did hurt like hell, the doctor put the ice packs back in place and made a few notes on my chart.

"It appears to be a moderate sprain," he said. "But I still want to send you down to radiology and have it x-rayed just to make sure there isn't a fracture anywhere. Assuming there isn't a fracture, I'll send you home with some painkillers and an anti-inflammatory."

He left with the promise that a nurse would be along shortly to take me to radiology. "Shortly" turned out to be the better part of an hour, and it was a full two hours after that before Dr. Bradshaw returned with his verdict.

While we waited for the doctor to come back, the time flew. Normally, being confined to a hospital room would have had me climbing the walls with boredom and impatience. I supposed it shouldn't have surprised me that that wasn't the case when Bastian was with me. After all, I had someone to talk to.

And whenever conversation fell into a lull, usually when fatigue had one of us starting to nod off, we still had those gentle, unhurried touches that had been going on since we'd been in this room. All night long, I was conscious of where and how our hands made contact. It was kind of odd, just touching like this, but the more we did it, the more comfortable—even habitual—it became. Up until tonight, we'd either been desperate to get each other's clothes off or we'd kept a paranoid distance to avoid rousing suspicions. Now that sex was off the table and there was no one around, we touched with neither worry nor urgency. Fingers loosely intertwining one minute, running along the side of a wrist the next. Occasionally he pressed his lips to the backs of my fingers or turned my hand over and gently kissed my palm. Though every bit of contact made my skin tingle, it was a side effect, not the intended effect. We touched just to…touch.

And so, even after hours of lying on this damned uncomfortable bed in pain, struggling to keep my eyes open and itching to just go home, I had to admit I was a little disappointed when the doctor came back. It was a rare opportunity for the two of us to be quarantined from the rest of the world with no way to pass the time but being together. I made a mental note that Bastian and I definitely needed to find some other place to do this under some other circumstances.

When the door opened, Bastian had his arms folded on the bed beside me, his head resting on them. He just barely remembered himself in time to sit back and make it look like we weren't "together." Not that it really mattered what the doctor thought; it was just habit.

Dr. Bradshaw flipped my chart open. "The X-rays don't show any fractures. It looks like a moderate sprain, but there's always the chance you've torn your meniscus, so I'd recommend a follow-up with your primary care doctor for a possible MRI."

I nodded, trying to mentally calculate how much time I had left before my current insurance lapsed and whether I had enough time to get an MRI before it did. That could be dealt with on Monday.

The doctor went on. "When's your next performance?"

"Tomorrow night."

Dr. Bradshaw pursed his lips. "Assuming you still go through with the performance, I don't think I need to tell you that you should stay on the stage this time."

Bastian laughed. "We'll tie him to an amp. He won't go anywhere."

"Well, be sure you tie the uninjured leg," the doctor said, chuckling.

"Don't encourage him," I growled.

He laughed again. "The nurse will be back with your discharge paperwork shortly." Dr. Bradshaw extended his hand. "Take it easy, and for your performance tomorrow, break—" He paused. "Well, I probably shouldn't say it, or you'll be back in here again tomorrow night."

I laughed. "Yeah, thanks."

Dr. Bradshaw left, and moments later the nurse showed up.

"Here's your discharge paperwork," she said. "And some instructions for taking care of your knee for the next few days."

While I went over the discharge paperwork and initialed wherever it was indicated, Bastian looked at the instructions and muffled a laugh.

"What?" I asked.

He held up the sheet so I could see it, and I had to laugh too.

On the bottom, under "additional instructions," the doctor had written in huge red letters: *NO CROWD SURFING.*

* * * * *

Bastian pulled up to the curb where I usually parked. The house was dark. It was after one in the morning, so everyone was most likely asleep, though Todd may have been out with Andre and Elena.

Thank God my bedroom was on the bottom floor. Just the thought of going up the stairs made me cringe.

Bastian shifted into park. "Need help getting inside?"

"You don't mind?"

He shot me a pointed look. "Aaron, don't ask stupid questions. Of course I don't mind." He turned off the engine and unbuckled his seat belt.

We got out of the truck and went inside. At least getting around wasn't so painful anymore, thanks to a pair of crutches. I'd tried to play the "I'm okay" card and say I didn't need them, but Bastian had threatened to make me walk home if I was that okay getting around. Much as I wasn't quick to admit it, he was right. They were a godsend.

When we got to the door, Bastian said, "Want me to unlock it?"

"I've got it." I rested my weight on the crutches while I found the right key. Behind me, as I unlocked the door, Bastian chuckled in the otherwise silent darkness.

I looked over my shoulder, just barely making out his silhouette. "What?"

He shook his head. "I was just thinking, this is probably the one time no one will care if they find out I'm in your bedroom."

I laughed. "Good point."

Once we got into my bedroom, I leaned the crutches against my dresser and hobbled to the bed. Short distances were doable without the crutches. Getting across the hospital parking lot or up the driveway? Yeah, Bastian was right.

"How're you feeling?" he asked.

"Like I fucked myself up stage diving."

"Huh, how odd." He laughed, then said, "Want me to get you some ice?"

The two flights of stairs between the freezer and me flickered through my mind. Shit, I hadn't even thought about that.

I nodded. "Please."

He gestured at the bed. "Need help putting your leg up first?"

"No, no, I've got it. Just need some ice."

"On it." With that, he left while I propped some pillows up so I could elevate my leg when I went to sleep. I listened to his footsteps going up the first flight, then the second. When he reached the second floor, there were voices. His and someone else's. Female. Must have been Lillian or Jennifer.

After a minute or two of voices murmuring over the sound of rattling ice and crinkling plastic, Bastian's footsteps started down the stairs again. A second later, he came through the door with a bag of ice.

"Thank you," I said as he handed it to me. "I have a feeling ice is going to be my best friend for a while."

"That and pain pills."

I shook my head. "Only if I really need them."

"Well, at least don't wait until you're in absolute agony before you take them, okay?"

I rolled my eyes like a petulant kid. "Yes, Mom."

"Stubborn shit." Bastian laughed and sat beside me on the bed. "You sure you'll be okay for tomorrow night?"

"I'll be fine." I rested my hand on his leg. "I'll just get a soft brace like the doc suggested, and I'll be okay."

"Just remember his orders." Bastian gave me a stern look.

"What? No jumping off the stage?" I clicked my tongue. "You're no fun."

"That's not what you said the other night." He winked, then nodded toward my knee. "How's the pain?"

"Present and accounted for." Was it ever. Even when it was iced and immobile, my leg throbbed relentlessly. Stage diving was definitely off the menu for a while.

Bastian put his hand over mine. "Need anything else before I go?"

I grinned. "*Anything* else?"

"And you say I'm always thinking dirty thoughts." He leaned down to kiss me. "I'm serious. Are you okay for the night?"

"I'll wake up one of my housemates if I need something." I ran my hand up and down his arm. "You going to be okay driving home when you're this tired?"

He gestured dismissively. "I'll be fine."

"Todd won't mind if you crash on the couch."

"I'll manage." He kissed me lightly. "Don't worry."

"I guess I'll see you tomorrow night, then."

"See you then."

We both paused, exchanging a long look like we both expected the other to say something more. When neither of us volunteered anything, he kissed me tenderly, resting his hand on the side of my neck while we, true to form, drew his kiss out as long as we could.

"Much more of that," he whispered, "and I *will* end up staying."

"I won't throw you out."

He laughed and kissed me lightly before standing. "We're liable to fuck your knee up even more if we do." Glancing at his watch, he sighed. "I'd better get out of here."

Reluctantly I nodded. "Okay, see you tomorrow."

My bedroom door clicked behind him. Footsteps faded down the hall. The garage door opened, closed. After a moment, the truck door banged shut and the engine rumbled to life. Then it too faded into the distance.

I managed to get ready for bed without jarring my knee too much and eventually settled in with my leg iced and propped up on a stack of pillows. As much as I could without moving my leg, I fidgeted. Tried to get comfortable. Failed miserably.

After about forty-five miserable minutes, I gave in and took a pain pill. In the darkness, I stared up at the ceiling, waiting for the painkillers and fatigue to kick in and knock me out.

I sighed and rubbed my eyes. Between the drugs and just being this damned tired, sleep should have come easily, but it didn't.

Without thinking about it, I put my hand on the edge of the bed, searching for Bastian's arm, and damned if I wasn't surprised to find nothing but cool, unoccupied sheets. I fidgeted even more. Why the hell did my own bed feel so fucking empty? It wasn't like we'd ever spent an entire night together.

An uneasy knot formed in my stomach. Bastian and I hadn't spent a single night together, so why did it feel so weird to spend *this* night alone?

CHAPTER THIRTEEN

My performance the next night was considerably more subdued than usual, at least as far as how much I moved around onstage. There was no way in hell I was going up on crutches, so I settled for wearing a soft knee brace under my clothes for some extra support, which helped. Painkillers fucked with my ability to enunciate and had been known to make it difficult to remember lyrics and cues, so I hadn't taken any in several hours.

By the time the show was over, I was in agony. I limped offstage, gritting my teeth, and found the nearest chair so I could take some weight off my leg. Now I was regretting leaving the crutches at home, but there wasn't much I could do about it now.

Todd pulled his guitar strap over his head. "How you holding up, kid?"

I grimaced. "I'll be a hell of a lot better once I've got some drugs in my system."

Andre laughed. "He sounds like a rock star already."

"Yeah, whatever." I laughed. "I have a prescription, damn it."

"So did Johnny Cash," Andre said.

"No, he didn't," Elena said. "Haven't you seen *Walk the Line*?"

While they discussed the ins and outs of Johnny Cash's addiction, I looked around for the water bottle I'd left back here earlier. I didn't see it. Someone must have thrown it out, damn it. At least there was a case over by our equipment on the other side of the room.

I started to get up, but a firm hand pressed down on my shoulder.

"Where do you think you're going, gimp?" Bastian raised an eyebrow.

I gestured at the case of water and pushed myself to my feet. "Just getting something to drink so I can kick-start my future drug addiction."

"Sit." He pointed at the chair. "I'll get it for you."

I opened my mouth to insist I was capable of walking ten feet for a bottle of water, but he didn't wait for objections. He came back with the water. I threw back the pain pill, chased it with a few long swallows, and sat back to wait for it to take effect.

"How's your knee?" he asked.

"Hurts, but I'll live."

"Think you'll be ready to stage dive tomorrow night?"

"*Bastian*," Elena growled from a few feet away.

He snickered. "Sorry, *Mom*." An empty water bottle flew through the air and hit his shoulder. "Hey, what the hell?"

"Behave yourself, Bastian."

"Would you two stop flirting?" Todd said. "It disgusts me." Another bottle, this time full, narrowly missed Todd's head.

"Okay, okay, get Elena away from the water before someone gets hurt," Bastian said.

"Why don't we all go out to the club and get some beers?" Andre said. "Beer solves everything, right?"

"Sounds good to me," Elena said.

Before going out to the rest of the club, I switched to a more solid knee brace that I could wear on top of my clothes. It was overkill if I'd just be sitting around, but a necessity if we got mobbed outside. We may have been just a local band, but our local fans were fans nonetheless and could get a little carried away in their enthusiasm. Hell, fans or no fans, it was nearly impossible to get through the crowd to the bar without being bodychecked a few times.

So with that in mind, I fastened the Velcro straps around my thigh and calf, securing some thick padding and a couple pieces of metal to my leg. With any luck, that would be enough.

"Ready to go meet your adoring public?" Elena asked.

I pushed myself up and gingerly put some weight on my leg. It hurt, but thanks to the brace and drugs, it was bearable. "Yep, I'm good. Let's go."

We made our way out to the main club, and the fans were waiting. Todd and Bastian stayed close to me at first, but this particular group didn't mob us like some did, so they relaxed. Before long, we'd all gotten separated and were each encircled by people asking us to sign shirts, tickets, and pictures. Occasionally a woman was brave enough—or drunk enough—to ask us to sign her cleavage. Such were the hazards of being a musician.

"So is it true about Bastian and Elena?" a giggling girl asked me.

"Bastian and Elena?" I looked up from signing a T-shirt. "What about them?"

"See?" The girl's friend rolled her eyes and elbowed her. "It's totally just a rumor."

"Oh come on," said the other. "They're totally dating."

I laughed. "What makes you say that?"

"Wishful thinking," the second girl said.

"Wishful thinking, hell," the first scoffed. "Wishful thinking would be saying he was dating *me*."

I smiled and signed someone's ticket. Oh, if they only knew.

"So are they?" the first girl persisted.

"If they are," I said, "I don't know about it."

I looked up from signing autographs and surreptitiously found Bastian in the crowd. He was a few feet away, a thick barrier of fans separating us.

He looked right at home, signing autographs and posing for photos like he was born to do this. And the fans, by the looks of it, adored him. He had a gentle charisma about him, attracting people with a warm, inviting smile and interacting with them like he was grateful to every last one of them. And he was; I was sure of it.

He was even a little shy with them sometimes, as if he didn't think he deserved this kind of attention. The women loved that too. All he had to do was blush or give that laugh-and-drop-his-gaze reaction, and every girl in a ten-foot radius swooned.

To them he was a local celebrity, an idol of sorts. Most likely a sex symbol to any red-blooded female—and probably more than a few of the males—in the audience. Had I not known him, if I'd been a fan of Schadenfreude, I could absolutely see myself vying for a second of his attention to get an autograph or a photo.

He looked up, and his eyes met mine for just a heartbeat. My breath caught in my throat.

I knew what it was like to meet a celebrity crush. Especially living in LA and being active on the music scene, I'd met a few over the years, and I knew that starstruck, weak-in-the-knees speechlessness that could tongue-tie even the most self-confident fan. It was a giddy, surreal feeling of being in close proximity to someone who'd previously only existed in the distance. Even meeting Schadenfreude, little more than a popular local band, reduced some people to nervous giggling and blushing.

That starstruck feeling was *nothing* compared to what I felt each and every time Bastian looked at me. That might have come close to describing what I felt when he'd walked into the garage the first night I sang with the band, but now it went far beyond that.

Being this close to him rendered some of the fans speechless.

Being this far away from him, even just a few feet, especially knowing what it was like to be in his bed, drove me insane.

Someone said something to him, and when he blushed, laughed, and dropped his gaze, the girls weren't the only ones getting weak in the knees.

I cleared my throat and returned to signing autographs for the other fans. Once everyone had cleared out, I rejoined the rest of the band in a booth in the corner. Not a moment too soon, either. My knee throbbed now, and I was more than a little thankful to take my weight off it for a while.

"I feel like dancing tonight." Rochelle elbowed Andre. "C'mon."

"I think I will too," Todd said. "Anyone else?"

"I'll pass." Bastian raised his beer. "I'm going to spend a little quality time with Sam Adams."

"Lucky bastard," I muttered.

"Don't you dare let me catch you drinking tonight." My sister glared at me.

"I won't, I won't." I picked up my glass. "It's just Coke, I promise."

"Good." She gestured at my leg with her beer bottle. "How's the knee?"

"Still sore, but it's getting better."

With a pointed look, she said, "Still planning on jumping off the stage again?"

"Eventually."

She rolled her eyes. "Well, I'm going to go join all the fun, able-bodied people on the dance floor." She looked at Bastian. "You sure you're not coming?"

He shook his head. "Not tonight."

"Oh come on," I said. "It'll just put more fuel on the rumors that you guys are sleeping together."

Elena groaned. "Oh Jesus, people are *still* saying that?"

Bastian scoffed. "They obviously don't know my taste in women, then."

She shoved his shoulder. "Yeah, they haven't figured out you prefer clingy psychopaths."

"She's got you there, Bastian." I winked over my beer.

"Eh, fuck you both," he muttered.

"Okay, I'm going to go have a good time." She gestured at me and said to Bastian, "You going to stay here and babysit the cripple?"

He chuckled. "Anyone going to buy me more beer for my trouble?"

"Hell no."

With a dramatic sigh, he said, "Fine, I'll stay here and keep an eye on him for free."

"Yeah, didn't figure I'd have to twist your arm too much." She shot me a look. A knowing look? A suspicious one? I couldn't tell. Then she nodded toward the dance floor. "You know where to find me if you need me."

She disappeared into the crowd.

"Don't mind me," I said to Bastian. "I need to stretch my leg out." I put my foot on the bench beside him, maneuvering it as best I could with the brace.

"Doesn't bother me any." His hand disappeared beneath the table, and all the air disappeared from the room when the backs of his fingers ran along the cuff of my jeans.

"Jesus…"

His hand stopped. "That doesn't hurt, does it?"

I shook my head.

A devilish grin pulled at his lips. "Doesn't cause the swelling to get worse, does it?" His fingertip trailed across my ankle just above my shoe.

I closed my eyes. "You're an evil, evil bastard, you know that?"

He laughed and took his hand off my foot, folding both his hands on the table in plain sight. "You know, I guess I could think of worse things than people thinking I'm sleeping with your sister."

I opened my eyes. "How do you figure?"

Shrugging, he said, "They think I'm with her, so they don't suspect I'm with you. Creates a convenient smoke screen, don't you think?"

I laughed halfheartedly. "Yeah, I suppose it does." I wasn't quite sure how to feel about the fact that, in theory, Bastian could date my sister with decidedly less backlash than if he were openly dating me. He was right about it being a convenient distraction from what was really going on, but I wasn't sure I liked being part of something that needed a decoy. I didn't know how much more of the secrecy I could handle. Why not just tell the damned band and get it over with?

"Anyway," Bastian said. "We—" He stopped and looked past me, doing a double take. Then he slammed his beer down and scowled. "Oh, for fuck's sake."

I looked over my shoulder. "What's wrong?"

"Fucking fan's messing with your sister again."

"Wait, *what*?"

"Come on." He stood and shouldered his way through the crowd. I got up and followed as quickly as I could, hobbling after him.

Elena was quite conspicuous thanks to the wild color of her hair, but as near as I could tell, she was just talking to someone. As we got closer, though, I realized she was doing her level best to back away from a heavily intoxicated dickwad in an AC/DC T-shirt. When he reached for her waist, she tried to sidestep him, but the dense crowd kept her from moving as much as she needed to.

Bastian picked up speed. In spite of my knee, so did I. A few people probably thought we were asses for shoving our way through, but I didn't particularly care at the moment. Someone was fucking with my sister, and he had about three seconds to find something else to do.

Either alcohol or a lame attempt to cop a feel sent the guy stumbling closer to her, and my temper surged to the surface as his hand went for Elena's chest.

Lucky for him, his hand didn't reach its mark because Bastian snatched his wrist. The drunk stared at him, eyes wide and jaw hanging open. Bastian took a step toward the guy, driving him backward, and I slid in between them and Elena.

"Is there a problem here?" Bastian snarled.

The drunk shook his head. "I...um...no, I just—"

"You were just leaving?" Bastian said. "Good, that's the right answer." He gestured toward the door. "Go on, out you go."

Over the music, I couldn't hear what else Bastian said to him, but the guy's widening eyes said it all, as did his clumsy, scrambling backward steps. Once he was satisfied the drunk had gotten the message, Bastian turned back to us.

I looked at Elena. "You okay?"

She glared at the retreating drunk, then ran a hand through her hair and nodded. "Yeah, I'm fine. Bastian saved me the trouble of having to kick his ass."

Bastian laughed softly, but then his expression turned more serious. "You sure you're all right?"

"Yeah." She smiled. "Thanks."

He glanced over his shoulder. "Is that the same douche who's pestered you before?"

She nodded. "Don't know what the fuck his problem is."

"Wait, this is something that's happened before?" I said.

Bastian glared in the drunk's direction, his lip almost curling into a snarl. "I'm going to go talk to security. I've asked them to boot this asshole out before, but he keeps getting in."

"Do you know his name?" I asked.

"Yep." She reached into her pocket. "Dumb shit gave me his phone number too." She held up a card and Bastian took it.

"Wes McIntyre," he said.

Under her breath, Elena said, "Fucking dick." She looked at Bastian. "Guess I'm not the only one around here who's flypaper for crazies."

"Ha, ha, very funny." He eyed the card in his hand. "I'm going to go talk to security. Why don't you two go hang out backstage? Just in case he decides to be an ass again."

"I'm fine, Bastian," Elena said. "He's not dangerous. Just really, really irritating."

Bastian pursed his lips. "Fine. But stick with Aaron for now at least, would you?"

She rolled her eyes. "Okay, if I must. Hopefully the one-legged man here can take on Douchey McDrunkass if he comes back."

"Hey!" I said.

Bastian and Elena both laughed. Then Bastian disappeared into the crowd while Elena and I worked our way to the other side of it. The booth I'd shared with him had been commandeered by someone else, and our half-finished drinks were MIA, so we found another table near the vacant stage. I propped my leg up as I had before, and we flagged down a waitress to order drinks.

"So this happens a lot?" I asked Elena after we'd gotten our drinks.

"Unfortunately." Then she looked at me, tilting her head slightly. "I have a question for you."

"Sure, what's up?"

"I'm just curious," she said, "and maybe this is none of my business, but..." She glanced in Bastian's direction, then looked at me, eyebrows raised.

I blinked. "What?"

"Is there something going on between you and Bastian?"

Panic caught my breath in my throat, but I forced it out in a cough that hopefully sounded like a startled laugh. "Last I checked, Bastian's not gay."

Her lips thinned and her brow furrowed. She glanced at him again.

"Why?"

She looked at me again. "Because you're the first thing I've seen without four strings and an amp that can hold his attention like that."

My mouth went dry. "Like what?"

"Please, Aaron." She raised an eyebrow. "I know what I've seen."

I showed my palms. "Honestly I don't know what you're talking about." I paused. "I mean, don't get me wrong, I would. I totally would."

"*Aaron.*"

"If he was gay and he wasn't in the band, I mean," I said.

"Emphasis on 'if he wasn't in the band.'" She shot me a pointed look. "The last thing we need is—"

"*Elena.*" I put a hand up. "Every member of this band is either related to me or not gay. Or both. It's a moot point. You have nothing to worry about."

She held my gaze, and I swore she could see right through me. Right through to all the dirty thoughts of Bastian, all the bruises under my clothes, even that stolen kiss in the emergency room.

Finally she said, "Okay. I believe you."

I forced myself not to release a relieved sigh. "Do you think he is, you know"—I inclined my head—"one of my kind?"

She pursed her lips. "Oh, I've had my suspicions from time to time."

"What about Denise?"

"Maybe he swings both ways."

Oh, how very astute you are. "What makes you think he is, though?"

"He doesn't set off your gaydar?"

Well, he certainly did when my cock was in his mouth. I coughed. "I, uh, no. Can't say he does."

"Huh. Maybe I'm wrong." She shrugged. "I can't really figure out what it is. I've just…gotten that vibe." She leaned forward a little and in a conspiratorial voice, just loud enough for me to hear over the club's noise, said, "That and at a show a few months ago, I could have sworn he was checking out the opening act's keyboardist."

"Seriously?"

She nodded. "Not that I blame him. The man was shit hot. Once he took his shirt off, Rochelle and I were both drooling, and I swear to God, so was Bastian."

I chuckled. "Well, well, well. Maybe he does—"

"Hands. Off."

"You mean I can't even look?"

"You can look all you—"

She stopped abruptly when the allegedly bisexual bassist in question slid into the booth beside her. He set his drink on the table, then put his arm around her shoulders, and she squealed, trying to shove him away.

"Oh eww, what are you doing?"

He laughed. "Just keeping up appearances."

"Bastard," she muttered. "Even if you were my type, our brothers would kill us. Now move over."

He lifted his arm off her shoulders and put a more platonic distance between himself and my sister. His eyes met mine briefly, and a knot twisted in my gut. The band would be livid if Elena and Bastian started sleeping together. If they found out about us…

The hairs on the back of my neck stood on end. Okay, so maybe keeping it quiet *was* a good idea, even if running stealth was a headache and a half.

"So," Elena said. "Did you tell security about that Wes douche?"

"Actually I ran into the guy outside."

Her eyes widened. "Oh God, you didn't hurt him, did you?"

"No, I didn't hurt him."

"What did you do to him, then?"

He grinned. "Took care of the situation."

Elena cocked her head. "Bastian..."

"I told him he's been coming on too strong and that tends to put women off."

"Why, Bastian," she said, grinning. "I didn't know you had that kind of maturity. What did he say?"

"He said he'd back off. Especially after I gave him your number."

Her smile fell. "Bastian Koehler..."

He chuckled. "Okay, I didn't give him your number."

"You'd better not have."

"I didn't." His trademark devilish grin made my spine tingle. "I gave him Denise's."

Elena and I both stared at him, wide-eyed. Bastian looked at me, at her, at me again. Then he rolled his eyes.

"Oh come on, I'm kidding. I wouldn't do that." He shook his head and picked up his drink. "The guy wasn't *that* much of an asshole."

CHAPTER FOURTEEN

The longer I was with the band, the more songs we added to the set. In the beginning, I'd learned the core songs, the hits that the fans demanded at every show. As the band and I got a feel for working together, we expanded into some of their older songs as well as the new pieces Rochelle and Bastian had written. At least that meant we could change the set around from night to night if we felt like it, not to mention balancing out the songs between Elena and me.

"We doing anything new tonight?" Todd asked at rehearsal.

"I was thinking, assuming Aaron's up for it," Bastian said. "Maybe we could run through *(Un)Fading*."

Todd blinked. "Seriously? We haven't played that one in ages."

"Of course we haven't," Bastian said. "I couldn't stand listening to Derek's voice mutilating it."

Andre said something in German. Bastian snickered and replied in the same language. Both brothers laughed.

"Hey, hey, what have I said about jabbering in Swahili around us?" Elena said. "Come on, what did he say?"

"Never mind." Bastian chuckled. "Okay, so, *(Un)Fading*. You all still remember how it goes?"

Andre's eyes lost focus, and he tapped out a rhythm on one of the snare drums with his fingers. Then he looked up and nodded. "Yeah, I think I remember. Might be a bit rusty."

"What about you?" Bastian asked Todd.

Todd did a similar mental run-through, staring into the middle distance while his fingers pantomimed a few chords. After a moment, he too nodded. "Yeah, I'm good."

"So we're really going to play this one, huh?" Elena said. "I thought you'd given up on it."

Bastian shrugged. "New singer. Worth a shot, right?"

"We haven't performed all that many ballads, though," Andre said. "Think the fans will go for it?"

"He's got a point," Elena said. "Some of the clubs, maybe, but the Anarchy crowd might not be down with something slow."

"Only one way to find out," Bastian said. "We'll see how it goes in rehearsal, try performing it, see what the fans think, and go from there. Even if the House crowd isn't into it, we've got plenty of gigs at other places where they might like it."

"You're the boss," Andre said.

"Let's give it a go," Todd said.

Bastian smiled at me. "You sure you're ready to try this one?"

I nodded. It was definitely one of the more challenging pieces he'd written, and it had taken me quite a bit of practice to get it right, but I was pretty sure I was ready. And what could I say? I was a lead singer. I wasn't without my ego, and a song that gave me a chance to really work my voice? Oh hell yeah.

"Let's give it a run, then." Bastian leaned down to adjust his amp. "Everyone ready?"

Andre counted us off. The bass line started the long intro. After a few bars, Andre and Todd joined in, bringing to life the slow, powerful beat and melody.

Then I came in.

The goose bumps prickled to life on my arms and back before the first line was off my tongue. I didn't know how many times I'd practiced that song at home, in the car, in the shower. I'd been through the lyrics a hundred times until I knew them inside and out. I knew them in my sleep, just like the myriad other songs in the band's usual set.

But tonight, singing them with Bastian's bass thrumming right beside my own heartbeat, the lyrics hit me in places they hadn't before. Like two seemingly benign substances combining to create an explosive chemical reaction, the words and the bass came together to change the meaning of the song completely.

"You lift me up, don't fade away, no one else, only you…"

Every line, every verse, may as well have been pulled straight out of me. It was like Bastian knew, like he'd channeled everything I didn't know I'd felt for him. Like I'd written every word myself.

Hadn't he written it years ago, though? This wasn't new material. It wasn't a new song. And it wasn't like he could read my mind, so how could—

I cut off that line of thought when my voice faltered.

"No one sees, you see right through me…"

Chancing a look over my shoulder during Todd's guitar solo, I met Bastian's eyes.

The intensity in his vivid blue eyes struck me just like every word of the song. Whatever I felt, I couldn't tell if he felt the same, but he felt something. Something about this song resonated with him now, even if he'd written it ages ago and had played it hundreds of times before there was an "us," and he looked just as surprised as I was.

His fingers slipped off a string. He looked away from me and tried to recover, but after a few beats, the bass and percussion fell too far out of synch. Andre stopped, so we all did.

Todd chuckled. "You know, for someone who was asking the rest of us if *we* remembered the song…"

"Shut up," Bastian laughed. "So I'm rusty."

"That old age kicking in," Andre said. "Starting to forget shit."

"Yeah, yeah, yeah." Bastian glanced at me. He instantly dropped his gaze and cleared his throat, but not before I caught the extra hint of red in his cheeks. "Anyway, why don't we pick up at the beginning of the second verse and try again?"

We tried it again. Todd probably could have played it in his sleep. Andre had the percussion part down pat. If Bastian didn't fuck it up, I did. Whenever I got it, he screwed up. And with every fleeting glance we exchanged, I was less convinced it was my imagination, this intense reaction to the lyrics. It wasn't my imagination, and it was anything but one-sided.

We finally got through it twice in a row without having to stop and restart.

"Okay, this definitely needs some work," Bastian said. "But I think we can do this. It'll just take some time."

"Well, all the screwups notwithstanding," Rochelle said. "Your voice was made for that song, Aaron; I'm telling you."

My gaze flicked toward Bastian. He focused on his bass, and I swore his cheeks colored. I cleared my throat. "Hopefully I can iron out the screwups then."

"We'll hold off on performing it for a while," Andre said. "But I'm with Rochelle. Once we really get it, this one's a keeper."

Bastian shot me another quick look. I tried not to shiver. It was probably just as well we'd have to spend some time rehearsing this one before adding it to our show. I needed some time to get used to singing it in Bastian's vicinity before I could think about taking it onstage.

"So what's next?" Andre asked.

"I haven't liked the sound of the chorus on 'Serrated' at the last couple of shows," Bastian said. "Why don't we run through it a few times, see where the problem is?"

That was one of Elena's songs, so I sat while she took her place at the mic. And my God, was it ever a relief to take some weight off my knee. It had been a week or so since my little stage-diving mishap, and while I could get around with almost no difficulty, the pain still acted up from time to time. The hazards of being a rock star, I thought, chuckling to myself.

Once Bastian and Andre were satisfied with the chorus of "Serrated," we decided to call it a night.

"We're going out for drinks," Andre said to me. "You coming?"

"Is Todd?" I asked.

"There's beer involved," Elena said. "Of course he is."

"Then I guess I am too since he drove me here."

"Bastian, what about you?" Andre said.

Bastian looked up from putting his bass away. "There's beer. Like you need to ask."

"Well, I know," Andre said. "But it *is* getting late, and—"

Bastian shot back something in German. He and I exchanged glances. The last thing I wanted was to go hang out with the band and have a few beers. My veins still tingled with the bass line of that song, and I was sure if anyone got close enough, they'd know. I wasn't even sure I wanted to be this close to him because *he* might catch on.

To what? Catch on to what, Aaron? It's just sex.

And (Un)Fading *is just a song.*

Right.

As everyone put gear away and migrated toward the cars, I found every reason I could to stay in the garage. Bastian didn't seem to be in much of a hurry to leave, taking his time putting his bass and amp away.

"You comin'?" Todd asked, one hand on the doorknob.

I nodded. "Yeah, yeah, I'll be right there. I'll meet you outside."

"Hurry up. I'm thirsty." Todd left, pulling the door shut behind him, and Bastian and I looked at each other. Swallowing hard, I kept one ear tuned to the noise outside, listening for the telltale crunch of gravel beneath approaching feet.

Bastian looked up from putting his bass in its case. "How's your leg?"

"Sore, but it's getting better."

"Good, good." I couldn't be certain, but I wondered if he was deliberately moving as slowly as possible, making sure his bass sat just so, securing it. Killing time, giving him a reason to stay in here. He glanced at me again. "Think you'll be stage diving anytime soon?"

"Not if my sister has anything to say about it."

Bastian laughed softly. Unusually awkward silence fell between us.

I cleared my throat. "Guess we were both having a bit of trouble with that song."

"Yeah." He swallowed, dropping his gaze for a second. "It's never been that hard for—" He paused, wincing. "I mean, that one's never been that difficult for me."

I forced a quiet laugh. "Yeah, it was always pretty easy for me until I actually played it with the band."

He smiled. "Well, it'll just take some practice, I guess."

I nodded. "Think we'll be able to perform it?"

"Oh definitely." He met my eyes, looking at me through his lashes. "I definitely think so."

"Assuming we can get it right." I held his gaze, barely even hearing what I'd said.

"I think we can." He sounded just as uninterested in the conversation. I wondered if the only reason we spoke was to give ourselves an excuse not to touch. *Keep talking, don't touch, don't risk getting caught in an embrace.* But with every passing second of disengaged small talk, I had less and less success convincing myself to stay an arm's length from him.

Bastian cleared his throat. "Well, I guess we should—" He cut himself off midsentence. Chewing his lip, he glanced at the closed door. Voices still murmured outside.

Dangerously close but safely separated from view by a wall and a door.

"Bastian, do—"

"Fuck it." He put both hands on the sides of my neck and kissed me, and oh God, his kiss was intense tonight. Desperate, like that first time in the alley and every time we'd stolen a kiss since then, but somehow different. Needy, hungry, but...tender? Fuck, I couldn't tell what was different. It was. Somehow it was. And whatever it was consumed my senses, my awareness, any brain cell that might have had any hope of trying to analyze it and figure out if something had changed and *Jesus Christ, Bastian, I need you so fucking bad.*

"Fuck," he whispered, running his fingers through my hair. "Do you know how hard—" He caught himself again, laughing softly against my lips.

"Oh, I think I know."

He kissed me again. "I need you tonight, Aaron."

I shivered. "Then come over." I licked my lips. "We'll go have a few drinks, keep up appearances. Then...come over."

He glanced over his shoulder toward the door. "What about—"

"I don't care. We'll be quiet. We've been quiet before."

He licked his lips, hesitating for a moment before he whispered, "Sure your knee can handle it?"

"I'm sure we can manage."

Bastian nodded, eyes once again darting toward the door that still divided us from the rest of the band. "Good, because I really, really want you tonight."

"I'll leave the side door unlocked."

"I'll be there as soon as I can."

CHAPTER FIFTEEN

Over the next couple of weeks, a heavy rehearsal schedule kept us in close proximity most nights, but all the nonsense relating to real life and being responsible, productive members of society kept us out of each other's beds. Job interviews, doctor's appointments, and an MRI for me; overtime, ex-fiancée drama, and some family commitments for him. Though it had been less than twenty-four hours since we'd seen each other, it had been almost two weeks since we'd *really* touched. By last night's rehearsal, we could barely look at each other, and we didn't dare exchange more than the briefest platonic fist bump before parting ways afterward.

Tomorrow our schedules were clear, which meant there was a good chance we could sneak off somewhere after the show tonight and relieve a little tension. Tonight, come hell or high water, I had to have him as soon as humanly possible.

But first I had to get through sound check, a performance, and whatever socializing we had to do to keep up appearances afterward. And before any of *that*, dinner. We had another show at the House of Anarchy, so we'd gathered at the restaurant across the street for dinner and a few beers. I stepped into the restaurant and looked around. Todd waved at me from the back, and I nodded to acknowledge him before meandering through the maze of tables to the corner booth where the band sat.

When I caught sight of Bastian, he was engaged in a conversation with Andre and Rochelle. His head was turned away from me and tilted slightly. The thought of kissing that exposed side of his neck, just below his ear, made my breath catch and very nearly knocked my feet out from under me. Yeah, I needed him. Like, *now*.

Then he looked up and smiled at me, turning my spine to jelly. Staying as casual and nonchalant as I could, I greeted everyone before sliding into the booth, taking a seat beside Rochelle and opposite Todd. Not a moment too soon, either. I sat before anyone else caught on to what Bastian's very presence did to me. It was probably just as well I didn't sit directly across from or beside him. The desire to touch him was overwhelming enough as it was.

"Sorry I'm late," I said, trying not to focus all the things I wanted to do to Bastian as soon as we were alone.

"Fashionably late, as always," Todd said with an exaggerated sigh.

"Guess that's better than coming too soon," Rochelle said.

Elena elbowed her and said in a loud whisper, "Oh, be nice, you'll give them all complexes."

Rochelle gestured dismissively. "Please. They're all too simple for complexes."

Andre and Todd scowled, then laughed. Bastian just grinned behind his pint glass and gave me a mischievous look, a wink without actually winking.

"So, cripple, what did the doctor say?" Elena asked.

"MRI didn't show a tear in the meniscus, so just a sprain." I grinned. "And it's just about healed, so he says I'll be in stage-diving shape in another couple of weeks."

My sister gave an exasperated sigh and muttered something under her breath before taking a drink.

"Just don't do it at the Battle of the Bands," Andre said.

"Why not?" I asked.

"Because the security guys for that show are dicks," Bastian said. "They throw fans out for crowd surfing, and they've threatened a few times to throw performers out for it too."

"Bastards," I said.

Todd raised his glass. "Hear, hear."

Bastian and Andre both raised theirs and said, "Amen."

Andre peered into his own glass. "Hey, I'm outta beer."

"Me too," Rochelle said.

Bastian shoved his own empty glass toward Todd. "Go score us some more, McClure."

Todd scoffed. "What? Why me?"

"Because you were flirting with the waitress," Rochelle said. "So as long as you have her attention…" She nodded at the glasses.

I laughed. "Todd, you were flirting with a waitress again?"

"I did no such thing." Todd sipped his beer.

"No shit," Bastian said. "Flirting actually requires a bit of tact and originality."

Andre and Rochelle laughed. Todd slammed his beer down, pretending to be indignant. "I *beg* your pardon! Those pickup lines were one hundred percent original."

"I'm sure they were," Bastian said in a patronizing voice. He patted Todd's arm. "That's why you got her number so easily, isn't it?"

"Fuck you," Todd muttered.

"You know, I may have to have a little chat with Lillian and let her know you're flirting with the waitstaff," I said.

He shrugged. "How do you know she doesn't have me out looking for someone else to, you know, 'join' us?"

Elena and I both grimaced and covered our ears.

"No," I said. "Don't want to know."

"Then stay out of my personal affairs," Todd said.

Bastian rolled his eyes. "McClure, shut up and go get us some more beer."

After another round of drinks, a light dinner, and an hour or so of shooting the breeze, Todd pulled back his sleeve and made an exaggerated gesture of checking his watch.

"Well, folks, looks like it's time to get to work."

We settled up the tab and left the restaurant. On the way across the street to the House, I cast a surreptitious glance at Bastian, who was talking with Andre and Todd. He met my eyes and tripped over his speech and feet. He recovered quickly, cleared his throat, and resumed his conversation, his eyes flicking once more in my direction.

The look he gave me, however fleeting, was almost enough to melt the clothing right off my body. That wink without winking again. The look that told me he was thinking what I was thinking.

Goddamn it, this show can't be over soon enough.

Backstage, onstage during sound check, and backstage again, we kept looking at each other. Just surreptitious glances here and there, nothing that would tip off the rest of the band, but more than enough to drive me out of my mind. Around the time the opening act went on, I wasn't even sure I could remember the lyrics to a single song in our set. All I could think was *Bastian, Bastian, I want Bastian.*

While we hung out backstage during the opening act, I threw one of those inconspicuous glances toward him, but he was gone. I looked around. The rest of the band was accounted for. Bastian? Nowhere to be found.

Probably just as well. Now I could—

My phone vibrated, and I looked at the screen. The name didn't screw with my blood pressure nearly as much as the three words of the message itself:

Meet me downstairs.

My heart jumped into my throat. I shoved my phone into my pocket, afraid someone would see. Downstairs. *Where* downstairs? The lower level of the club was a labyrinth of hallways, closets, and various rooms. Grinning to myself, I guessed Bastian had already thought that far ahead.

I casually got up. To my sister, I said, "I need to run out to my car. I'll be right back."

She nodded. "The other band won't be long, so hurry up."

"I will," I said over my shoulder. "Don't worry."

The second level of the club wasn't as crowded as the main floor, but a few people milled around, mostly caught up in their own conversations or wandering out the back for a cigarette. I didn't see Bastian though.

"Come on, where are you?" I muttered.

Someone brushed past on the stairs and a hand paused momentarily on my lower back, the contact lingering a second longer than a silent *pardon me*. I glanced up and caught Bastian's eye as he walked past. He smiled, then casually continued on his way, turning down one of the side hallways.

After a moment, I followed.

The side hallway, unlike the area by the stairwell, was deserted. I turned the corner just in time to see Bastian disappear into one of the many rooms, and I resisted the urge to break into a run. The hallway was right below the stage and thrummed with the muffled thumping of the music above, but the air crackled with something that had nothing to do with bass or percussion.

Glancing back to make sure no one saw, I slipped through the door marked JANITOR.

As soon as the door shut behind me, Bastian shoved me up against the wall and kissed me. His hands were in my hair, his mouth devouring mine, and my body melted against his.

"It's been too fucking long," he said in a throaty growl.

Oh, he was right about that. It had been too long. Entirely too long. And here, now, we didn't have nearly enough time.

"Bastian, we—" I closed my eyes, groaning softly when his clothed cock brushed over mine. I licked my lips. "We're on soon."

"I know. We don't have a lot of time, but I…" He held my face in both hands, his heavy, unsteady breaths warming my lips. "God, I just need to touch you." He kissed me again, sliding his hands into my hair and pressing his cock against mine again.

When he dipped his head to kiss my neck, I dug my fingers into his shoulders just to keep myself from collapsing. Fucking hell, he knew how to turn me on. If I survived tonight's show, the sex afterward would probably kill us both. After two long weeks together but apart, and the way his lips teased my neck just now, by the time I was done with him tonight, there would probably be nothing left of the man but a pile of ashes and the faint twang of a bass line.

I licked my lips. "I want you so fucking bad right now."

Bastian shivered, releasing a low growl against my neck. "If I could, I would fuck you right here, right now."

"Oh God…"

"I've been dying to feel you again," he whispered. "There is no way I can get through another show without touching you." I shivered when his fingertips found my zipper. A mixture of arousal and panic flooded through me. I wanted him, I needed him, but every pulse of the opening band's beat above us reminded me we had somewhere else to be and not a lot of time to get there.

"Bastian, we don't have time." I bit my lip when his fingers closed around my cock. Another song ended above us, and in spite of every fiber of my being ordering me to shut the fuck up, I said, "We don't…we don't have time."

"I know we don't." His voice was unsteady with a degree of desperation I'd never before heard from him. "But we don't have a choice."

The panic in my mind, the voice telling me I needed to get back upstairs and get ready to go onstage, faded when Bastian knelt in front of me. The moist warmth of his mouth on my cock took my breath away. My spine straightened as he took all of me into his mouth. He pulled back slowly until only the head of my cock was between his lips. Then he suddenly took the whole thing again.

"Jesus, Bastian..." I'd been on edge ever since I'd arrived at the restaurant, and now his mouth was almost too much. The tremors intensified. The shock waves surging up my spine with each stroke of his hand and mouth nearly knocked me off my feet.

"*Oh...fuck...*" I barely choked the words out. My entire body shook with the power of an orgasm that wasn't even fully realized yet. I was close, right there on the edge, the tension long since past what I thought was the breaking point, and still it built. I grabbed the metal shelves on either side of me for balance as my legs threatened to buckle. I moaned, the world spinning around me in time with the rapid, gentle circles his tongue and piercing made on the head of my cock.

Above us, the music tapered, then drowned in the sound of applause and shouting. One more song down. Two to go if I knew their set. The music started again, the deep thumping of the bass and the percussion vibrating through the ceiling and down the metal shelves, into my hands, pulsing straight through my body to my cock. I couldn't tell if I felt the drum solo or if it was simply the rapid, rhythmic touch of Bastian's tongue stud across hypersensitive nerves, but it didn't matter.

"Oh God, Bastian, don't...don't stop," I murmured. My body tensed, my hands seizing around the shelves, making them creak like old bed frames. The music crescendoed toward its climactic final chorus, echoing the intensifying orgasm that swelled within me, and as the song reached its heart-stopping peak, the tension broke.

My back arched off the wall, and I gasped for breath, my body convulsing and shaking against him as he drew my orgasm out. When I finally begged him to stop, he stood. His mouth was vaguely salty, and he was as breathless as I was. My knees trembled, threatening to buckle, but the need for balance wasn't why I put my arms around him. I couldn't get close enough to him. Not here, not with so many clothes between us and somewhere else we needed to be, but I tried anyway.

Above us, the music faded and the shouts of the crowd took over. We both released frustrated sighs, breaking our passionate kiss. We had less than ten minutes to get onstage.

"We should go," he whispered.

"But what about you? I—"

"We definitely don't have time for that."

"You're an evil tease, you know that?"

He laughed and kissed me. "I got you off, didn't I?" He gasped when I cupped his hard-on through his jeans.

"Yeah, you did," I said. "But I haven't done anything for you."

"Then that'll just give me something to look forward to after the show, won't it?"

I shivered. The music changed again. Not much time.

Bastian muttered something in his native tongue, probably something as profane as everything running through my mind, and stepped back. We both straightened our clothes.

"You go up first," he said.

I nodded and reached for the door. "See you onstage."

"Wait." He caught my arm.

"Hmm?"

He took a breath. "Listen, later tonight…" He shook his head. "There's no way in hell I can deal with staying quiet."

My heart sank. God, I needed him. He couldn't bail on me now.

He slid an arm around my waist. "I was thinking, why don't we get a hotel room for the night?"

"Are—" I blinked, then cleared my throat. "Are you serious?"

He nodded, not a trace of humor in what little of his face I could see. Leaning in to kiss me, he stopped a hair's breadth from my lips and whispered, "It's either that, or we take the chance of someone hearing us, because I have a feeling I'm going to fucking lose it tonight."

All the air left my lungs in one sharp exhalation.

He kissed me gently. "You game?"

"You'd better believe it."

Against mine, his lips curved into a grin. He teased my lips apart with his tongue. I desperately wanted to surrender to his kiss, but I knew us. *Just one more kiss* would have us down here for half an hour, so I broke away.

"We should get onstage," I whispered, even though I didn't want to let go.

"Yeah, I know." He released me. "You go ahead after the show. Find a place, check in, text me the address and room number. We'll split the cost."

I nodded. "Works for me."

"Good. Now go. We have a show to nail."

I kissed him lightly, then made a quick escape before we gave in to the temptation for *just one more kiss*. On the way back up the stairs on shaking legs, barely aware of the protests of my nearly healed left leg, I tried not to let our plans for the evening distract me. A hotel room. All night with Bastian. Nowhere else to be, no one to overhear us.

There was probably some reason why it was a bad idea, but I sure as hell couldn't think of it. Being involved with him in the first place was a bad idea, so why not just jump in with both feet, get a room, and fuck like we really wanted to?

"Hey, Aaron." Denise's voice startled me out of my thoughts. She leaned against the wall a few feet from the stairwell.

I stopped. "Oh. Denise. Uh, hey." I wanted to ask how the hell she got back here. Last I'd checked, Bastian had asked security not to let her backstage. But I didn't have time for her explanations, nor did I really have time for small talk. "Hate to run, but I need to get backstage. Band's going on soon."

"Right, of course." She paused, and something about the way she narrowed her eyes unsettled me. "Have you seen Bastian, by chance?"

I swallowed, pretending I couldn't still taste his kiss. Or myself in his kiss. "Um, no. Can't say I have. He might have gone out to his truck, though." I nodded toward the club's back door, which was in the opposite direction of the room where Bastian and I had stolen away.

She smiled. "Great, thanks." With that, she turned on her heel and went in the direction I'd indicated. I watched her go, wondering what it was about that conversation that had made me so uneasy.

Then I shook my head. Of course she unnerved me. She was Bastian's crazy ex-fiancée.

I kept walking toward the backstage area, counting down the seconds until we had that hotel room.

CHAPTER SIXTEEN

After the show, once our gear was squared away, I showered, changed clothes, and got the hell out of there.

Still trying to cover our tracks so the rest of the band wouldn't catch on, I left first. About fifteen minutes later, Bastian texted me to let me know he'd gotten held up. Twenty minutes after that, he called to tell me Andre had stopped him to ask about the new songs we were adding to the set for our upcoming shows and some other shit relating to rehearsals. Then the club manager headed him off with some contract questions that were really Rob's domain, not Bastian's. Everyone seemed to be conspiring to keep him in the club and out of this room.

By this point, I'd already checked into a cheap motel just north of Seattle and tried to occupy nervous hands with channel surfing while I lay back on the bed. Every time my phone beeped, my heart skipped, certain the next delay would be one that kept him from getting here at all. I swore if one more person tried to keep him from me, I was going to drive back and drag Bastian out of the club.

Finally he texted me with: *Leaving now. Thank fuck.*

I sent back: *I'll be here.*

My phone stayed silent after that. Every time a car pulled into the parking lot, I muted the TV and craned my neck, trying to decide if it was the familiar purr of his truck's engine or just another guest. Finally I turned off the TV. I wasn't paying any attention to it anyway, and any sound that wasn't Bastian's truck or voice just annoyed me.

I closed my eyes and let out a long, ragged breath.

It had been too damned long since we'd been in bed together. I'd gone months at a stretch without getting laid before, but not when the guy I wanted was in close proximity. Not when that guy was *Bastian*.

Every time with him felt just like the first time, and the anticipation still drove me mad just like that first night. And tonight there was no one around. No need to hold back. Quiet sex was hot, there was no doubt about that, but there was too much pent-up desperation between us. The blowjob backstage hadn't even begun to take the edge off.

I needed to let go. I needed to know what he sounded like when he let go.

An engine outside raised the hairs on the back of my neck. Was it?

A second later, a text message came through. Fumbling with my phone, I finally got the message open, and the three words on the screen had me on my feet and halfway across the room before the phone had even clattered onto the table:

Open the door.

I threw the door open just as Bastian, bass case slung over his shoulder, cleared the top step.

"Jesus, I couldn't get here fast enough." He pulled me into a deep, passionate kiss, gripping the back of my neck while his tongue demanded access to my mouth. I grabbed the front of his shirt, not quite sure if I was trying to drag him through the door with me or just keep him as close as possible. Either way, he didn't protest. He put his hands on my hips and pulled me with him, taking me away from the door frame but not allowing even an inch of space between our bodies. He kicked the door shut behind us, then quickly shrugged the case strap off his shoulder and set his bass down. Once that was out of the way, I shoved his jacket off his shoulders and we stumbled across the room. He kissed my neck, panting against my skin as he slid his hands under my shirt. His hips pressed against mine, and just having his hard cock this close to mine after such a maddening wait was enough to throw my world off its axis.

He broke the kiss long enough to pull my shirt over my head, then his own, and when we came back together, I gasped at the heat of his body against my skin. Our hands were all over each other, running through hair, grasping shoulders, loosening clothing.

Shoes thumped against the wall, furniture, wherever the hell they landed. Clothes fell on top of them. We were too busy kissing to speak, and the only sounds were our shuffling footsteps, the rustle of bodies struggling free from clothing, and sharp breaths punctuating our desperate, unending kissing.

He tried to unbuckle my belt with unsteady hands. "Too many clothes," he muttered against my lips. "Fuck, too damn many..."

"Here..." I stepped back and finished what he'd started, though I wasn't much steadier. With trembling hands, we got out of our clothes as fast as we could, stopping every few breaths for a deep, hungry kiss. There was no rush to be finished, but damned if we were going to take our time getting started.

With every last thread of clothing out of the way, we gave in to need and gravity, sinking onto the bed together in a breathless kiss. The bed frame creaked beneath us, but it only barely registered in my senses. There was no one around to hear us, and even if there were, it didn't matter. The whole damned world could have been within earshot and I just. Didn't. Care.

He kissed my neck, my collarbone, my chest. I squirmed under him, running my hands up and down his arms. My fingers traced the edges of his tattoos, following lines I'd long since memorized, just to remind myself this was really happening, because everything about it—the warmth of his body, the taste of his kiss, the touch of his hand—was too good to be real. Like no one else I'd ever dated, I constantly had to convince myself this was happening. Most of the time, I still couldn't believe Bastian Koehler was my lover, even when it was his name rolling off my lips at the peak of an orgasm.

I wanted to be as close to him as possible. "Bastian..." I licked my lips. "Come back up here."

As soon as he did, I pulled him down to kiss me, and he took over, parting my lips with his tongue while he pinned one arm, then the other, to the bed beside me. I was completely at his mercy, completely surrendered to him, and I didn't fight.

I shivered when his piercing glided over my tongue. It wasn't the thought of all the things he did with the piercing that gave me goose bumps; it was the fact that each time I felt it now, each time my tongue brushed against it, it subtly emphasized that I wasn't kissing just anyone. I was kissing *Bastian*. And every time he touched me, it was *him*, and it was *right*. Everything about this was right.

His mouth left mine and once again went to my neck. His tongue made a circle at the hollow of my throat, and I sucked in a hiss of breath.

"We've got all night," he murmured, pausing to kiss my collarbone before continuing downward. "Nowhere else to be." His lips brushed the center of my chest. "And no one to hear us." He ran the tip of his tongue around my nipple and looked up at me. "And I intend to take full advantage of that."

I groaned, biting my lip and closing my eyes.

"Sucking you off backstage just made me want you that much more," he whispered. "I wasn't kidding at all when I said I would have fucked you then and there if I could have, and now"—he pressed his hips against mine—"I can fuck you."

I opened my eyes. "No."

Bastian raised his head, lips parted in surprise.

I licked my lips. "I want to fuck *you*."

Surprise turned to more surprise, which quickly turned to arousal. He grinned, then came down to kiss me. "I'm not going to argue with that."

We both sat up. Out of habit, I reached for the bedside table but froze. Oh shit. In my rush to get here and all the time I'd impatiently waited for him to show up, one tiny detail had slipped my mind.

I looked at him. "Did you bring condoms?"

He raised his eyebrow. "Didn't you?"

I groaned. "Fuck..." There was a convenience store a few blocks away. Open twenty-four hours, I hoped. All we had to do was get dressed, leave this room, walk or drive, *fuck, fuck, fuck, how could I forget condoms on a night like this?*

Bastian laughed and kissed my cheek. "Relax, I was just kidding. I brought plenty."

"You bastard."

He got up and went to get his jacket from the other side of the room. "What are you going to do about it?"

"Guess I'll just have to fuck you, won't I?"

Tossing me an unopened box of condoms, he grinned. "Guess you will."

"I assume you brought lube too?"

"No, I was thinking we could try it without lube tonight."

I glared at him while I opened the box. He pulled out a bottle of lube and smirked.

"Smart-ass." I pulled one condom free from the pack and left the rest on the bedside table. While I put the condom on, Bastian poured some lube into his palm. Then he stroked it onto my cock, laughing softly when I closed my eyes and moaned.

"Thought you could use a hand," he said.

"Oh, I don't mind."

"Didn't think you would." He stroked a little faster, a little harder, and even through the condom, his hand drove me insane.

"Don't you fucking dare make me come yet," I whispered.

He kissed me lightly, then grinned. "I've already made you come once, remember?"

The memory of my orgasm backstage sent another shiver through me, and I grabbed his wrist before he sent me past the point of no return again.

"Get on your knees," I said through clenched teeth. "Now."

He exhaled hard against my lips. Though he couldn't move with me holding his wrist, that didn't stop him from squeezing, releasing, squeezing, releasing.

"Oh God, Bastian," I moaned. "Fuck, you're… Get on your goddamned knees."

His thumb ran up and down the underside of my cock. "Ask nicely."

"Please get on your goddamned knees."

A breath of laughter warmed my lips. "Come on, Aaron. Ask nicely."

I growled with frustration. "Will you *please* get on your knees so I can fuck you?"

"That's more like it."

He released my cock. I released his wrist. He kissed me once more, then shifted onto his hands and knees, and I knelt behind him. The temptation to tease him was there, but to hell with it. If I wasn't inside him in the next few seconds, I was going to set off the hotel's fire alarm.

Slowly, calling on every last bit of self-control I had, I pushed into him one inch at a time. I swallowed hard, barely breathing as I watched my cock slide into him, as I watched myself fuck him in slow motion.

"That's perfect," he whispered, letting his head fall forward. "Just like that, that's—"

"Like this?" I withdrew just as slowly, then pushed back in.

He groaned. "Just like that."

"Sure you don't want it"—I thrust all the way inside him—"harder?"

He gasped. A shudder began between my hands and ran the length of his spine, rippling up to his shoulders just before he threw his head back and moaned. "Holy...fuck...Aaron..."

I took another deep, hard thrust. "Like it like that?"

He said something. I couldn't understand the words, couldn't even tell what language he'd spoken. I understood the desperation in his trembling voice, though, and fucked him deep and hard, just the way I knew he wanted it. He whimpered and moved with me, slamming back against me as he alternately spoke in slurred German and profane, growled English.

I watched my own hands sliding up and down his sides while I fucked him slowly, watching myself touch him in ways any man in his right mind would sell his soul to do. Looking down at him, watching myself slide in and out of him, watching him come undone, I felt like one of his starstruck fans: reduced to breathless silence just by being in the same room with him.

I sucked in a ragged breath, struggling to stay in control. A tremor nearly knocked me off balance. My eyes rolled back, my fingers dug into his hips, and I held my breath, hoping for just another second or two, a few more thrusts, whatever it took, just *not yet*.

"Oh God, oh my God..." The low thrum of his voice sent tremors through me as if he'd spoken right to my nerve endings. Then I heard his name and realized it wasn't his voice at all. "Oh fuck, Bastian..." I tried to cry out, tried to breathe, tried to comprehend it was possible to feel this fucking incredible.

White light crept into the edges of my vision as he took me higher, higher, still higher.

A heartbeat before I lost control, he moaned, "Oh my fucking God, Aaron..." The unrestrained lust in his voice was more than I could take, and all at once, the world around me—the world *inside* me—exploded. I gripped his hips tighter, drove my cock deeper into him, and still he rocked back and forth, sending me deeper into perfect oblivion with each powerful stroke. I sucked in a breath, tried to roar, tried to cry out, but nothing, not even a silent breath, came out as everything around me and inside me melted. Shattered. Erupted.

And with one last powerful shudder, it was over.

I pulled out, rocking back on my heels while I tried to catch my breath. Bastian turned around and shot me the most mouthwatering grin just before he grabbed the back of my neck and kissed me.

"My turn," he murmured.

All I could do was exhale and shiver with anticipation. I managed to get up long enough to get rid of the condom, and when I got back into bed, Bastian kissed me.

"Why don't you get on your back?" He ran his fingers through my hair and kissed me again. "That way I can see your face while I'm inside you." Didn't take much to get me to obey that suggestion. My spine had pretty much turned to liquid at this point, and when he gently nudged me with his body weight, I sank to the bed.

"Don't move." He kissed me again, then reached for the pack of condoms. I supposed I could have teased him like he'd teased me, stroking the lube onto his cock and threatening to make him come, but that would have required some semblance of a steady hand. My hands were barely steady enough to find their way to his shoulders when he rejoined me in bed.

He pressed his cock against me. Into me. A little more. Back out, farther in. It didn't matter how many times we'd fucked, I still couldn't believe how good his cock felt inside me.

"Oh God, that feels…" He groaned, screwing his eyes shut and pushing himself a little deeper. "I've been thinking about this all damned day. The whole way down here."

"You aren't the only one." I closed my eyes as he withdrew slowly.

"Oh God, Aaron," he whispered, closing his eyes. His brow furrowed. "Oh my God..." He held me tighter. "*Aaron...*" With a throaty groan, he fucked me even harder, and I gripped his sweaty shoulders as my body shook beneath his. I didn't know what the hell he did with his hips, how he managed to twist them just so with every thrust, but he did, and it was perfect. Jesus Christ, it was perfect. If I hadn't already come, I wouldn't have lasted like this. No way in hell.

"That's amazing," I moaned. "What you're...that thing you...with your hips...Jesus..."

"Oh fuck, I'm gonna come," he whispered, releasing a ragged breath against my skin. "You feel so good, so...fucking..." A deep, primal growl emerged from his throat. His body shuddered against mine, and he picked up even more speed. His shoulders trembled with each stroke, the muscles bunching and quivering beneath my hands. "Oh fuck, Aaron," he whispered, his voice shaking as badly as his body. His brow furrowed, and he grimaced as if in pain. His breath caught. He screwed his eyes shut. "Oh God, I'm gonna come..."

He growled, then roared, and that uncensored, unbridled release of powerful, insatiable lust instantly raised goose bumps along every inch of my skin, and when he shivered, so did I.

The roar fell to a moan that was so soft I never would have heard it had he not been so close, and finally he sank down to me, resting his forehead on my collarbone. My grip on his shoulders relaxed. The tension in his muscles melted away. He released a long breath that cooled my sweaty skin. Slowly, silently, we separated.

Once he'd gotten rid of the condom, we both collapsed into bed. We shifted onto our sides, facing each other. For a while, we just looked at each other, the satisfied but disbelieving expression on his face mirroring what I felt. His hand rested on my hip, absently stroking my skin with his fingertips.

After a long silence, his lips parted as if he was about to speak, but instead he gently lifted my chin with two fingers and drew me into a gentle kiss. His kiss was tender, languid, even lazy, but there was intensity just beneath the surface, a degree of need that he could restrain but not completely hide.

"If I didn't know any better," I said, struggling to catch my breath, "I might think you were still horny."

"Just can't get enough of you, I guess."

"You're not the only one." *That would be the understatement of the century.*

He kissed me lightly. "I can honestly say I have never been as desperate for anyone as I am with you every fucking time." His fingers drifted into my hair, and his lips brushed mine again. "And it's not getting any better. Every single time I have you, I want you that much more."

We were definitely on the same page. Holy hell, were we ever. I wasn't so sure how I felt about that, but I grinned in spite of the way my chest tightened. "I suppose I should take that as a compliment."

He laughed. "That or a safety warning." He kissed me lightly. "With the way you turn me on, I can't be held responsible for what happens if I completely lose control."

"Are you threatening to hurt me?"

"Do you want me to?"

"I want whatever you've got, Koehler."

"Careful what you wish for." He kissed me again, forcefully this time. "You just might get it."

CHAPTER SEVENTEEN

My eyes fluttered open. Slipping between the thick brown curtains over the hotel windows, the harsh light of day invaded my senses. After blinking a few times, my eyes adjusted.

I was nestled against Bastian, his hand clasping mine on top of his chest, my head resting on his shoulder. His arm was around me, his fingers gently grasping my shoulder. We held each other exactly as I'd remembered doing just before I'd drifted off to sleep, and judging by the ache in my back and the tingling in my other arm that was bent and tucked between us, neither of us had moved all night. Every muscle screamed at me to get up, move, stretch, but I wasn't about to break this gentle embrace just yet.

I smiled to myself as last night replayed in my mind. He did everything right: sensual and tender, rough and wild, everything in between. We hadn't had to keep an ear tuned to anything beyond our surroundings, hadn't needed to listen for anyone who could overhear us or come home at an inopportune moment. For once it was just us, and we'd taken full advantage.

Without the need for silence, Bastian was deliciously vocal. Sometimes English, sometimes German, sometimes sounds that transcended the need for translation.

Getting a hotel room was definitely a good idea.

Bastian's fingers twitched on my arm. He murmured something, then turned his head. When he looked at me, he smiled and squeezed my shoulder gently.

"Morning." He kissed my forehead. Then he grimaced, his hand lifting off me. "Ow, ow, my arm..."

"Oh, sorry." I propped myself up on my elbow, wincing when the blood rushed back into my own arm.

"You okay?" He shifted onto his side, gingerly rubbing his wrist.

"Yeah, I think I just had my arm in the same position for too long."

He flexed his fingers. "Tell me about it." Then he winked and kissed me gently. "Well worth it, though. I had to hold on to you. Make sure you didn't go anywhere."

"I wasn't going anywhere." I draped my arm across his chest. "Not if there was a chance of a repeat performance of last night."

"There's always a chance of that when I'm in bed with you." He grinned. "You know, you have a very foul mouth when you're that turned on."

"No worse than yours. At least I only swear in one language."

"Okay, fair enough," he murmured. "To be honest, in between all the cursing, I thought you were having a religious experience."

I furrowed my brow and cocked my head. "What? Why?"

"I don't think I've heard God's name more times in one night in all my life. Well, and my name." His eyebrows jumped. "Wait, does that mean *I'm* a god?"

I laughed and rolled my eyes. "Yes, Bastian, clearly it means you're a god."

He chuckled. Then he sighed. "I suppose we should get out of here eventually."

"What time is it?"

He craned his neck toward the table between the beds. "Almost ten."

"Yeah, I suppose we should get moving."

Reluctantly we got out of bed, both pausing to work out a few aches and kinks.

For a motel that probably existed solely for liaisons like ours, this room had one *tiny* shower. Barely big enough for one person, not nearly big enough for two. Bastards.

Bastian took a shower first. Then we switched, somehow managing to avoid skipping my shower and tumbling back into bed. I knew us. If we started again, we'd end up staying past checkout time. Not that I minded paying for another night if that was the price for staying just a little longer, but we had to leave eventually.

After my shower, I opened the bathroom door to let some of the cool air in from the rest of the room while I dried off. I pulled on a pair of jeans, and a low vibration made me pause and listen. At first I thought it might be a booming car stereo somewhere outside or a TV in another room, but then I recognized it as the unamplified sound of Bastian's bass. It wasn't loud, but the deep sound resonated right through me, so quiet I felt it more than heard it.

I didn't blame him for bringing it in last night; this part of town was crawling with people who wouldn't hesitate to relieve him of his instrument if he'd left it in the truck. Since he had a few minutes to himself while I was in the shower, I wasn't surprised in the least he'd opted to pull the bass out and play it. Todd often did the same thing. A musician's idle hands always found their way onto an instrument.

Bastian finished one tune. Paused. Started another. After a couple of bars, the melody connected in my mind, and I caught myself quietly humming along to *(Un)Fading*. I shivered, a pleasant chill running up my spine beneath my warm skin. It didn't matter how many times we'd played that song, it still gave me goose bumps every time.

I stepped out of the bathroom, and his fingers faltered on the strings in the same instant my feet faltered in step. We both recovered quickly, though. He kept playing. I leaned against the door frame and just watched him, certain he could hear my heart keeping time with the song.

Like me, he'd put on a pair of jeans but hadn't bothered with anything else. He sat up against the headboard of the bed we'd shared, and his fingers nimbly manipulated the strings. I could barely imagine Bastian ever being anything other than sexy as hell, but this? Sitting half-dressed on a rumpled hotel bed with a bass across his lap and a night's worth of stubble on his jaw? Jesus Christ.

I cleared my throat and nodded toward the instrument. "Putting in a little overtime?"

He laughed. "Just one of those things I can't keep my hands off of." He inclined his head slightly and offered a mouthwatering, one-sided grin as his fingers slowed to a stop. "Sort of like you."

Fuck. Want. "So what ever do you do when you don't have me or the bass handy?" I knew before I'd finished asking the question that his grin would get even more devilish, that he'd laugh just like that, and I'd have one more filthy image of him in my brain. As if I needed any more of those.

"Do I even need to answer that?"

I rolled my eyes, hoping he'd blame any extra color in my cheeks on my hot shower, knowing full well he wouldn't. Fortunately he let the subject go before I got myself any more flustered and tongue-tied.

"You ever played?" he asked.

"I've picked up a guitar maybe once or twice. Years ago." I shrugged. "But I don't have a clue how to play."

"Ever wanted to learn?"

"I've always wanted to try it. Asked Todd a few times, but he would never let me anywhere near his guitar."

Bastian smiled. "Understandable. We're all a bit overprotective of our instruments. Paranoid bastards, every last one of us." He paused, looking at the bass, then at me. "Well, if you're up for it, I can show you a few things."

"I'm always up for learning something new." I shifted my weight. "But we should get going, shouldn't we?"

"We've got plenty of time. Checkout isn't until eleven, and I have nowhere else to be today." He ran his fingers down the bass's neck, letting them hiss across the strings until I shivered. "You game?"

I thought about all the times I'd caught myself watching him play. Who was I to turn down an opportunity to be with Bastian and his bass? "Why not?"

Pulling the strap off his shoulders, he nodded toward the edge of the bed. "Sit."

I gave him a playful smirk. "How do I know you're not just trying to get me into bed, Herr Koehler?"

"Because I don't *have* to try to get you into bed." He winked and I laughed.

I sat on the bed, and he joined me, lifting the strap over my head and letting it come to rest between my shoulders. The weight of the instrument settled onto my legs and against my torso. I expected its smooth surface to be cool against my bare skin, but it wasn't. Of course it wasn't. It was still warm from Bastian's body heat.

I gulped. "You actually trust me with this thing?"

He chuckled as his arm slid around me. "I wouldn't let you leave the house with it, but as long as I'm supervising..."

"Hey!"

"Kidding." He kissed my cheek. "Of course I trust you with it."

It was awkward in my hands, which probably had less to do with my lack of familiarity with the instrument than it did with the warmth of Bastian against me. He sat close, one arm around my waist, and we were skin to skin. Just like we'd been all—

The bass. Focus on the bass, McClure. Carefully I took the bass's neck in my left hand. I was partly afraid of damaging it—ridiculous, I knew, given the way Bastian and Todd brutally played onstage without incident—and partly worried about looking stupid, clueless.

"It's been years since I've even held one of these," I said.

His face was right next to mine, his voice soft. "Just let it rest in your hand, so the pads of your fingers are on the strings."

I scowled, turning my hand in different directions, trying to find a comfortable position. It didn't help that simply being this close to him always made my hands shake.

"Here." His hand gently covered mine and guided it to the right position. "You're going to hold your hand against it with your thumb." He put his thumb over mine and hooked it over the bass's neck. "Now your hand will be able to slide up and down so your fingers can press on the strings." Cupping my hand in his, he guided it down the neck, slowly, then back up.

I swallowed.

"Then when you want to play a different note," he said, barely whispering, "just press on the strings, like this." He pushed my index finger against one. "You want to do it between the frets, not on top of them, or it won't sound as good." One by one, he pressed my fingers against different strings, gently guiding my hand up the neck, down, back again.

The strings were abrasive beneath my fingertips, but it was the soft warmth of his hand over mine that occupied my senses. I fought the urge to shiver when the tip of his thumb drifted down the back of my own, then up again, mimicking the motion of our joined hands on the bass's neck.

"See? It's not hard."

Oh, it most certainly is *hard right now, Bastian.*

"Now your other hand." He nodded toward my right hand. I looked down, swallowing. His face was almost touching mine now, every breath cooling the side of my neck and sending my body temperature soaring. He put his right hand on mine and moved it to the body of the guitar.

"Relax your hand. Rest your thumb here." He guided it into place, and damned if he didn't run the tip of his thumb across the back of mine again.

This time I couldn't mask the shiver.

He nuzzled my neck and whispered against my skin as he put my index finger against one of the strings. "And to pluck a string, just roll it like this." He rolled my fingertip across the string, pulling it toward my body—toward *us*—before letting the string go, and a satisfying vibration thrummed through the instrument. Then he did the same with my middle finger. After showing me a couple of times, he pulled his hand back, resting it on my forearm.

His lip brushed my neck. "You try it."

I took a breath, trying to focus on the strings beneath my fingers, not the fingers on my skin. "You make it look so easy."

"It just takes practice." He kissed behind my ear. "After a while, it becomes second nature. And then you can start playing other notes and chords." His other hand squeezed mine on the bass's neck, the gentle reminder of that contact drawing a startled breath out of me.

I kept plucking the strings, if anything to give my fingers something to do so they wouldn't shake. While I did, he guided my other hand over the frets, pressing a string here, another there.

The deep sounds resonating from the bass were unsteady and timid, not bold and unafraid like they were when Bastian played, and it wasn't just because of the lack of an amp. I could barely hear it anyway over the gentle whisper of his breath and his soft voice next to my ear as he said, "See? You're a natural."

His right hand drifted from my forearm to my upper arm, then up to my shoulder, tracing a gentle path along goose bump-covered skin. His lips pressed against the side of my neck while our joined left hands slid up the neck of the bass.

Then he stopped our hands, holding just tightly enough to keep mine from moving or releasing the instrument.

"Your fingers will get sore if you play too much just yet," he whispered, running his fingers along the backs of mine. My breath caught, the sound echoing in the stillness, and I wondered how long ago my other hand had stopped moving on the strings.

Bastian kissed my neck. "Look at me."

I turned my head, and as soon as I did, he met my lips with his. I took my hand off the bass and reached for him. My skin tingled at the coarse warmth of his jaw, and when the tip of my tongue found his piercing, I shivered.

As one, our hands let go of the bass's neck and came to rest between us, fingers still laced together. Then he whispered, "Maybe we should get this thing out of the way." Releasing my hand, he shifted, picking up the bass. I ducked my head as he pulled the strap over. Carefully lifting the bass off my lap, he leaned away just long enough to set it on the other bed.

"Now that that's gone," he whispered. He put his arms around me and kissed me, lowering me onto the bed as he did. His lips went to my neck, his unshaven jaw brushing my skin and raising more goose bumps all over me.

"This is what you had in mind all along, isn't it?" I murmured.

He laughed. "I *always* have this in mind." Then he raised his head and caressed my face. "But that's not what I was thinking when I offered to show you how to play."

I kissed him lightly. "Is that so?"

He nodded. "What I was thinking was that I have always hesitated to let anyone play it. Overprotective, I guess. But with you"—his fingertips trailed down my neck—"I didn't think twice."

I touched his face, looking into his eyes. I tried to will myself to speak, but he kissed me before I could.

For the longest time, we simply kissed. Touched. Held each other. His hips pressed against mine, leaving no doubt he was as aroused as I was, but he was in no hurry at all. Even when he kissed his way down my neck to my collarbone, he paused for every single gentle kiss like we had all the time in the world to do this. His mouth moved slowly across my skin, as if memorizing every inch of me, pausing to discover the contour where my shoulder met my neck. Teasing my nipple with his tongue and stud. Letting his lips tease goose bumps to life on my abs.

He came back up to kiss me, and it was a long, hungry kiss caught somewhere between desire to take it slow and frantic need to have each other *now*.

Pushing himself up, he looked at me, and the intensity in his eyes echoed that need and desire. He rested his weight on one hand and reached for me with the other.

Two fingertips began a slow, gentle path down the side of my face, and the world stopped turning. His touch was featherlight and electrified, commanding my full attention and the stillness that suddenly thrummed between us like the notes from his bass. His lips were parted, his brow creased above wide eyes that watched his own fingers with something between fascination and disbelief. The lack of warm air against my skin told me that he, like me, held his breath.

When his fingers reached my collarbone, he stopped and his eyes rose to meet mine. His eyebrows jumped slightly, and when he released his breath, it came out in a single, uneven huff like something in my expression had knocked the wind out of him.

We held each other's gazes for a long moment. I didn't know what he saw in my eyes. I didn't know what I saw in his. There was something there, though, and it made me want him that much more.

He came down to kiss me again, and our hands made frantic, clumsy work of getting our jeans off. At least we hadn't had a chance to put any more clothes on, and in fairly short order, what little we had to remove was on the floor and our naked bodies were in each other's arms again.

With my fingertips, I traced every inch of his back, following the ridges and grooves of his spine along the downward curve from his lower back to the upward sweep that led to his powerfully sculpted shoulders. His stubble hissed across my neck and jaw, and cool air rushed past my skin as he inhaled deeply through his nose as if he was taking in my scent.

When he came up to kiss my mouth again, his hand ran down my side and, when my spine arched in response, slid under my back. I'd never been so close to him, to anyone, and I couldn't get close enough. Our every move and touch happened together, no clear line between action and reaction. Did I arch my back because his hand slid beneath me, or did his hand slide beneath me because my back arched? I didn't know. I didn't care.

It was only a matter of time before one of us reached for the stash of condoms and lube on the table between the beds, and Bastian finally did. I sat up while he tore the wrapper and put the condom on. My mouth watered. Didn't matter that my body still ached from last night. I needed him *now*.

Once the condom and lube were in place, Bastian looked at me and grinned. "Lay on your side." He licked his lips. "With your back to me."

I did as he said, and it was mere seconds before his body was against mine again. He propped himself up on one arm and guided himself to me with the other. It was a little awkward to start with, but with a little fumbling and laughing at our own clumsiness, he was inside me.

"Oh God, that feels good," he whispered, pushing deeper.

I couldn't find the words to tell him how amazing he felt. Not just the slow, smooth strokes he took inside me, but everywhere we touched. His body was molded against mine, moving only from the hips while his hand kept my own hip still. Hot skin touched hot skin. His foot slid over my ankle. His chest pressed against my back. His lips and unshaven jaw explored the exposed curve of my neck.

I turned my head toward him, and he leaned forward enough to kiss me over my shoulder. It wasn't the most comfortable position for my neck, but damned if I was going to pull away from his mouth. I reached up and ran my fingers through the fringe of his hair. We both moaned when he slid deeper, but we kept right on kissing, especially while he withdrew, slid in again, withdrew. Fucking hell, he was amazing. Nothing else in the world existed except for us. Nothing broke the silence except for ragged gasps of breath and the whispers of skin on skin and skin on sheets. For once we didn't have to worry about staying quiet, but we were silent nonetheless.

He started at my shoulder and let his hand drift slowly down my arm, his palm warming every inch of skin in turn until he reached my hand. He curled his fingers between mine, then guided our joined hands down to my cock. I couldn't begin to tell whose hand acted and whose reacted, who determined how fast, how hard, but together we stroked my cock while he fucked me.

I broke the kiss, turning my head away from him only to ease a cramp in my neck, but he didn't mind. He bent to kiss my neck, and between the warmth of his breath, the coarseness of his jaw, and the softness of his lips, I was in heaven.

"I can't get enough of you," he murmured behind my ear. "Every time...every fucking time...I just want more." I moaned, the only response that was possible when he spoke that way, touched that way, moved our hands that way, moved inside me just like that.

With every touch and every stroke, I was coming apart at the seams, and we were coming together. Through the dizzying oblivion, I'd never felt closer—physically or otherwise—to anyone. I'd never wanted to be this close to anyone, and with Bastian, I welcomed it.

"Oh God," I breathed.

"Like that?"

"Fuck, yes."

He thrust harder. Not faster, just...harder. His breath rushed across the side of my neck. Our hands mirrored his hips: squeezing my cock harder, but moving no faster, and I neared the verge of losing my goddamned mind.

"Just like that," I murmured. "Fuck, just..."

His unshaven jaw grazed my neck as he whispered, "Come for me, Aaron," and there wasn't a damned thing I could have done to hold myself back. Bastian held me, kissing my neck and stroking my cock with my own hand and moving deep inside me, and I came. I came hard, and I came completely undone in his arms.

As if my orgasm had been his own, Bastian groaned. "Oh God," he whispered, his breath cool on my neck. "I can't...I can't wait... This is..." A shudder drove him deeper, and a groan vibrated against my skin. "You feel so...fucking good..." His hand released mine and went to my hip, steadying me, and he pulled in a deep breath, held it, kept going, kept going...

The air around us was alive with his almost-there tension, with the roar he held in his lungs, the roar that was ready to be released the instant he surrendered. Closing my eyes, I bit my lip, silently begging him to let himself go. *God, yes, let me feel you come, Bastian. Let me hear you come.*

His lips brushed the side of my neck.

His fingers pressed into my hip.

He thrust deep inside me.

And he released the most arousing sound I'd ever heard: a ragged, near-silent rush of breath across the side of my neck.

It was only when his orgasm had peaked and fallen, when his fingers had eased their death grip on my hip and his body had relaxed, that he let out a long, low groan.

"We have *got* to remember this position," he slurred. He kissed behind my ear.

"I don't think we'll have any trouble remembering this one."

"Damn right we won't." He sank against me, burying his face in the side of my neck and panting against my skin. I reached back to run my fingers through his hair, and he shifted just enough to let me turn my head so he could kiss me. And oh God, did he kiss me. Even as the aftershocks passed, as the trembling ceased, we didn't let each other go. He held me just as tightly, his body still pressed against mine, and he didn't stop kissing me. Though the frantic urgency had dissipated, there was no less passion in his kiss now than when we'd first fallen into bed together last night.

For the longest time, we just held each other. Whether it was because we were simply too overwhelmed to move or if we both just wanted to let the moment linger a little bit longer, I couldn't tell. All I knew was that I had never felt like this before.

Eventually we moved, and after he'd gotten rid of the condom, we settled onto our sides, facing each other. I ran my fingers along his jaw and just looked at him. Disheveled, sleepy-eyed, with a sheen of sweat on his face and that dusting of dark stubble on his jaw, he was fucking gorgeous. I couldn't stop looking at him or touching him.

Being here like this was right. It had to be. Everything about this moment made sense. His presence, the way we touched, the taste of his kiss on my tongue. It was...natural. As if the cosmos sat back and gave us a nod of approval, an unhesitating *yes, this is as it should be.*

It was right, but it unsettled me. And more than that, I wondered if he felt it too.

He stroked my cheek with his fingertips, then let them trail down the curve of my neck and over my shoulder, pausing to make soft circles on my arm. His other fingers were clasped in mine between our chests, and he ran his thumb across the side of my hand. "What's on your mind?" he whispered.

I moistened my lips. "Just thinking."

"About?"

I hesitated, swallowing. "Us, I guess."

His eyebrows jumped a little as if in alarm, but he masked his reaction with a smirk and said, "Does it involve us being naked?"

Rolling my eyes, I laughed. Then my smile fell. "I don't know, I'm just…" I trailed off.

He touched my face again. "Not sure what's going on?"

"Yeah."

He exhaled. "I know what you mean." He looked at me silently for a moment, then said, "But I'm starting to think this is going beyond just sex."

I swallowed hard. "So am I."

Kissing our clasped fingers, he lifted his eyebrows. "So where do we go from here?"

"I was going to ask you the same thing."

He gave me a devilish grin, but there was a hint of uncertainty in his eyes. "I asked you first."

Shrugging, I said, "I don't… I guess I just don't know. But…"

His eyebrows lifted again. "But?"

I took a breath. "I don't want to rush anything, but…" I paused. "At the same time, I don't want to stop it if it's happening on its own."

Smiling, he leaned in and kissed me gently. "Obviously we're on the same page, then."

My heart raced. "So you're not going to run screaming for the hills if I say I'm okay with things getting more serious?"

He laughed. "No, but I might pin you to the bed and make you come again."

"You're insatiable, aren't you?"

"Guilty as charged." Kissing me again, he let his lips linger against mine for a long moment. His hand moved to my waist, his skin warm against mine as he pulled me closer to him. "Honestly, Aaron, I don't know where this is going, but I do know I don't want to stop."

Looking away for a moment, I drew a breath. "But with everything with the band, with our siblings, all of that…" I trailed off, scowling.

"I know," he whispered, running his fingers through my hair. "I've thought about it too."

"So what do we do?"

"We take things a day at a time," he said. "And we'll figure it out as we go."

"I'm just worried that if we do take this any further, things could get"—I chewed my lip—"complicated."

"Then let them get complicated." Stroking my hair, he kissed me.

I touched my forehead to his. "Do you think we should still keep it quiet?"

Bastian sighed, stroking my cheekbone with the pad of his thumb. "For the time being. With the Battle of the Bands coming up, and possibly the Rock-out after that, the band isn't going to need any added stress." He kissed me lightly. "And let's face it, this could cause some problems."

"Yeah, I know." I closed my eyes, exhaling hard. "Which is why I'm still worried about it."

"Me too. But I don't want to stop doing this. Right or wrong, I…" He trailed off.

I opened my eyes. "Hmm?"

Bastian swallowed hard. Then he touched my face again and held my gaze. In a whisper so soft it almost didn't register at all, he said, "*Ich liebe dich.*"

Something about his eyes told me he meant every word I didn't understand.

"What does—" I licked my lips. "What does that mean?"

He took a breath. Started to speak. Then he shook his head and swallowed hard as he drew me closer to him. "Nothing."

I didn't argue. I just surrendered to his kiss and let everything else be.

But I had no doubt it meant something more than nothing.

This was going to get complicated.

CHAPTER EIGHTEEN

As we often did, the band went to the local bar to wind down after rehearsal. I was tempted to have more than one beer, but I still had to drive, so I resisted. I'd just have to deal with the unsettled, unnerved feeling in my gut.

I swore the band knew something. Maybe I was just paranoid—the nervousness of the guilty accused—but with every benign comment, every shift in the conversation, I was certain they knew.

"So what about *(Un)Fading*?" Andre asked. "It sounded great tonight, and I really think it's ready to add to the set."

"Might not be a song for the crowd at the House, though," Elena said. "They get bored during ballads."

"What about the Battle of the Bands?" Todd said.

"Are you kidding?" Andre looked at him over his glass. "Dropping a new song at something like that?"

"Well, why not?" Bastian's eyes darted toward mine but quickly shifted away. "We've got it down. I have a feeling it'll be a hit, and bands play ballads at the Battle all the time."

"Good point," Elena said. "We can have, what, four songs in our set?"

"Five," Andre said. "Maybe two faster pieces with Aaron pulling lead, two with Elena, and *(Un)Fading* in the middle."

"It's a bit of a risky move," Bastian said. "Adding a song we've never performed before. But I really think this one is worth taking that chance."

"I agree," Todd said. "Something like that will blow the judges away, not to mention the fans."

"And hey, play a sappy little ballad, maybe it'll make all the girls swoon." Rochelle grinned. "Then maybe we can find one to take Bastian's mind off Denise."

Bastian laughed, his cheeks coloring a little. "I don't think that'll be a problem."

"What?" Elena elbowed him. "Bastian Koehler, are you seeing someone?"

My heart stopped.

Bastian coughed behind his hand. "No, I meant I don't need any help getting my mind off Denise."

"He's got a point," Andre said. "I think she's the one who needs help getting over him."

"She just needs help," Elena muttered into her drink. "Period."

"I'll drink to that." Todd raised his glass.

"You'll drink to anything, you fucking drunk," Bastian said.

"Hey, I resemble that remark." Todd sipped his beer.

Andre picked up his beer but didn't take a drink just yet. "I think she's finally over your ass anyway, Bastian. When I've tended bar at the House, I've seen her there hanging all over the lead singer of Flogging for Coffee."

"Oh, thank fuck," Bastian said. "I mean, if that's true, it sucks to be Bruce, but maybe she'll leave me alone."

"God, I hope so," Rochelle growled. "I can't stand that fucking cunt."

Andre laughed, nearly choking on his drink. "Tell us how you really feel, Chelle."

She shrugged. "What can I say? She's an evil bitch who needs a swift kick in the box." We all howled with laughter. Then Rochelle looked at Bastian. "So when are you going to find a new woman, anyway?"

I took a long drink, hoping the low lights masked any color in my face. They knew. They knew. They knew. I was fucking sure they knew.

Elena sighed. "Chelle, the poor man has only been paroled for a month or so from the Denise Bauer Maximum Insecurity Prison. Give him some time to enjoy his freedom, you know?"

Rochelle shrugged, grinning. "I just figured he might want to get the taste out of his mouth."

"Oh, don't you worry about that." Bastian winked at her.

"Bastian Koehler," Elena said. "Have you been getting some on the side and not telling us?"

"Maybe I have, maybe I haven't." He shot her a playful grin. Part of me wanted to panic, sure they'd catch on. He picked up his drink and grinned. "Maybe I just want to fuck a few groupies for a while before I let myself get tied down again."

Elena rolled her eyes. "You're such a pig, Bastian."

Bastian just grinned and took a drink. His eyes flicked toward me, and there it was, that wink without winking. That son of a bitch. He knew exactly what he was doing. Putting his alleged "activities" out there, and in doing so, throwing up a smoke screen over what he was really doing.

It worked. They didn't catch on. But I was still sure they knew.

On the way to our cars, Bastian and I stopped. We didn't touch. To anyone nearby, we were just two guys having a conversation. I had to force myself not to fidget, shift my weight, and look around warily. Just be cool. No one would know we were talking about anything other than the band and the music.

And we were talking about the band and the music. Sort of.

"So you really think we're ready to play that song?" I asked.

"Definitely." He hooked his thumbs in the pockets of his jeans and casually rested his weight on one foot. "It just took some practice, but we're there."

The conversation faded. Neither of us moved to leave. Something unspoken hung in the air, and it did nothing to settle my nerves.

Bastian sighed, eyes flicking toward the bar. "I'm not sure how much more of this my blood pressure can take."

"Being with me or the secrecy?"

"The secrecy." He winked. "Being with you has other ways of nearly killing me." We both laughed but halfheartedly. Silence fell again, and I didn't let it linger this time.

Keeping my voice low, I said, "We have to tell them sooner or later."

He nodded. "I know. I just...I'm not sure I'm ready to tell Andre about..." He swallowed hard. "Hell, about me. Then I get to drop the bomb that I'm dating someone in the band."

"We'll do it a little at a time. Let me come out to my family. See how that goes, let the dust settle."

"Think your family will freak?"

"My parents will. Guaranteed. Todd? Don't know." I chewed my lip. "It's a necessary evil, though. I'll deal with it. But the longer we keep this to ourselves, the longer we have to stress ourselves out with flying under the radar and keeping it quiet."

"True."

I resisted the urge to put a reassuring hand on his arm. "Let me talk to my family. I'm going over to my folks' place tomorrow night."

Bastian nodded. "Good luck with that."

"Yeah, thanks." I laughed humorlessly. "They'll be thrilled."

He chuckled. "I can imagine."

More nerves tangled in my stomach. Neither of our families would be thrilled about us not being heterosexual, but I couldn't decide if I was more worried about them or Schadenfreude. One way or the other, though, we couldn't keep this a secret forever. That and the longer we tried to keep it a secret, the more likely the cat would get out of the bag on its own.

It needed to happen on our terms.

And whether we relished the idea or not, it needed to happen *soon*.

CHAPTER NINETEEN

Since we lived in Seattle and our folks' place was almost forty miles away in Monroe, not far from where the band rehearsed, I rode in with Todd.

Thanks to excuses about work schedules, getting settled in after my move, and recovering from a nebulous injury I hadn't fully explained to them, we'd avoided coming over for dinner for weeks. But things like this could only be avoided for so long without causing more headaches than they were worth, so tonight we gave in.

This was going to be fun. I hadn't yet broken the news to them about my involvement with Schadenfreude, and I wasn't looking forward to that. Our parents barely approved of Todd's involvement in the band. Though they'd put on sympathetic faces when I said my own band had dissolved, their relief had been obvious. Most likely they thought I'd moved back to Seattle to give up that ridiculous hobby and find a respectable job.

They'd always frowned on any professional musician who didn't play in symphony halls and opera houses, which is what they'd always expected us to do. It didn't help when someone's friend's neighbor's cousin's ex-boyfriend's ballet instructor's eldest sister had dropped out of college to run off to the East Coast with a starry-eyed musician. A musician whose dreams turned out to be—literally and figuratively—pipe dreams. Two kids and a lot of heartache later, he left with his guitar and drug habit and hadn't been seen since.

Since then, our parents were certain all rock musicians were drug-addicted losers and users, in spite of the fact that their sons and daughter were clean, sober, and fairly successful. They'd grudgingly let us all go through our "rock and roll phases," thinking we'd get it out of our systems, and they were none too happy when all three of us had opted to stick with this path. I shuddered to think what they would say if they knew I was not only in Schadenfreude, but so was my boyfriend. Even if they had known Bastian since he was a teenager. He may have been the kid they'd known since he was in high school, but now he was a musician—that kind of musician—so he had fallen a few notches in their eyes.

My stomach coiled into knots. I wondered which would bother them more: that I was gay or that I was in Schadenfreude. Not that I needed their permission, but there wasn't much in the world more unsettling than the anticipation of parental disapproval.

Todd glanced at me. "Ready for the inquisition?"

"Ready as always."

"You going to tell them about the band?"

I took a breath. "Might as well get it over with."

"They'll be thrilled."

I rolled my eyes. "You'd think they'd be over it by now."

"You would think." He shrugged. "I don't know, maybe I should just do what they think I'm going to do and develop a drug habit and knock up some random chick."

I laughed. "Yeah, that's so you. Just let me know when you're going to tell Lillian so I can take cover."

"No shit."

"I don't know how you put up with it, honestly. From a thousand miles away isn't so difficult, but this close by?"

He glanced at me and shrugged again. "There comes a point when you stop living your life for the approval of others, even Mom and Dad."

"How very philosophical of you, Todd," I said. "But I can't imagine it's easy."

"It's not." He cursed under his breath at a driver in front of him and changed lanes. "But I'm not going to give it up. Sometimes you just have to do what's right for you and let the rest of the world go fuck themselves."

Somehow, I don't think you'd be saying that if you knew what—or rather, who—I've been doing. I cleared my throat. "Fair enough."

The conversation moved to lighter topics, and before I knew it, Todd pulled into the driveway in front of our parents' two-story blue house on the outskirts of Monroe's farm country. The familiar house didn't look nearly as inviting as it usually did.

We were right on time for dinner, and we'd barely taken our seats at the dining room table when they started.

"So, Aaron, are you enjoying being back in the area?" My mother looked up from cutting a piece of meat and smiled at me.

I nodded, swallowing. "Yeah, so far."

"Any luck finding a job?" my father asked.

And it begins. "Not yet." I tapped my foot against the leg of my chair. "Still looking."

Todd smirked. "Maybe if you spent less time pursuing all that music nonsense, you'd have a job by now."

I resisted the urge to kick him under the table, instead casually rubbing my eye with my middle finger.

Our parents exchanged silent looks. Maybe it was just disapproval. Maybe it was their typical nosiness and worry. Whatever it was, I couldn't help but feel like they knew something, even though they couldn't possibly. It seemed ridiculous to expect an interrogation over something they didn't know about, but such was their vehement disapproval of Schadenfreude; it wouldn't have surprised me if they could simply sense that I was involved in it now.

Just like I was sure the band somehow knew about my involvement with Bastian. Oh, the tangled webs we weave…

I anticipated more questions, but our mother turned her attention to Todd. "And how are things with the band?" She said the last two words with her usual sour demeanor. I had long since stopped rolling my eyes at it, as had Todd.

Todd set his glass down. "Things are fine."

The disapproval on our parents' faces, in the looks they exchanged, was palpable, but neither spoke. There had been countless discussions about our music careers at this table, and some time ago, everyone had more or less agreed to a cease-fire. We all still played, they still disapproved, and the potatoes were passed in tense silence.

It drove me crazy. Especially now that I was about to drop the disappointment bomb on them. They were elated I was no longer in a band. They were about to find out that wasn't the case. My stomach twisted and turned. Christ, the thought of coming out to them bothered me less than telling them I was in Schadenfreude.

He glanced at me. "We fired our male lead recently, but we've got a good solid replacement now."

"Well, that's good to hear," my father said without an ounce of enthusiasm.

I gritted my teeth as the family ate in taut silence. I knew it drove Todd crazy, and having been far away from it for several years, it made my blood boil now.

Fuck it. I kept enough of my life out of their sight.

"I'm the new lead singer, by the way," I said.

My mother's head snapped up. My father's eyebrows jumped. They looked at each other, then scowled at their plates. Unspoken comments hung in the air. Too talented for a band like that. Wasting your talent on that kind of noise. You're both too talented for that garbage. None of it was said, but it was felt. Though Todd and I were adults and didn't need our parents' permission, their disapproval grated on both of us.

And Todd, being Todd, didn't want to let it go this time. "With him singing, I think there are big things in store for us. He's really good, and it's getting us a lot of attention from some important people."

"Well, that's good," my mother said dryly. "Assuming you can call anything you do with that kind of music 'big.'"

"A Grammy or a platinum album would qualify as big, don't you think?" I asked.

"Not to mention playing for thousands of people," Todd said.

"It isn't exactly Carnegie Hall," my father muttered.

I looked at Todd across the table. We both rolled our eyes. There was no sense arguing about it. Maybe one day when we had that Grammy or platinum album, they'd change their minds.

For now, we kept passing the potatoes in silence.

* * * * *

On the way home, I couldn't quite tell where the heartburn from my mother's cooking ended and the self-loathing began. I tried to tell myself it was a wise move to keep my sexuality to myself and save that particular bit of news for another night. After all, my parents had had enough on their plates with disapproving of my involvement in that band when they'd been so certain I was finally through that phase.

I sighed and looked out the window.

"You okay?" Todd asked. "Dude, I don't think Mom meant anything by what she said. You know how she is."

"Oh, I know. Trust me, she does it by phone when you're too far away to do it in person."

"Well, damn, there goes my plan to move to Bolivia to avoid it."

I laughed. "Yeah, good luck with that."

"Eh, I'm pretty much immune to her crap."

"Lucky you. Being a thousand miles away didn't do much for immunity."

He chuckled. "Trust me, a few more dinners and you won't feel a thing anymore."

"We'll see about that."

We rode in silence for a little while. We had almost half an hour ahead of us now, so I figured this was as good a time as any to talk. Even if I hadn't worked up the nerve to tell my folks, I did still have time to tell Todd before the evening was over.

I took a breath. "Listen, there's, um…something I haven't been entirely truthful about."

He glanced at me, eyebrows up. Then he shook his head and sighed. "Damn it, I knew it."

My heart skipped. "What? What do—"

"You son of a bitch." Another sharp sigh.

I gulped. "Uh…"

"Fuck, all those years." He clicked his tongue, shaking his head again. "Mom and Dad said you weren't, but I knew it."

I stared at him, slack-jawed.

He turned just long enough to give me a pointed look. "You really *are* an alien, aren't you?"

I burst out laughing, hoping my relief wasn't obvious. "Jesus, Todd, you haven't changed a bit."

He chuckled. "Okay, so what's really going on?"

Clearing my throat, I shifted in my seat a little. "Uh, well, it's about my last band."

The humor faded from his expression, and I couldn't help noticing his hand gripping the wheel a little tighter. He pursed his lips. "Okay…"

"I told you I dated the drummer." I paused. "I…didn't."

Todd furrowed his brow and looked at me. "Why would you say you did?"

"Well, I *did* date someone in the band," I said. "Just…not the drummer."

The look he shot me said *go on*.

I took a deep breath. "I was dating the guitarist."

"The guitarist?" He cocked his head. "But all the pictures and videos you sent me, the guitarist was—oh my God." His eyes widened. The car veered slightly but recovered before he put our lives or anyone else's in danger. Once the car was between the lines, he glanced at me. "Are you telling me you're...gay?"

I swallowed. "Yes."

Todd rested his elbow below the window and thumbed his chin. For a long moment, he just looked out the windshield, furrowing his brow while God only knew what went through his mind. I didn't speak, just let him digest it.

Finally he took a breath. "Wow. I... Wow. How long have you been? Or, well, known?"

"Since I was a teenager."

Shaking his head, he said, "I honestly didn't have a clue." He paused. "Wait, does..."

"What?"

He chewed his lip. "So you're not, like, going to redecorate my house or something, are you?"

I laughed aloud. "No, I'm not going to redecorate your house." *Might sleep with one of your best friends, but your decor is safe.*

He chuckled. "Color me shocked, bro, believe me. I had no idea."

Since he'd taken this pretty well, I thought I'd test the water a little further. "It's kind of your fault I figured it out so young, by the way."

"What?" He laughed. "What do you mean?"

"You kept bringing Andre around, you asshole."

He laughed harder. "Oh God, you had a thing for *Andre*?"

I shrugged. "I never claimed to have good taste in men."

"Yeah, no shit." He shook his head. "Well, no going after him."

"Wasn't planning on it. He is straight, after all. And Rochelle might hurt me."

"Okay, yeah." He glanced at me, and there was no humor in his expression. "But he's also in the band."

I gulped. "Right. Of course."

"Even if Andre was gay, Schadenfreude is way, way too close to making it for something like that to fuck it all up."

I gritted my teeth. "Look, hypotheticals aside, two band members dating—"

"Is *always* an epically bad idea." Todd shook his head again. "I know it's a moot point with this group. I'm just saying, you know from experience it's a bad idea."

"It's a bad idea when two people can't separate the band from the relationship, but—"

"And sooner or later, when shit goes south with a relationship, it takes the band with it." He tapped his thumb on the wheel. "I've seen plenty of bands fall apart over it and rarely seen one last. It's just…not a good idea. Ever."

I bit my tongue. The temptation to argue was there, but if I got too defensive about it, he'd think I was defending more than just my past relationship. I shrugged away the irritation, and said, "Well, band member or not, getting involved with Jason was a bad idea."

"Jason?" He swallowed. "That's your ex…uh…"

"Boyfriend. My ex-boyfriend."

"Right. Ex-boyfriend." He cleared his throat. "So, um, I assume Mom and Dad don't know? About you?"

I laughed. "Are you insane?"

"You going to tell them?"

I shrugged. "Eventually."

His thumb tapped out a rapid, nervous beat on the edge of the steering wheel. "Well, when you do, remind me to take cover."

"You're so supportive."

"Hey, I'm supportive, but I do *not* want to get caught in that cross fire." His thumb stopped, then tapped again. I couldn't decide if he was unsettled because of what I'd told him, or if it was the thought of our parents' reaction that made him fidget.

"Guess I can't blame you for that."

The conversation moved to lighter subjects, but my gut was still knotted with worry. Though it would take time to really sink in, my brother accepted me. One obstacle down, plenty to go. I wondered, though, what would happen once Bastian came out. Would anyone suspect anything? And even if they didn't now, what happened when we eventually dropped the bomb?

Shit. Now what?

CHAPTER TWENTY

Holy shit.

I'd performed for big crowds before. A few decent-sized festivals, some larger venues, that sort of thing.

Looking out from backstage at the crowd that had gathered for the annual Battle of the Bands, I willed my heart to keep beating. From here, it looked like fucking Woodstock. I thought I'd heard there were ten or fifteen thousand people here. The amphitheater seated something like twenty-five thousand, and it didn't look like there was a hell of a lot of room left.

"Get used to it, kid." Todd elbowed me. "We make it into the Rock-out, it'll be fifty thousand or more."

I swallowed hard, then went back to where the rest of the band hung out, waiting for our turn to go onstage.

"Ready for this?" Elena asked.

"Yeah, I am." *I think.*

"You sure you're ready to play *(Un)Fading* live?" Bastian asked.

I nodded. "Yeah. Yeah, I can play it."

"In front of a crowd that big?" He grinned.

My worries about performing that particular song had nothing to do with the thousands of people in front of the stage. Just one who'd be standing a few feet behind me. I smiled in spite of my nerves. "You doubting my ability?"

"Not in the least." He grinned. "Guess we'll see how they like the song."

"Guess we will."

In no time at all, the band onstage was finished and the emcee announced our entrance. I took a deep breath, let it out, and walked out onto the stage.

More than stage lights ever were, the sun was blinding. I squinted at first, but then my eyes adjusted. Our first song had a long intro, so I had a chance to drink in the view before I needed to sing.

Holy shit, indeed.

Row upon row of screaming, jumping, waving fans, each row of faces a little harder to see than the one in front of it. A sea of people continuing so far I couldn't even see the last row.

Stage fright drowned in adrenaline. This was what I'd always wanted. This was what I'd lived for. And we were here. Fuck *yes*.

The intro ended, and I gave the song everything I had. By the next song, my heart was pounding, the crowd was going crazy, and it just didn't get better than this.

Then it was time for that song. The bass line gave me chills, and just like every time we'd rehearsed it, the lyrics raised goose bumps on my skin. I almost forgot about the thousands of people watching and listening, and for a moment I was only aware of the one behind me.

At first, the crowd wasn't quite sure what to make of the song. It was a dramatic shift from our first two hard-rock pieces, and this wasn't usual Schadenfreude music. But before the end of the first verse, they were on their feet, screaming and begging for more.

The song ended, and I left the stage, high-fiving my sister as she went on to take over for the rest of the set. Backstage, I dropped into a chair, my hands and knees shaking and my heart pounding. It wasn't just the exhilaration of a hugely successful performance in front of thousands of people. The lyrics of *(Un)Fading* lingered on my tongue like the tingle of a kiss cut off too soon, and the only thing that would bring me back to something close to sanity was Bastian.

My heart in my throat, I thumbed a quick message into my phone and sent it before I could think twice: *I want you.* He wouldn't get it until he was offstage, but just sending it made my pulse speed up even more.

I didn't know when or where or how we could do anything now. We were hundreds of miles from home. We'd checked out of hotel rooms this morning. We still had hours to hang around the amphitheater before the awards ceremony. Then there was the long drive home.

Somehow. If I didn't have him soon, I was going to lose my mind.

The show ended. The band came backstage. We congratulated each other on one of the best shows we'd had yet, and everyone quickly cleared gear out to make room for the next band. All the while, I kept glancing at Bastian, wondering when he'd get my text.

Finally I caught him looking at his cell, brow furrowed. His thumb moved rapidly across the keypad. Then, without looking at me, he slipped his phone into his pocket. A second later, mine vibrated.

I cast a quick glance around to make sure no one read over my shoulder when I looked at the message. Then I read:

I can't wait.

Seconds later, another message came through: *Meet me here. Half an hour.* Below that was the main street through town and a cross street.

The only problem? I didn't have my car. Fortunately there was an easy solution to that little dilemma.

"Hey, Todd, you mind if I borrow your car?" I asked. "I need to eat something other than concession stand shit."

He tossed me the keys. "Don't wreck it."

"Want me to bring anything back for you?"

He shook his head. "Concession stand shit is fine by me."

I laughed and took off, hurrying out to the parking lot before anyone could question where I'd really gone and why.

Though hundreds of people swarmed the parking lot, a flicker of movement caught my eye. I glanced up, my heart jumping. The most fleeting glance of a woman disappearing into the crowd stopped me in my tracks. I searched the sea of faces, certain I'd seen her.

It must have been my imagination. I shook my head and walked on. Like the rest of the band, my wariness of Denise had grown to a low level of paranoia; we all tried to keep a buffer between her and Bastian whenever we could, and she had a tendency to show up at random times. It wouldn't have surprised me if she'd driven all this way to fuck with him at an event this big.

I scanned the crowd again. Didn't see her. Kept walking. I found Todd's car and drove out of the parking lot. I didn't bother with the GPS. The town's main drag was scored with evenly spaced, consecutively numbered cross streets, and I figured it wouldn't take much to find Fourteenth Street.

I was right. In minutes, I passed Fifteenth. As I approached the cross street that I knew was Fourteenth, Bastian's truck came into view parked on the shoulder. I slowed down to pull over, but he pulled out, so I followed him.

He put on his right blinker and turned down Thirteenth. We drove for a while down a narrow, unlined strip of crumbling asphalt between thick, untouched forest, following it until the pavement ended and the dirt road began. Clouds of yellow dust played in the sunbeams and the only sounds were gravel crunching beneath tires and the low purr of the engine. We were as far out in the middle of nowhere as it was possible to get around here.

Then his blinker came on again and we turned down another dirt road, one that probably hadn't seen vehicular traffic in months, judging by the plants encroaching on the narrow road.

And there he stopped.

My heart pounded. I shifted into park. By the time I'd turned the key and killed the engine, he was out of his car and heading toward mine. I unbuckled my seat belt as he got in on the passenger side.

He closed the door, and we stared at each other. The space between us lingered in spite of my nearly irresistible need to kiss him. Equal parts caution, restraint, and disbelief kept me back. Were we really doing this? Did we really just sneak away to relieve some tension? Was he thinking what I was thinking?

"You know," he said, finally breaking the stillness and moving a little closer, "I should be able to go two days without touching you." He put his arm around my shoulders and drew me to him. "And I should be able to wait another day until I can take you home and fuck you, but I can't." His other hand shook when it trailed down the side of my neck, and he whispered, "I just fucking *can't*."

"Then don't."

Restraint and caution vanished as soon as he kissed me. Even when it was only his lips against mine, as we just touched and breathed each other, everything about his kiss was desperate. The unsteadiness of his breath, both in its sound and its warmth across my skin, screamed *insatiable*. Restraint and caution may have fallen by the wayside, but disbelief held fast, tingling in my fingertips as I found the familiar coarseness of his jaw and the cool softness of his hair.

His hand left my face and ran down my neck, my chest, my abs. When he hooked a finger under my belt, my back arched off the seat. A cool rush of panic swept through me. What if someone knew we'd both gone? Figured out why? And where?

"Bastian, should we—"

"Probably not. We probably shouldn't, but I'll be damned if I want to stop."

"But we're—" My belt buckle jingling free sounded an awful lot like shattering inhibitions.

"We're about as far from anyone as we can get." He started to draw my zipper down, then stopped. "Tell me you want to stop, and we will." Drew it down a little more. Stopped. "It's your call, Aaron."

I moved my fingers into his hair, and kissed him even more passionately than before. When he wrapped his hand around my cock, I broke the kiss with a gasp and let my head fall back against the seat. His lips were instantly on my neck.

I breathed exactly in time with his hand's slow, smooth strokes, inhaling on every upstroke, exhaling on every down. My hips tried to join in his rhythm, but this position kept me passive, letting me do nothing more than surrender to him.

"Did you really think I could get through this weekend without doing something?" he said, pausing to kiss my neck.

Closing my eyes, I licked my lips and slurred, "I didn't think we—" *Oh fuck, Bastian, that feels so damned good.* "I didn't think we had much choice."

He laughed softly, the huff of breath on my neck making me shiver. "The last few days have been fucking torture," he said in a hoarse whisper as he drew his fingertips along the underside of my cock. "Every time I've looked at you…" The words trailed off into a half moan, half sigh. "Every time, all I could think of"—he kissed me, letting it linger for a long moment before he breathed—"is how much I've wanted to have you again." Our eyes met. He swallowed hard and whispered, "Especially after today's show."

I touched my forehead to his. "Fuck, Bastian, I can't wait until we're home and can actually get some time to ourselves."

"With a bed to ourselves."

"Exactly."

"For now, I guess this," he said, kissing his way down my neck, "will just have to do." And in the next heartbeat, his mouth was around my cock and I was almost instantly on the verge of coming. Only Bastian could get me so close, so fast.

"Oh God," I moaned, gripping the headrest with both hands as he sucked my cock. "Oh God, that's..." My breath caught, and I clenched my teeth, trying to hold out just a little longer, just a few more seconds, just a little—*oh God I am too damned turned on to last when your tongue does that.*

The entire world went white, and my hips tried to thrust upward as electricity surged through my veins and up my spine. I was vaguely aware of my own voice crying out something I couldn't understand, thought I should worry that someone might hear, but I didn't care. As long as Bastian heard me and knew how much he turned me on, I didn't care.

He sat up and kissed me, his hands trembling against the side of my face, and the taste of my own semen on his tongue made the world spin even faster. I nudged him back, using my body weight to lead him back to the passenger seat. He growled into my kiss as I trailed my hand up his inner thigh.

"You had to know I'd return the favor, right?" I squeezed his cock through his clothes.

"I was hoping you would," he said with a grin. Cupping my jaw, he kissed me again and pressed his erection against my hand. "Because I fucking love what you do with your mouth."

"Do you?" I teased.

He nodded slowly, closing his eyes and sucking in a breath when I unbuckled his belt. "Oh my God..." When I drew his zipper down, deliberately dragging my fingertips along his clothed cock, he let his head fall back and whispered, "There's no way in hell I'm going to last long."

"Quickie now." I kissed his neck and stroked his cock. "We'll take our time tomorrow night."

His fingers ran through my hair, twitching against my scalp as I leaned down and circled the head of his cock with the tip of my tongue. I thought for a moment he'd have second thoughts, realize we shouldn't stay out here too much longer in case someone had noticed we were both gone, but he made no effort to pull me away. He wanted to come, not come to his senses.

"We'll definitely take our time tomorrow night." His voice edged closer to a moan with every syllable, and when I deep throated him, his entire body trembled.

The fingers in my hair did nothing to stop me, so I kept going, finding that perfect rhythm that kept his voice wavering somewhere between a moan and a whimper. There existed no sexier sound than Bastian when he was just like this, when all he could do was release the helpless moans of a man so close to the brink he couldn't decide if it felt too good to stop or too intense to go on.

I ran my tongue around the head of his cock again, and his back arched off the seat.

"Oh my God, Aaron," he moaned. "Fucking hell, don't stop, don't stop, *do not fucking stop.*"

I couldn't stop if I wanted to. I squeezed a little harder and moved faster, every pulse against my fingers and tongue urging me to give him a little more, a little more, a little—

"Holy...*fuck*..." His cock twitched, his breath caught, his back arched, and a tremor rippled through him so violently I swore I tasted electricity just beneath his skin. In the next instant, he came, hot, salty semen hitting my tongue just seconds before he begged me to stop.

I sat up and kissed him. We both struggled to catch our breath in between kisses, panting against each other's lips. Eventually he stopped trembling and we both breathed in a steady, slow rhythm.

"I think we might have to come out here again," he slurred, "next time we have a show at the amphitheater."

"Tell me when. I'll be here." I looked around at the forest outside the car. "How the hell did you find this place, anyway?"

He laughed softly. "Well, at least Denise was good for one thing."

"You two used to come all the way out here?"

He nodded, running his fingers through my hair. "We've been to the amphitheater for a couple of performances, plus we've come out to see some other concerts. And sometimes you just can't wait."

"Yeah, I know the feeling."

Bastian smiled and touched my face, trailing the backs of his fingers along my jaw, and we just looked at each other. Neither of us spoke, and all I could hear was my heartbeat and the phantom melody of *(Un)Fading*.

No one else, only you, my own voice echoed in my head.

No one else. I ran my fingers through his hair. *Only you.*

In front of ten or fifteen thousand people, I could belt those words out, but here in the woods in a car with only him, I was mute.

"Come here," he whispered. He pulled me to him and kissed me, just his lips against mine for a long moment. His tongue parted my lips, and he breathed me in.

His kiss made me dizzy, and only in part because of the lingering saltiness on both our tongues. I just couldn't get enough of him. Much more of this, though, and we were never going to make it back before someone noticed we were gone.

Panting against his mouth, I rested my forehead on his and whispered, "We should get back."

"I know," he said. We started to come together for another kiss, then backed off. Then again. Lust and reason vied for dominance, and he granted lust the victory when he whispered, "One more kiss and we'll go."

As they always did, that last kiss went on for almost ten minutes, but we finally managed to separate. I left first, my lips still tingling from Bastian's kiss as I followed the winding road back to the main drag.

Up ahead, tendrils of yellow dust twisted and twirled in the air. Odd. We'd been back here long enough, any dust we'd kicked up should have settled by now. Must've been the wind, I told myself, though the trees and bushes didn't look disturbed.

Just being paranoid. No one knew we were out here. No one knew "we" existed at all.

I stopped at the car wash on my way back and ran Todd's car through it. If we both showed up with dust all over our cars, people might get suspicious. Chances were no one would notice, especially since the entire town was coated with similar yellow dust, but I wasn't taking any chances. That and it gave me a few minutes to straighten my clothes and slightly mussed hair.

With my appearance looking less disheveled and all the incriminating dirt swirling the drain at the car wash, I headed back to the amphitheater. Traffic was hell with all the concertgoers trying to get in. Another easy way to explain my lengthy absence.

Returning to the Battle of the Bands was like stepping onto another planet. It was surreal, walking among concertgoers and performers, security guards and vendors, knowing where I'd been, what I'd done, and with whom, with none of them being any the wiser. Especially when I rejoined my own band, casually falling into conversation with my sister about this or that while no one had a clue. The thrill of secrecy, the smug *if only the rest of you knew*, just made everything about this hotter. Riskier but hotter.

I passed Bastian near the lot where the bigger bands' tour buses were parked. He stood with Andre and Todd, discussing something I couldn't hear, and as I passed him, we both pretended not to notice each other. I kept my eyes down to avoid eye contact.

WITH THE BAND

In my efforts to keep from looking right at him, something caught my eye that would have otherwise escaped my notice.

I shivered and grinned to myself because no one else knew the story behind that whisper of yellow dust on Bastian's boot.

CHAPTER TWENTY-ONE

The setting sun found Schadenfreude chilling in the back parking lot by the vans, buses, trucks, and trailers of all the various bands who'd come to perform.

Bastian and Rochelle sat on the tailgate of his truck. Andre leaned against the van parked beside the truck. Elena, Todd, and I sat on the pavement, and the whole group dined lavishly on whatever we could find at the concession stands that looked more or less fit for human consumption.

With our performance over, we all relaxed. The only thing left to give any of us nerves was the awards presentation, which was still an hour or so away. Other than that, we could kick back and take it easy.

Well, we could until the moment Todd glanced past me and pursed his lips. "Somebody order some crazy?"

Bastian flipped him the bird. "Funny, McClure."

I looked past my brother, and my blood turned cold. "Uh, I don't think he's kidding."

Bastian groaned. "Please tell me you're both—"

"Hey, guys!" Denise's voice sent a collective wince through the band, as if feedback had just shrieked through an amplifier. "Great show."

"Thanks," Todd said dryly. "What's that? You were just leaving? So sorry to hear it. Good-bye, Denise."

She glared at him. "No, actually I wasn't."

"How the fuck did you get back here?" Bastian asked.

"Seriously, Denise," Rochelle said. "You don't have a pass, so—"

Denise cut her off, pulling her sleeve up to reveal one of the blue bracelets that performers and crew wore.

"How the hell did you get one of those?" Andre asked.

"I have my ways."

Elena fidgeted, eyeing Denise uneasily. Something in my gut twisted.

Bastian hoisted himself off the tailgate. "Denise, why don't we go someplace else and talk about this, okay?"

Denise stood her ground. "I'm here to congratulate the whole band. Not just you."

Rochelle exhaled hard. "Denise, have you ever looked up the word 'stalker' in the dictionary? Or do you need me to spell it for you?"

Denise glared at her. "Ever looked up the word 'bitch'?"

"I have." Rochelle sipped her drink. "Had a picture of you next to it."

Bastian laughed, which made Denise's posture that much more hostile. On some level, I wanted to feel sorry for her, but the band had made it abundantly clear she wasn't welcome, particularly around Bastian. *So Todd was right. She is a slow learner.*

Rochelle opened her mouth to speak, probably getting ready to unleash another snide comment, but Todd stood and said, "Listen, Denise, you've got about ten seconds to get the fuck out of here before I go get security."

She looked at Bastian, and the way she narrowed her eyes screamed cunning and evil. "Are you going to let him talk to me like that?"

Bastian shrugged. "Wasn't planning on stopping him, no."

"Right, I forgot," she growled. "You're an asshole."

"Which begs the question, why the fuck do you keep showing up?"

Everyone looked at her, waiting for an answer.

Denise took a breath and squared her shoulders. "Well, you should know I'm dating the lead singer of Flogging for Coffee now anyway. You know, a *signed* band?"

"Good to know." Bastian unscrewed the cap on his water bottle. "I'll be sure to send the poor bastard a sympathy card."

"Oh, fuck you."

He muttered something under his breath as he lifted the bottle to his lips. My gaze flicked toward Denise just in time to see her eyes narrow again. Her mouth twisting into a grin, she watched him, calculating, timing, waiting, and just as Bastian took a drink, she said, "Well, fine. I guess you're just happier fucking your lead singer, then."

Bastian choked on his water. He narrowly avoided spitting it on Rochelle and turned his head away, coughing a few times.

"Okay, that's enough, I'm getting security." Todd glared at her. "You and Bastian can argue all you want, but you leave my sister out of this."

With a smug sneer, Denise said, "Oh, I wasn't talking about your sister."

"Uh-huh, then what—" Todd glanced at me, then Bastian, and for a panicked second, I thought he believed her. Then he rolled his eyes. "Denise, you're fucking high."

"Am I?" She looked at me. Her eyes widened, and she put her hand over her mouth in mock horror. "Oh, did they not know about that?" My blood turned to ice.

"Shut up, Denise." Bastian paused to clear his throat. He coughed a couple more times, then glared at her. "Just shut the fuck up and get out of here."

"That sounds like a damned good idea," Andre said. "Denise, out."

She looked at me again. "You're not going to tell them?" To Bastian, she said, "Too embarrassed by your boyfriend to tell anyone?"

"Fuck you," he growled.

Elena and I exchanged glances. Her posture straightened just slightly, and when I bit my lip, her eyes widened.

"And that's enough out of you." Andre put his hand up and started toward her, herding her away from us.

"Tell them, Bastian," Denise said over Andre's shoulder. "I saw the two of you at the House of Anarchy. And before the show this afternoon. I fucking saw you. Don't deny it."

"You were also miraculously pregnant with his kid," Andre said. "And now you're leaving." He led her away, but she didn't go quietly.

"Didn't you guys notice them sneaking off for an hour?"

"Yes, God forbid any members of the same band leave at the same time," Andre said. "Come on. You're leaving."

He escorted Denise away, and the rest of us remained in tense silence. I looked anywhere but at Bastian. Or my sister. Or my brother.

"Aaron," Elena said, her voice low and even. "Where did you go earlier?"

I looked at her. "I...went out to lunch." She saw right through me. Oh God, she fucking did.

"Wait." Todd shifted his weight. "She *was* lying, right?" I met his eyes, and his were full of an unmistakable plea of *please tell me she was.*

Before I could stop myself, I glanced at Bastian. He glanced at me. Between the split second of eye contact and the way we both quickly dropped our gazes, the secret was out.

"You lied to me," Elena growled, stabbing a finger at me. "You fucking looked me in the eye and told me there was nothing going on between the two of you."

Bastian looked up. "She asked you about us?"

I sighed. "Yeah, after one of the shows."

"You suspected this?" Todd said. "What the fuck? Why didn't you tell me?"

"Because he said there was nothing going on," Elena said.

"Obviously there was."

Elena threw up her hands. "Oh, do forgive me for not hooking him up to a fucking polygraph."

"Enough," Bastian growled. "Get off her case, Todd. She didn't know any more than you did."

Todd took a deep breath, then turned to Bastian. "And since when are you gay anyway? What about Denise?"

"I'm bi, Todd."

"You're *what*?" Andre came around the row of vehicles and stopped in his tracks.

Bastian rolled his eyes and exhaled sharply, then said something to his brother in their native tongue. They went back and forth a few times. My name slipped in there at some point, and Andre took a step back, eyes widening.

"Are you…" Andre looked at me, then Bastian, then me again. "You're serious. You two are… You're…"

"We're dating, okay?" Bastian snapped.

Andre pinched the bridge of his nose. "Are you fucking kidding me?"

"How long has this been going on?" Todd asked. "I mean, the two of you. Not, not each of you being gay, just…you know what I mean."

"Awhile," Bastian said.

"Define 'awhile,'" Andre growled.

Bastian glared at him. "Do you want a list of every time and place we've ever—"

"That's enough," Elena snapped.

"We've been seeing each other since I joined the band," I said.

Todd blinked. "Like, right from the beginning. From the get-go." He rolled his eyes. "Christ, you two didn't wait around, did you?"

Bastian and I looked at each other for a second but said nothing.

"So, you've..." Todd shook his head. "Wait, have you been fucking my little brother in my own goddamned house?" Before either of us could answer, he put his hands up and shook his head again. "Never mind, never mind, don't want to know."

"What the fuck were you two thinking?" Andre growled. "Fucking a band member?"

"Of course, Andre," Bastian said. "That's exactly what we were thinking about. Hey, let's start screwing each other and fuck up the band while we're at it."

Todd looked at me, lips curling into a snarl. "We talked about this. *Specifically* this. Do you mean to tell me you were seeing him"—he pointed at Bastian—"when we had that conversation?"

I swallowed. "Yes. I was."

"So you just lied to me about it?"

"Oh yeah, can't imagine why I wasn't forthcoming about it, since you were raking me over the coals for dating Jason."

"Jason?" Andre cocked his head. "Who the fuck is Jason?"

"The guitarist from his last band," Todd said. "His ex-boyfriend."

Andre glared at me. "I'm seeing a pattern here, you know."

"Since when do I need to clear my private life with all of you?" I said.

"Since your private life involves another member of the band," Elena said through her teeth. "I don't give two shits who either of you are fucking, except when it could adversely impact the band."

"Exactly," Andre said. "Okay, fine, you're gay, that's..." He barely masked a shudder that made me want to deck him. "Whatever." He looked at me. "But didn't your last band fall apart because of something like this?"

I exhaled. "Yes, but—"

"Hey, hey," Rob appeared, stepping between all of us. "What the hell is going on here?"

"Just sorting out some personal shit," Andre said through clenched teeth.

"Seems a couple of band members have a little 'thing' going on," Todd growled.

Rob furrowed his brow, eyeing all of us. "Who?"

Bastian sighed. "Me and Aaron."

Rob blinked, eyes shifting back and forth between Bastian and me. Then he made a dismissive gesture. "Okay, whatever. Right now, I don't care what y'all are doing on your own time. However, you guys need to get out there for the awards presentation." He stabbed a finger in the air at each of us in turn. "Put on your fucking game faces. I don't want to hear another word about this until after the awards. Got it?"

We all nodded.

"Good. Now *go*."

* * * * *

"And the winner of this year's Battle of the Bands is…" The presenter made a huge theatrical gesture of unfolding the piece of paper with the results on it. She looked at it, then leaned down to speak directly into the microphone. "Schadenfreude."

A mixture of excitement and *oh shit* ratcheted my heartbeat up to an insane speed. The high fives and congratulations weren't nearly as intense as the icy tension between us all.

We went onstage to accept the award, and we did a damned good job of keeping up appearances: smiling for the crowd, shaking hands with the emcees and presenters, posing for photos. But the tension was there. It was there and wouldn't be denied.

Bastian and I looked at each other, both shifting uneasily.

Winning this competition was a huge step for the band. The Rock-out would provide excellent exposure, look great to record agents, and could be the start of some big things. But the timing. Shit, the timing. Just what we needed: three high-pressure, back-to-back performances coming up fast with no time for the band to settle our personal issues.

There was no doubt in my mind Denise had deliberately timed it this way. We'd been a crowd favorite, and there'd been speculation for weeks that we'd win this year. The bitch had known exactly what she was doing.

But what was done was done. Now to face the music.

After posing for some promotional photos and signing autographs, we all went backstage again. Everyone was tense, poised for another fight, but Rob's icy glare told us not to even think about starting again.

"Listen, guys," he said. "You can all sort out this personal shit on your own. I really don't give a fuck who's dating who, who's doing what, anything like that. We don't need any bad publicity when we've got record agents sniffing around. Get this shit sorted and keep it out of sight. That means offstage, behind closed doors, and I'd better not hear a *peep* about it anywhere near the End of Summer Rock-out. Am I clear?"

Nods and murmurs all around.

"Good. Now everyone pack your gear up and let's get the hell home. I suggest everyone get a good night's sleep, then deal with whatever bullshit you need to."

I wasn't going to argue with that. We were all exhausted, and we had a long drive ahead of us. There was no sense spending half the night fighting. There would be plenty of time for that at our next rehearsal.

I'd ridden in with Todd the other night but, for the sake of peace and harmony, decided against riding back with him. Of course, the band wasn't thrilled about me hitching a ride with Bastian, but at least it wouldn't be five hours of icy silence with him.

Not that Bastian and I were terribly talkative, but that was more out of nervousness, distraction, and worry than hostility.

After a while, I said, "Well, that wasn't what I expected this afternoon."

"You're not the only one." He sighed. "Fuck, I knew she'd turned into a fucking psycho, but that…"

I put my hand on his knee. "How do you think the dust will settle with this one?"

"I don't know," he said, practically whispering. He rested his hand on top of mine, squeezing gently. "I really don't have a clue."

"You don't think we should—" I paused. Swallowed hard. I didn't want to go there. Band in shambles or not, there were some things I was afraid to suggest.

He glanced at me. "Hmm?"

I gulped. "Should we…keep…" I coughed. "Keep doing what we're doing?"

"Should we?" He shrugged. "I don't fucking know what we should do." He squeezed my hand again. "But I don't want to stop. Not even with all the drama that's probably going to start. Why? Do you?"

"No, no, I don't want to stop." I paused. "Just…wondering."

He put on his blinker and pulled into a gas station. At the pump, he parked and turned off the engine but didn't get out. He didn't speak, didn't look at me.

"What's wrong?" I whispered.

He turned to me, the bright lights of the gas station illuminating one side of his face. "Are you worried I'll want to call things off because of the band? To keep the peace, all of that?"

My heart thundered in my chest. I nodded.

He pursed his lips, dropping his gaze for a second. "That's probably the only solution I haven't considered and wouldn't consider. The thing is, I—" He cut himself off and looked into my eyes, his expression so full of emotion it made my breath catch.

My heart pounded. I touched his face. "What is it?"

"There is—" He caught himself again, looking away for a second and furrowing his brow. Finally he swallowed hard, looked into my eyes, and whispered, "Ich liebe dich."

My breath caught. Even the harshness of his accent and the German language couldn't temper the unsteadiness in his voice. I didn't understand the words, but I understood his eyes.

Without another word, he pulled me close, kissing me gently.

When he broke the kiss, he watched me for a moment as if searching my eyes for something. He caressed my face with the backs of his fingers. "Aaron," he whispered. "I mean it. I love you."

I touched his face and smiled. "I love you, Bastian."

He kissed me gently. "When we get home, as much as I'd love to stay, the rest of the band will be along sooner or later. We've got some damage control to do, so it would probably be best if we spent the night apart."

"Yeah, I guess if someone comes home at the wrong time, it would just throw gas on the fire."

He nodded. "Exactly." He touched my face. "But, soon. I promise."

"At least we don't have to keep it a secret anymore."

He laughed softly. "No, I guess not." He kissed me gently. "I love you," he whispered.

"I love you too."

CHAPTER TWENTY-TWO

The following night, all my housemates except Todd were home when I pulled up to the curb. At least they were all upstairs, since the lower half of the house was dark while the upper half was brightly lit. Good.

Tonight's rehearsal had been excruciating. The hostility remained in the air, but the band had tried to put it aside. Though no one was particularly thrilled with recent events, it was done and rehearsing was more important, particularly with the Rock-out coming up. Bitterness lingered, but professionalism prevailed. We'd played; we'd rehearsed; we'd all said to hell with our customary trip to the bar afterward. Everyone went their separate ways, no doubt looking for a way to escape, break, relieve, ignore the festering tension.

That's what I assumed everyone else had gone to do, anyway. I didn't particularly care where any of them had gone or why, with the exception of one.

The one who, thank God, had just pulled up to the curb on the other side of the driveway. I was out of my car before his headlights had dimmed, and he'd barely gotten out of the truck before I'd crossed the expanse of pavement that divided us.

He elbowed the door shut. "I've been dying for—"

Before he could finish, I grabbed the front of his shirt and pulled him into a passionate kiss, nearly knocking both of us off balance.

He caught himself with the truck and steadied us, his kiss matching the hunger in mine. The tongue stud grazed my lip, and I moaned, my body melting against his. To hell with what the neighbors could see. It was the kind of deep, sensual kiss that made me forget what day it was, never mind what kind of day it had been. *He's here*, the piercing's presence told me. *He's here, and he's not going to let you go until you forget why you needed him here in the first place.*

Pulling me closer, he went for my neck, panting in between kisses as his fingers combed through my hair. I pressed my erection against his, and he released a sharp breath across the side of my neck.

"Fuck," he whispered. "Do that again and we won't make it to your room before I fuck you." It barely registered in my mind that there was anything wrong with him doing just that. To hell with the rest of the world.

But Bastian must have been at least somewhat more rational, because he gently pushed me away and nodded toward the house. "Come on," he said. "The longer we stay out here, the longer it'll be before I'm inside you."

I shivered. "In that case…" I slid my arm around his waist, and we started up the driveway. He followed me to the side of the garage. At the door, I handed him my keys. No sense even trying to convince my hands to unlock the door. Even Bastian was a little unsteady this time, fumbling with the key the first couple of times before he finally got the door open.

Safely inside my bedroom, we didn't hold back anymore. My jacket hit the floor, and my keys landed somewhere nearby. Shoes landed wherever they landed. As he shrugged his jacket off, I grasped his shirt and pulled him toward me. The bastard had worn a button-down shirt today, damn it. How the hell was I supposed to work buttons when I—

Oh, fuck it.

I grabbed his shirt and pulled it apart, a flying button narrowly missing my face before clattering against the wall behind me.

We both froze.

Bastian looked down at his shirt, then looked at me through his lashes, and I couldn't remember ever seeing him look so fucking ready to just lose it.

He licked his lips. "So it's gonna be like *that*, is it?"

I pulled the rest of his shirt apart. "Yeah. It is."

"Good." He shoved me toward the bed. I pulled him with me and took another step. We fell onto the bed together, kissing and panting and grabbing handfuls of clothing, trying to get close to each other.

"Fuck me, Bastian," I moaned and pushed his shirt off his shoulders. He growled softly, kissing my neck and shifting his weight as he reached between us to unbuckle his belt. I fumbled with my own belt. Then I lifted my hips so he could pull my jeans off and out of the way. When he sat up and got rid of his jeans, a powerful shudder rippled through me, the sheer anticipation of having him inside me nearly making me come.

"Fuck me," I heard myself say, only vaguely aware that I'd finally willed myself to speak.

He couldn't get the condom and lube on fast enough, and when I got on my hands and knees, my arms shook so badly from anticipation I could barely hold myself up. When he pressed against me, slowly sliding into me, I closed my eyes and moaned, leaning back to pull him just a little deeper.

He groaned softly, dipping his head to kiss the back of my neck as he drove his cock deep inside me. With every thrust he took, the reasons I'd needed this tonight faded into irrelevance. I needed him, and it didn't matter why.

"Oh God," he whispered. He shuddered, exhaling against my neck. "Oh God, I…"

I thrust back, drawing him deeper, and he groaned something I didn't understand. His hands gripped my shoulders, and he fucked me harder. Deeper. Faster.

Then he stopped. Pulled out. Panic tried to ripple through me, but it was quickly replaced by arousal when he whispered, "Get on your back."

I did, and once he was inside me again, he leaned down to kiss me, and everything slowed down.

He took long, deep strokes, moving only his hips. Everything happened in slow motion. Even my heartbeat seemed to slow down as our bodies moved as one fluid being. Neither of us spoke, neither so much as moaned, but the ragged breaths and trembling muscles said all that needed to be said. I wasn't sure I could have put into words what I felt at that moment anyway; the powerful sensations defied language, went beyond anything that could be contained in a cry or a whimper.

I swore I felt every nuance of his building climax as if it were my own—the shuddering gasp, the shiver that straightened his spine, the tremor that nearly forced him off balance—and when the tension released, I realized it wasn't his orgasm at all, but my own. His name and a dozen or so expletives were right on the tip of my tongue, but I couldn't muster anything more than a groan. Only as my orgasm tapered did I finally manage to whisper, "Oh my *God*."

"I'm gonna come," he moaned. "Oh God, I'm gonna..." He held on tighter and drove himself into me, screwing his eyes shut and baring his teeth as his body shuddered with the force of his orgasm. After a moment, he let his head fall beside mine, releasing a long breath on my sweaty skin.

He pulled out but didn't get up. We just held on to each other. With his body over mine, the weight of the world lifted off my shoulders.

"This was exactly what I needed tonight," I said, my words slurred.

"Me too." He wiped sweat from his brow. "I could go for a shower, though."

No one in the house would be downstairs anytime soon, so we left our clothes in the bedroom and went across the hall to the bathroom. Not a moment too soon, we stepped into the shower.

Hot water and Bastian's hands ran through my hair and down my back. I was vaguely aware there were things wrong in my world, but the water soothed my unsettled nerves, and his touch washed away my uncertainty. Whatever went on outside this room, everything in it was right.

Stepping back, he lifted my hand out from under the water and uncurled my fingers with a single upward sweep of his thumb. One by one, he kissed the ends of my fingers, looking right at me as he sucked my index finger into his mouth. I bit my lip when he kissed the center of my palm and made a slow circle with the tip of his tongue. Then he did the same on the inside of my wrist, sending a tingling ripple of goose bumps up my arm and down my back.

One kiss at a time, he inched toward my elbow. As he drew closer, I could barely breathe, my entire body tensing in anticipation of something I couldn't quite identify, some sensation that my body remembered even if I didn't.

His lips paused on my inner elbow, and when his tongue made that same slow, gentle circle there, my spine straightened with a shiver and I sucked in a breath.

"Jesus," I whispered.

"Like that?" he murmured, keeping his lips close enough to my skin that the coolness of his breath and the hum of his voice teased nerves that had just discovered they were erogenous.

"I love it." Closing my eyes, I exhaled slowly and let my head fall back. The touch of his hand on the side of my neck made me suck in a startled breath, but the gentle warmth of his lips beneath my ear knocked that air right back out. The water was tepid compared to the heat of his lips and skin on mine.

His hand left my neck and drifted down, pausing to tease my nipple with his thumb before continuing down my abs to my hip. There his hand stopped, resting just inches from my cock. For the longest time, he was still except for his lips and tongue moving with mine, but the gentle pressure of his palm didn't escape my notice.

As he kissed my neck again, his hand started moving, trailing slowly downward.

"Already getting turned on again?" he whispered, running a single fingertip up and down my hardening cock.

My skin tingled with a pleasant chill that came from within, his touch creating the kind of goose bump-raising shiver the hot water couldn't begin to temper.

"Jesus Christ, Bastian," I breathed. He laughed softly, his cool breath on my wet skin making my breath catch. "Oh my God…"

"I love it when you get like this," he growled. "The more turned on you get, the more turned on I get."

I sucked in a breath. "If you're anywhere near as turned on as I am right now—"

His fingers closed around my cock, and my speech turned into a moan. He stroked slowly, liquefying my spine with his touch.

"Oh, I am," he whispered. "I have been all day, and now…" He exhaled hard against my neck, then raised his head and kissed me passionately. "Christ, I've already had you once, and…fuck, look what you're doing to me." He guided my hand to his own erection, and I couldn't help exhaling when I realized he was as hard as I was.

"Fuck, I can't get enough of you," I whispered, shivering as my hand slid up and down his hard cock.

"Likewise," he murmured. He exhaled against my lips as I matched his rhythm, stroking him just as he did me.

His free hand was against the wall behind me. Mine rested on his arm. When he moved his hips closer to mine, the backs of his fingers touched the backs of mine, our hands moving slowly together. His downstroke was my up, and mine was his.

We tried to kiss but couldn't quite remember how. Every time our lips came close to meeting, one of us gasped or the other shivered, and we lost whatever ground we'd gained. Instead I let my head fall beside his, the coarseness of his stubble brushing against mine as water slid from our hair into the nearly nonexistent space between his jaw and mine.

Our hands stroked faster now, no longer moving in tandem but turning each other on just the same. Every squeeze of his fingers sent me closer to insanity, and every motion of my hand made his breath catch.

A throaty moan rose above the white noise of rushing water, and while I couldn't be sure whose voice it was, the sound seemed to bring us both to life. We sought each other's mouths and found the desperate, sensual kiss that I didn't even realize I'd craved.

I broke that kiss as a whimper escaped my throat.

"Oh Jesus, Aaron," he moaned, the sound almost disappearing into the water. "That is so…fucking…perfect…" He tried to kiss me, but his spine straightened in the same instant his cock twitched in my hand. He threw his head back, and I watched him, completely mesmerized as he screwed his eyes shut and his lips parted with a soundless cry. Water fell down the sides of his face and neck like sweat, tracing every contour of his jaw and throat before sliding over his quivering shoulders.

His hand faltered, but just the sight of him like this kept me right on the edge with him.

"Oh God," he said. "Oh God, I'm—" He gasped, and his eyes flew open, meeting mine with a look of such undeniable, unbridled lust, it pulled the air right out of my lungs. His hand tensed around my cock, and it was my turn to gasp. He glanced down as if suddenly aware of his own hand again. Even through the tremors of his building orgasm, he found his rhythm again, stroking my cock rapidly and *perfectly*.

It was impossible to tell who came first or whose orgasm triggered whose. All I knew was that his helpless, surrendered moans mingled with mine and through my electrified haze of oblivion, I couldn't tell when I felt his cock pulsing in my hand or when mine pulsed in his.

My knees were ready to buckle, so I used the shower wall for support, the cold tile jarring me back to reality. Then Bastian's body was against mine, his breath cooling the side of my face as he kissed me.

It was well after midnight when we collapsed, exhausted, breathless, and satisfied. After Bastian fell asleep, I lay awake in his arms for a little while.

It struck me as ironic that our relationship was, in a way, the catalyst for all the tension and stress tonight, yet it was also the cure. The poison and the pill.

Lying in his arms, it seemed absurd to even worry about what the rest of the world might think about our relationship. The thought of wanting to be anywhere but here was incomprehensible. Whatever the rest of the world thought of it, this was *right*. We'd figure everything else out in time, but my feelings for Bastian—physical and otherwise—weren't going anywhere.

And I didn't want them to.

CHAPTER TWENTY-THREE

With all our rehearsals and gigs, the band was forced to ignore my relationship as much as possible. There was a definite undercurrent of *we'll talk about this later* in every conversation, every encounter, every exchange. I couldn't wait to see how things went after the Rock-out.

I doubted we'd make it that far before some of the tension broke, though, and facing my siblings across my parents' dinner table one Thursday night, I had a feeling we were close to that breaking point.

Todd barely looked at me. Elena picked at her food—though, to be fair, it *was* my mother's cooking—while glancing back and forth between my brother and me. I gritted my teeth and tried to decide whether to feel guilty or be pissed they'd taken it this badly.

"So this award," my father said, oblivious to the hackles going up at the mere mention of the Battle of the Bands. "I assume this is a good opportunity for you?"

"Definitely," Todd said through his teeth. "Could mean a record deal on the table, all kinds of opportunities." He paused, narrowing his eyes. "Assuming no one fucks it up."

"Todd," our mother said, shooting him a disapproving look.

"Todd, don't start," Elena said.

"Don't start?" He laughed bitterly. "Am I the one who started this whole thing?"

"You really want to get into this now?" I snapped.

"Seems like as good a time as any."

"Todd, Aaron, I'm not fucking around," Elena said. Our parents exchanged dumbfounded looks but wisely stayed quiet.

"Neither am I," Todd said. "Unlike—"

"Shut the fuck up," I snarled.

"Okay, okay," our father said. "You're all adults. Enough of this."

To Elena, our mother said, "What is going on here?"

"What's going on," Todd said, "is a band member who can't seem to get his priorities straight when it comes to the band and his personal life."

"Todd, not here," I said.

"Then where? My house obviously isn't the place, since that's where—"

"*Enough.*"

"Todd, drop it," Elena said.

"It's done," I said to my brother. "What do you want me to do about it?"

Todd slammed his glass down. "I want you to tell me what the fuck you were thinking when you started fucking Bastian."

All three of us froze. My heart stopped. Elena let her forehead fall into her hand. Todd swallowed, glancing back and forth at our parents.

"Why don't we take this outside?" I said, keeping my tone as calm as I could.

Todd said nothing. He pushed his chair back. Without a word, so did I, and we left the dining room. Behind us, our parents bombarded Elena with questions, and I made a mental note to buy her several beers. I didn't like leaving her to them in this situation, but it would only get worse if Todd and I stayed in the dining room.

In the foyer by the front door, I spun on my heel and glared at him. "Thanks for outing me to Mom and Dad," I growled. "Really. That's how I always wanted them to find out I'm fucking gay."

"Wasn't my intention." He almost sounded apologetic. Almost. "But your relationship has the potential to fuck up all kinds of shit, so forgive me if I wasn't thinking about that."

"Oh, my heart fucking bleeds." I rubbed the back of my neck. "Jesus, Todd, this is getting out of hand. Seriously. I get that you guys are pissed we're dating, but—"

"If you didn't think it was a problem, why did you keep it a secret?"

"I never said I didn't think it would be an issue," I said. "We didn't set out to do this, Todd. It…happened."

"Yeah, I'm sure. And when exactly were you going to tell us, anyway?" he asked.

I exhaled. "We were planning to tell the band after the Battle. After the Rock-out, as the case may be. When things had settled down a bit." I wet my lips. "And after Bastian had a chance to come out to his family. Especially Andre. We both figured he'd be a hell of lot more shocked than you were. We just didn't want to drop the whole bomb on the band all at once."

"Okay, yeah, it was a shock. Look, date whoever the fuck you want," Todd said. "But look what happened to your last band. How the hell can we be sure that won't happen to my band?"

"*Our* band, Todd."

"Oh yeah, you've certainly stepped right in and taken a piece of it, haven't you?"

"I'm an adult. I don't need to justify who I'm dating or why." I glared at Todd. "And you and Andre might as well learn to deal with it too."

"Right. We'll just sit back and watch it rip the band apart."

I rolled my eyes. "Melodramatic, much? You guys know we're seeing each other, so just accept it and let's move on. As a band."

Todd snorted. "Why don't you tell that to the Brothers Grimm who can barely be in the same room with each other right now."

"Oh honestly," I said. "They aren't that bad off."

"They're getting there fast," he said. "Have you seen them since the Battle? I'm just waiting to see who ends up with a black eye first. All because you and he—"

"Look, it's not up for discussion. I'm seeing Bastian. I'm in the band. Get over it."

"Get over it?" Todd's eyes narrowed, and I very nearly drew back in spite of the distance between us. "Aaron, mark my words, when—not if, *when*—things start going sour with Schadenfreude, you had damn well better have a plan for fixing it. I'm not going to lose my band or a friend over this."

"That's not going to happen," I said.

He eyed me for a moment. "We'll see how sure you are when you're saying that in hindsight."

I kept a stoic face, but something in his tone resonated. Worry coiled in the pit of my stomach. What if he was right?

Todd shifted his weight, looking anywhere but at me. After a moment, he spoke through clenched teeth. "You still haven't answered me. I want to know what the fuck you were thinking. Getting involved with a band member."

I resisted the urge to roll my eyes. "It's none of your business what I was thinking."

He laughed. "None of my business?"

"None of your fucking business."

"Right. Okay." He glanced toward the dining room, where our sister still tried to appease our progressively more freaked-out parents. Turning back to me, Todd said, "Can we take this shit outside, or should I invite Mom and Dad into it now?"

"Fine." I grabbed my jacket and followed him out onto the porch, fully intending to leave as soon as this conversation was over. Or sooner, depending upon whether or not Todd had finished speaking by the time I finished listening to him.

For a full minute, we simply stared at each other in silence. The porch light illuminated one side of his face, leaving the other almost completely in shadow except for the hint of a sparkle in his eye from the streetlights.

Finally he spoke. "You say it's none of my business, but I don't think you get it, Aaron. There's a lot on the line right now, and you two don't seem to give a shit."

"That's not true, Todd."

"Isn't it?" He folded his arms across his chest, leaning on the porch railing.

"Look, it happened," I said. "I told you, we've been trying for a while to figure out how to address it without causing problems with the band."

He let out a long breath. "Yeah, glad you were on top of that. Really kept the peace, didn't it?"

"I didn't know Denise was—"

"*Fuck* Denise. She was a cunt to tell us, it was none of her business, but the fact is, you guys shouldn't have been involved with each other. The last thing we need is two band members so wrapped up in each other—"

"So wrapped up in each other that *what*, Todd?" I shifted my weight. "If we were so wrapped up in each other that it affected the band, wouldn't everyone have caught on to us sooner? Maybe noticed that one or both of us wasn't putting our all into the music?"

His lips tightened. He opened his mouth to speak, but I cut him off.

"Don't you think if this was actually a problem—beyond you and Andre being assholes about it—that something would have come up sooner? Missed rehearsals? Distraction? Lack of focus? If it was affecting our performance, I could understand, but it's *not*."

"Not yet."

"Jesus, Todd, you—"

"You two have been trying to keep it a fucking secret all this time, but now that it's out, what now? How long before you two start taking off to fuck before performances, or—"

"We've been doing that since the beginning," I snapped. His flinch gave me a feeling of triumph and satisfaction, which in turn made me feel guilty. My tone softening, I said, "Look, the bottom line is that my relationship with Bastian hasn't done a damned thing to the band."

"That doesn't mean it *won't*," he said.

Through my teeth, I said, "Maybe if you and Andre learn to live with it—"

"Fuck, Aaron, don't you get it?"

"Evidently I don't. Enlighten me."

He pushed himself off the railing and paced on the porch. "Listen, I want you to be happy. I'm not pissed about this because I don't want you dating or because you're gay or because I don't think you should be sleeping with someone." He paused, grimacing. "Though I'd just as soon not know about it." The glare he shot me was completely devoid of humor. "Where I draw the line is when your relationship has the potential to threaten something I've worked the better part of my life for."

Gritting my teeth, I said, "You're assuming it has that potential."

"It does if things go south." His tone changed from angry to…something else. Worried? Hurt? "You of all people know what something like this can do to a band. And I mean, even if the band wasn't a factor, he's my friend. I don't want to see you get hurt, I don't want to see him get hurt, and I sure as shit don't want to have to take sides if you guys split." The anger returned to his face and voice. "But there's more on the line here than just you and Bastian, Aaron. Who you love is none of my business, but my career is hinging on the two of you staying in each other's good graces."

I avoided his eyes.

He went on. "Think about it. If you two break up, do you think you could still face him every day? Go onstage with him? Sing lyrics he writes for whoever comes after you?"

Swallowing hard, I said, "I don't know, Todd. I won't know unless it happens."

He straightened, almost looming over me. "That's what I thought. Thanks for thinking this far ahead. Your relationships are none of my business, but this one could hurt more than just you and Bastian."

I opened my mouth to speak, but the door slammed behind him, cutting me off and leaving me alone on the porch. For a long moment, I stood in the heavy, unsettling silence, my brother's words echoing in my mind. I let out a long breath, rolling my shoulders as if I could shake off the tension.

The door opened behind me. I cringed, certain it was either Todd coming back for more or my parents coming out to discuss me, well, coming out.

"How you holding up?" Elena's voice relieved some of the tension in my shoulders.

"Great."

"Are you going to talk to Mom and Dad?"

I shuddered.

She put her hand on my arm. "You need to talk to them. They're upset, and—"

"I'm sure they are." I sighed. "This wasn't how I wanted them to find out."

"I know. How did it go with Todd?"

"It was lovely." I sighed. "Fuck, I swear, Elena, I didn't set out to get involved with a band member. Especially after what happened with Jason. It just...happened." I dropped my gaze. "It happened, and I...we..." I trailed off, shaking my head.

Elena watched me quietly for a moment. "You're in love with him, aren't you?"

I swallowed hard, then nodded.

"Shit." Her shoulders dropped a little. "Look, I wish you both the best. Honestly. I don't have any ill will against you two or whatever it is you have going on. But relationships come and relationships go. You two haven't been together nearly long enough to know if you'll be in for the long haul. And even if you had been, shit can happen. Look at Bastian and Denise." She shifted her weight. "The thing is, Schadenfreude *is* in for the long haul, so if the two of you come apart, then what?"

I shook my head. "I don't know."

"Guess we'll play it by ear, then. Not much else we can do."

I nodded.

"And I'm trying to be cool with this, Aaron, I really am. But I have to admit, it's..." She laughed softly. "Look, from where I'm standing, it *is* a little weird."

"Elena, you've known for years that I'm gay."

"That's not what I mean. Bastian is like a surrogate brother to me." She showed her palms and shrugged. "So I'm sure you can imagine it's a little odd having my baby brother dating my surrogate big brother?"

I laughed. "Okay, I see your point. And I'm sorry I lied to you about it. You understand why I did, right?"

"Yeah. I guess I probably would have done the same thing." She shifted her weight.

"Guess I should probably talk to Mom and Dad."

Elena pursed her lips, then nodded slowly. "I guess you should face *that* music sooner than later. Do you want me to come with you?"

I swallowed. I hated imposing on her, but I needed someone to have my back for this. I nodded. "Yeah, I do."

She smiled and gestured toward the front door. "After you."

CHAPTER TWENTY-FOUR

An hour and a half away from Seattle's perpetual glow and Schadenfreude's hostile tension, down some dead-end country back road I doubted I could find again to save my life, Bastian and I stared up at the stars from the bed of his truck.

I couldn't say how long we'd been out here. Maybe an hour, maybe more. Neither of us had spoken in a while. I'd rested my head on his arm for some time, but we'd separated when his arm started going numb and I got a crick in my neck. We didn't touch now. Not out of any aversion to touching, it was just how we'd ended up. We were inches apart but alone with our thoughts.

In the darkness, I could just make out Bastian's fingers flexing and straightening, tapping on his thigh, pressing unseen strings into the chords of some unheard tune. Ever the musician, seeking refuge in notes and rhythm. My own fingers drummed, in some crude Morse code no one could hear but me, the chorus of *Terra Firma*. Tried to, anyway. Every time my mind started wandering, my fingers crept into *(Un)Fading*.

My eyes tracked the tiny silver speck of a satellite moving across the sky. I followed it until it disappeared behind some trees, then looked for something else to hold my half-interested gaze.

Bastian sighed and fidgeted, his leather jacket creaking in the stillness.

"You okay?" I asked.

"Just getting comfortable." He rested his hand on my arm. *Ah, contact.*

"I don't think truck beds were made for comfort." I reached across and put my other hand on top of his.

He laughed. "No, I guess they weren't." Leather protested softly when he turned his head toward me. "How do you think this will all work out?"

I swallowed hard and turned onto my side to face him. Propping myself up on my elbow, I said, "I guess we'll just have to ride it out. See what happens."

Bastian exhaled and looked up at the sky.

I touched his arm. "What do you think will happen?"

"I don't know." He sighed. "I don't think it could have come out at a worse time, though."

"Yeah, can't argue with that."

He rubbed his eyes with his thumb and forefinger. "I can't fucking believe she outed us like that."

"I didn't even think she knew."

"Neither did I." He muttered something in his native tongue. "The very fact that she kept it quiet until the Battle of the Bands surprises the shit out of me. I would have expected her to have come screaming out of the woodwork when she caught us in the act."

"Think she really caught us?"

He nodded. "Probably. She mentioned the House of Anarchy and after the show at the Battle, so it was either a really, really well-timed bluff or she saw us."

In my mind's eye, yellow dust hung in the air, twisting and spinning in slow motion, the ghosts of unseen tires.

"Somehow I don't think she was bluffing," I said quietly.

"No, I don't think she was. And obviously she was keeping that ace up her sleeve until it was the perfect time to fuck with me," he growled. "I'm surprised she didn't drop the bomb *before* the show at the Battle."

"Still did plenty of damage either way," I muttered.

"No shit."

We both went quiet for a moment. Then I said, "I gotta know, what on earth did you see in her?"

He sighed. "Honestly, she used to be a lot easier to get along with."

"Really? What changed?"

He chuckled. "I stopped drinking quite as much."

"I suppose that would help." I laughed. "Really, though. I just can't get my head around the two of you, not with the way she's treated you."

"Okay, okay, seriously." He lifted his head long enough to run his fingers through his hair, then laced both hands behind his head. "The first few months or so, everything was fine. She really is a nice girl. All you've seen is the manipulative, backstabbing side of her."

"Hard to believe someone like that has any *other* side."

He laughed, but it was halfhearted. "Honestly we had a really good thing for a while. I mean, I thought we did, anyway." He sighed. "I loved her, I really did. But after a while, our relationship was nothing but stress. And it shouldn't be like that."

I bit my tongue, withholding my concern that recent events might turn our relationship into something like that. After a moment, I said, "And she never knew about…this? You being bisexual, I mean."

"No. I never told her."

"In six years, you never told her?"

Bastian sighed. "I wanted to. It killed me to hide that from her. I guess that should have been a sign we had no business getting married when I couldn't tell her something like that."

"So why didn't you?"

"I was afraid she'd buy into the stereotype that bisexuality and monogamy aren't compatible." He took a deep breath. "She had enough trust issues where relationships were concerned. I didn't think I'd ever be able to convince her that even though I'm attracted to both men and women, I'm not a cheater."

"Did she think you'd cheat anyway? Even without knowing you were bi?"

"She accused me a few times." Blowing out a breath, he shook his head. "Christ, a relationship like that is exhausting. If I wasn't trying to convince her of my fidelity, she was trying to convince me not to leave."

"I think the lack of trust would have pushed me right out the door."

He laughed quietly. "Yeah, looking back, it should have. But I stuck around. In the beginning, I really did love her. Toward the end, I was just afraid she'd make good on her threats to off herself."

I looked up at him, blinking. "You really thought she'd do it?"

He rolled his eyes and nodded. "I fell for it a few times, yes, which is why it was her favorite way to twist my arm. Aside from claiming she was pregnant, anyway."

"Sounds like she needed help, not a fiancé."

"Oh, you don't know how right you are."

"So, outing us to the band," I said. "What did she think she was going to gain from that?"

He shrugged. "Probably just some smug satisfaction that she got the last fucking word. She couldn't have me back, so she threw a Hail Mary to try to hurt me as much as she could."

"I've never understood people like that," I whispered.

"Tell me about it." He slipped his hand into mine. "But I've quickly learned there are better relationships out there."

"You're not the only one." I looked at him, and though it was dark, I could just make out his smile. He raised his head and kissed me gently.

"I want you to know, whatever happens, with the band, with our siblings, whatever..." He ran his fingers through my hair, then gently drew me to him. "None of that changes the fact that I love you."

"I love you too," I whispered and kissed him. "Nothing's going to change that."

After another gentle kiss, Bastian sat up. He pulled out his phone. The screen lit up. Then he scowled and closed it. "We should probably get out of here."

"What time is it?"

"Almost midnight."

I let out a breath. "Do we have to leave right now?"

He shrugged. "We might be paying for it tomorrow."

"And if I said I didn't care?"

"Well, if you don't"—he lay back beside me again—"then neither do I." I moved a little closer to him, and he put his arm around my shoulders so I could rest my head on his chest. His jacket creaked in the otherwise still night, and the leather was cool against my cheek.

Eventually we did have to leave, though, and we finally got out of the truck bed and into the cab. The engine turned over, and the low rumble made my heart sink. Back to civilization. Back to the lights and noise and people and bullshit. Back to our respective homes with their respective hostility and tension toward us.

Bastian exhaled. Probably more to himself than me, he whispered, "Guess we can't stay out here forever, can we?"

He put the truck in reverse, but before he could release the gearshift, I put my hand over his. Furrowing his brow, he eyed our hands. Then he looked at me, and his piercing caught the dim glow from the dashboard lights when he raised his eyebrow.

"Aaron—"

Eyes locked on his, I pushed the shifter back into park.

He looked at our hands again, then back at me. When my seat belt clicked, then retracted with a low *whir*, he gulped.

"We can't stay out here forever, but we can stay a few more minutes, can't we?" I unbuckled his seat belt, and he pulled in a breath as the shoulder strap slid back toward the door. My hand was on his inner thigh, and when I drew it up in a straight, deliberate trek from his knee, he shivered.

His head fell back against the headrest, and he whispered, "Jesus, Aaron, let's get out of here."

"Not yet."

"Aaron, you're—" He sucked in a breath when I unfastened the top button of his jeans.

"I don't want to leave yet." I kissed the side of his neck. "That and I can't wait." I nipped his earlobe while my fingers drew his zipper down. "I just can't." I wrapped my fingers around his cock. A groan vibrated against my lips.

The engine fell silent. "Don't let me stop you."

"Didn't think you'd mind." I raised my head to kiss him, still stroking him slowly. "I was thinking maybe this will relieve a little tension." I teased the corner of his mouth with the tip of my tongue. "Maybe make it a little easier for you to focus on the road when we do leave."

He ran his fingers through my hair and kissed me, groaning softly when I squeezed him. "What road?"

I laughed. "The one that's going to take us to my place so you can fuck me."

He tensed when I stroked a little faster. "For now, you have my undivided attention."

"Good." I flicked my tongue across his lower lip. I squeezed his cock, and he closed his eyes, letting his head fall back against the seat.

"Oh God," he murmured, screwing his eyes shut. "Keep doing that and—*oh fuck...*"

I slowly took his cock into my mouth, one inch at a time, teasing him with my tongue the entire time. His hand rested between my shoulders, and every subtle twitch of his fingers through my clothes told me what I did was right. When I took his cock a little deeper, as close to deep throating as I could, his hand moved up to the back of my neck and then into my hair. Goose bumps rose beneath my shirt as his fingertips trailed along my scalp. I loved giving head, but my God, I'd never wanted to go down on a man as much as I wanted to go down on Bastian just then, and his hand in my hair and his cock against my tongue turned me on so much it was painful.

"Oh my God," he groaned. "Aaron...your mouth...your..." Another groan, quieter this time. "Fuck, where did you learn to *do* that?"

I took him a little deeper into my mouth. Beside me, something jarred the steering wheel. I assumed he'd grabbed it, probably just seeking something to anchor himself. His other hand was still in my hair, fingers twitching against my scalp while his cock twitched against my tongue.

"Oh Jesus, Aaron, that's incredible, you're..." He was breathless, panting. His back arched off the seat. "Fuck, don't stop, that's..."

I deep throated him again, and his words dropped to little more than a whimper. When I did it again, his voice crescendoed to a moan, and the third time, he roared my name, my name, my name... *Fuck, Bastian, I can't believe how hot it is to hear you say my name like that.*

I sat up, and he pulled me into a deep, frantic kiss.

"Oh my God, that was..." He finished the sentence with another desperate kiss, holding the sides of my neck in trembling hands.

"Hot," I murmured against his lips.

"That's the word. Jesus Christ." He let his head fall back against the seat again, closing his eyes and running the tip of his tongue along the inside of his lip. "Fuck, whatever it is you do with your mouth..."

"I think it's called sucking your cock."

He laughed. "Yeah, that." He kissed me again. His hand slid over my thigh, and I jumped.

"Don't you think we should go?" I asked.

"Absolutely not."

"Bastian, it's late, we'll—"

He silenced me with a long kiss. When he ran his fingertips along my zipper, teasing my hard-on through my jeans, I forgot why I'd protested in the first place.

Just before he went down on me, he whispered, "The rest of the world can wait."

CHAPTER TWENTY-FIVE

The next performance at the House of Anarchy was rife with hostility. The crowd was pleased and begged for more, but even if they didn't feel it, we sure did. The icy looks, the clenched jaws, the palpable anger in the air. There was no fucking escaping this tension.

As soon as we were backstage, cases started slamming, and no one spoke until Andre said, "All right, we need to settle this. Here and now. This is stupid."

"I could have told you that from the beginning," Bastian snarled.

Andre snapped back in German. The brothers went back and forth a few times, each comment getting progressively more venomous.

"Can we at least keep it all in one fucking language?" Elena growled.

"What is there to settle?" Bastian gestured at me. "We're dating. I'm bi. He's gay." He put his hands up. "What's left to explain?"

"Here's the thing," Andre said. "As long as you two are fine, everything's all right, whatever, then it's not an issue. But what happens when you get into a fight?"

"Or split up?" Rochelle asked.

"Sooner or later, shit's going to happen," Todd said. "And what happens then?"

Bastian dropped his gaze. I chewed the inside of my cheek. Of course we'd both known from the beginning that was an issue, and there was no shortage of guilt eating at me over it. The answer? Hell if I knew.

"Look, we can't afford to lose either of you," Elena said. "Losing Derek when we did could have been disastrous if we hadn't gotten Aaron, but if we lose Aaron now or Bastian, we're fucked."

"I'm not going anywhere," Bastian said.

"Neither am I," I said.

Todd laughed bitterly. "Easy to say now. You both still like each other."

"Well, at least someone in the band is getting along, then." Elena glared at him. "I'm with you guys, don't get me wrong. They shouldn't have started dating in the first place, but unless someone knows a way to change the past, we're stuck with it."

Bastian flinched.

I chewed the inside of my cheek. Elena was right, but was it really that simple? Much as I wanted to deny it, I'd known from the beginning I was taking a risk getting involved with Bastian. I hadn't expected us to be outed this way, but there was always the chance someone could find out.

Under normal circumstances, our siblings could get over the fact that we were dating. But these weren't normal circumstances. We were in a band that was quite possibly on the verge of making it. We would always be right in each other's faces.

"Okay, fine, we have to deal with it," Andre growled. He gestured sharply at Bastian and me. "But if things go to shit with the two of you—"

Before he could finish, the door opened and in walked Rob.

"What the fuck is the matter with all of you?" he snapped. "I swear to Christ, you guys brought the temperature in that club down by fifty degrees."

No one spoke. No one looked at each other.

"Here's the deal," Rob said, offering a stony glare to each band member in turn. "We're two days away from the Rock-out. I don't give a fuck who's dating who. I really don't. However, if I hear anything more about it, if I even *think* it's affecting you guys and your ability to perform, I will pull you from the shows myself. Understood?"

Nods and murmurs of "got it" went around the room.

"Night after tomorrow," Rob continued, "I expect the band I agreed to manage to be onstage at the Rock-out. You guys are way too good to let some personal bullshit fuck things up this late in the game. You've made it to the goddamned Super Bowl. Now is not the time to suddenly decide you don't like the rest of your team. Get it the fuck together."

He didn't wait for a response and stormed out.

"Well, you heard the man," Todd said. "Guess we focus on the Rock-out now."

We all finished putting gear away. No one spoke. Bastian didn't look at me. Once he paused to rub his forehead with two fingers, and the side of his neck was visibly taut with tension.

After all the gear was loaded, Bastian picked up his bass, and we walked out together. The secret was out, so we didn't bother leaving separately anymore. We were still quiet on the way out this time, and we didn't touch, both miles away in our own little worlds.

In the parking lot, we stopped. There was nothing I could do about the tension among my bandmates, but maybe Bastian and I could at least escape it for a little while.

I put my hand on his waist. "Feel like coming over tonight?"

Bastian took a breath, then nodded. "I'll follow you."

* * * * *

I don't think the drive from the House of Anarchy to my own house had ever been so long, but we finally made it. Out of the cars, up the driveway, through the garage, into my bedroom. We'd walked this same path countless times before, following the same steps and hallway from the madness of the world to the sanity of passionate, feverish oblivion. His body heat alone was usually enough to make me forget, or at least not give a shit about whatever went on outside this room.

Something was off, though. His hands made only halfhearted attempts to get past my clothes, and his kiss was tepid. He'd pulled me to him, held me close as I pressed him up against the door, but I couldn't help thinking his heart wasn't in it. Any of it.

I looked at him. "Bastian, what's wrong?"

I might have been able to believe it was my imagination, right up until he let out that long, resigned breath. He let his head fall back against the door and closed his eyes. I reached for his face, my heart skipping when he flinched at my touch.

Letting him go, I took a step back to give him some room to breathe. He ran a hand through his hair, still avoiding my eyes.

Finally he said, "What are we doing, Aaron?"

I chewed my lip. Normally a smart-ass response would have fit, but not this time. "What do you mean?"

He was quiet for a long moment again. Eyes fixed on something that wasn't me. Mind a million miles away. Brow furrowed. Then he whispered, "We can't keep doing this."

My heart stopped. "Bastian—"

"We've both known from the beginning this was a bad idea."

"Why not? Why can't it work?"

"Look at what's happening to the band, Aaron," he said. "Jesus, no one in the band is speaking, no one—"

"And what does that have to do with us?" I said, trying to keep my voice even.

"What *doesn't* it have to do with us?" With what looked like a lot of effort, he met my eyes. "If there hadn't been an 'us' to begin with, we wouldn't be in this."

"So are you saying you regret it?"

He rubbed his eyes, sighing. "No. No, I don't." His voice softened, but only a little. "But maybe we'd save ourselves a lot of heartache and headache if we didn't continue it."

My knees almost buckled. "What?"

He dropped his gaze, pressing his lips tightly together. Finally, he looked at me, but only for a second. "I love you, Aaron. I couldn't change that if I wanted to. But we can't keep doing this." He swallowed hard. "I can't keep doing this."

My tongue stuck to the roof of my mouth. "But, Bastian—"

He met my eyes. "Look at everything that's happened since we got together. Do you really think that's going to get any better?"

"Quite frankly, it doesn't get much better than some of the things that have happened since we got together." My voice wavered. "We can get through the bullshit with the band, but I don't want to lose you."

"And I don't want us to be cornered into staying together just to keep the peace in the band." His tone was unsteady. He rubbed his neck and was silent for a moment. "I don't know what else to do, Aaron. I don't know how we can make this work without making things worse."

My heart dropped into my feet. "You really want to do this right before the Rock-out?"

He shook his head. "I don't want to do it at all."

"Then why—"

"It needs to be done, Aaron." He forced himself to look me in the eye. "I'd rather do it now and walk away peacefully than wait until something happens and we fall apart."

"But you're cool with doing it right before the damned Rock-out?"

He moistened his lips. "And if I hold out until after the Rock-out, then what? Wait until we're signed? The first record? The second? I'd rather just do this now and be done with it than keep biding my time, leading you on, and waiting until everything else settles down enough to do this."

"Or until it's settled enough that we don't have to do this."

Bastian sighed. "I don't think that'll happen. There will always be this pressure for us to stay together to keep the peace."

I swallowed. "What do you want me to say, Bastian? I can't change the past. I can't change the fact that we did this and we're both in the band. Neither can you."

"I know." He walked past me, making sure there was just enough room between us that we didn't touch, accidentally or deliberately. I wanted to reach for his arm, to stop this train wreck with a touch, a kiss, *something*, but my body wouldn't move.

Bastian reached for the doorknob. Over his shoulder, he said, "I'm sorry, Aaron. I really am."

And he was gone.

The door clicked behind him, the sound echoing in the stillness with an eerie finality. The quieter *click* of the door at the end of the hall hit me in the gut. Garage door. Car door. Engine turning over. Each hammering home the reality that he'd really left, and still I couldn't grasp it, even as the engine's rumble faded into the distance.

"Bastian," I whispered. His name disappeared into the silence, slipping into nothingness, following him into the night like smoke through the keyhole. I sank onto my bed, eyes locked on the closed door, trying to comprehend what had just happened.

I'd costarred in the ends of numerous relationships, and most of the time, I knew the split was coming long before either of us finally said the word. The ends of all my relationships had been remarkably anticlimactic. Predictable, anyway. Ending one of those relationships was usually sad and disappointing, but in my mind, I always knew it was the right thing to do. Even my most heartbreaking split—when Jason and I had called it quits—had been a rational, foregone conclusion.

This moment, as the weight of his departure sank in, didn't make sense. It was wrong.

It was wrong, but it had happened.

* * * * *

I tried to sleep that night even though I knew I wouldn't.

The next morning, exhausted and completely numb, I trudged out of the bedroom. My feet were heavy on the way upstairs, like deadweight. The shock of Bastian's departure was still beyond my comprehension, and the click of the closing door kept echoing in my mind.

"Aaron?" Todd's voice stopped me in my tracks. I hadn't even seen him, even though he was right in front of me in the kitchen. He cocked his head. "You okay?"

"Yeah, I'm fine." My voice was flat. Lifeless. God, I hoped I could inject some life into it before the show tomorrow night.

"You sure?"

No answer.

"Wait, wasn't Bastian here last night? Where is—" He paused. "Aaron, tell me you two didn't get into it."

I looked at him, offering no words, not even a change in my expression.

His shoulders dropped, and he looked away, clenching his jaw. "How bad?"

"Bad."

"*How* bad?"

I moistened my lips, not that it helped. How bad, indeed? I sighed.

"Oh fuck. You broke up, didn't you?" He grimaced, his eyes taking on the same "please tell me you didn't" look they'd had when he learned about Bastian's and my relationship.

Dropping my gaze, I nodded.

"Goddammit," he muttered. "This—"

I put my hand up. "Todd, please. Not now." When I met his eyes again, he opened his mouth to speak, then stopped.

His expression softened. "What happened?"

"He couldn't deal with being pressured to stay together, so he…" I trailed off.

Todd scowled.

Folding my arms across my chest to still the shivering, I said, "I know what you're going to say, Todd. You saw this coming, you—"

"No." He shook his head. "I was afraid something would happen, but that's not like Bastian at all. Especially not right before a huge fucking show."

"Well, he did."

"Maybe he's just buckling under the pressure," he said. "He's always handled stress pretty well, but everyone has their limits."

"Can't imagine why our relationship has been a source of stress lately." I shot him a glare. He looked like he was about to come back with something snide but thought better of it.

He sighed. "Well, hopefully he'll come around. He's probably just freaking out."

I didn't want to get my hopes up that Todd was right, that Bastian had simply buckled under the weight of everything that had happened recently, but I knew that was futile. I loved Bastian too much to accept that this was really it. But maybe it was, and if it was, then we'd just have to learn to work together in the band.

Todd cocked his head. "You okay?"

I shrugged. "As okay as I'm going to be."

"You gonna make it through the Rock-out this weekend?"

I cringed. I was about to say I'd try, but when I looked at my brother, the lift of his eyebrow and incline of his chin warned me not to let him down. He was sympathetic about my breakup with Bastian, but the fact remained that he had a hell of a lot riding on my ability to get onstage at the End of Summer Rock-out. We all did.

I'd made my bed, and with or without Bastian, I had to lie in it.

Swallowing hard, I nodded. "I'll be fine."

CHAPTER TWENTY-SIX

I avoided Bastian backstage.

Less than forty-eight hours after he'd walked out, we had to go onstage together. His mere presence made it difficult for me to breathe, but I would get through this show. We were both professionals. We could both put our personal shit aside enough to do what we came here to do.

I tried to concentrate on the pressure of the show itself. The coliseum was huge, seating something like seventy thousand people. From the sound of it, ticket sales were through the roof and the stands were packed. That and the place was crawling with scouts from record agencies.

The last thing I needed to do was worry about Bastian. Or the strife between the rest of the band members, for that matter. The air was frosty between all of us. I only hoped that chill didn't spill onto the stage.

Before I knew it, the emcee was calling us onstage. As soon as I joined the rest of the band, nerves twisted in my gut. The air was taut with that hostile tension. It resonated in every note, every chord, every beat. In the way we glanced at each other. In the way we moved, particularly when we were close to one another.

Fuck, I thought. We still nailed all our songs, still brought the crowd to their feet, but the tension was palpable.

And there was still one thing left that I dreaded.

Another song ended, and I knew it was coming. I braced myself. I held my breath. I tapped into every well of professionalism as a performer and a musician, willing myself to just get through it. *Just sing it. Don't think about it. Don't feel it.*

But when the deep, haunting timbre of the bass signaled the beginning of the song, of *that* song, my knees almost buckled. A lump rose in my throat. I swallowed hard, forcing it back. *Come on. Get it together. It's just a song.*

As the guitar and the drums joined in for the melody, as everything led up to the moment when I would start singing, I knew full well it wasn't just a song.

My voice wavered going into the first verse, but I forced myself to keep singing. I tried to focus on the notes and the sound, not the lyrics, like I did with every other song in the damned set, but each word hammered itself into my consciousness. I may as well have ripped my own heart out with each passing line.

(Un)Fading wasn't a confession of love or a tribute to our relationship anymore. With every line, I used his own words to plead with him, to get it through his head that I loved him and needed him.

During Todd's guitar solo, I chanced a look at Bastian and instantly regretted it. His lips were tight, his jaw set, and the pain in his eyes was palpable. It was hard to tell in the flashing, flickering stage lights, but I swore his eyes were wet.

How was I going to finish this song now? If it was painful before, it was agony now. The guitar solo neared its end. I swallowed my emotions. I had to finish this because I needed him to hear it.

"I'm here again, but your eyes don't see me," I sang. "You fade from me, my unfading love can't bring you back…"

Please hear me, Bastian. You have to hear what I'm saying to you.

I swore he faltered on a note, but I couldn't be sure if it was his mistake or my wishful thinking. If I'd imagined that hesitation or that note that didn't quite ring true.

When the song finally, mercifully ended, I slipped offstage to let Elena take over for a couple of songs. Bastian kept his eyes down while I walked past. On one hand, I wished he would look at me—*just be a man and fucking look at me, Bastian*—but on the other, I didn't think I could handle the weight of even the briefest glance from him.

Offstage I took a few deep breaths, closing my eyes and trying not to feel the vibration of Bastian's bass thrumming through every fiber of my being. I had to pull myself together. There was too much riding on this performance. Willing myself to be professional, I pushed my feelings aside as much as I could and returned to the stage to finish the set.

When the show was finally over, I went backstage and released a long breath. I rubbed my eyes with my thumb and forefinger as my stomach wound in knots.

Behind me, a case slammed. The latches snapped into place. A moment later, the case slid violently across a table's surface, and I turned my head just in time to see Bastian storm out. The door banged shut behind him, and to my surprise, some of the tension in my shoulders released. As much as I desperately wanted to talk to him and sort things out, I just couldn't handle being this close to him. Not now.

A hand touched my shoulder. "You okay?" Elena's voice was soft and gentle.

"No," I whispered. I jerked my arm away and went outside to get some air, hoping Bastian wasn't going to the same place to do the same thing.

* * * * *

Right about the time I'd managed to walk off some of the tension and started to gather my thoughts, my phone vibrated. Muttering under my breath, I picked it up and found a new text message.

It was from Rob: *Backstage. Now.*

Great. Just what I needed. I started toward the backstage area. There was probably another ass chewing awaiting me, along with the rest of the band. Too much tension, letting our personal shit interfere with our performance, all the same crap I'd already heard. He must have been thrilled to hear Bastian and I had split up, assuming he knew by now.

When I came around the corner, I almost tripped. Rob stood with his arms folded across his chest and his lips twisted into a scowl. Beside him, leaning against a table, was Bastian.

There was no one else in the room.

I cleared my throat. "Still waiting for everyone else?"

"No," Rob said coldly. "Just you two."

Wonderful. "Okay." I took a seat in a metal folding chair. "Well, we're here."

"Yes, you are," he said. "And I need the two of you to get it together."

I avoided Bastian's eyes. Most likely he did the same.

"I'm going to leave you alone," Rob said. "I really don't care how you do it or what you have to do, but sort it out." A second later, the door slammed behind him, and I was alone with Bastian.

For half an eternity, neither of us moved or spoke.

Finally I said, "So how do we settle this?"

Bastian shook his head. "I don't know."

"Well, we might want to think of something."

"Yeah, I know. If you come up with something, do let me know."

"This was *your* choice, Bastian," I snapped.

He glared at me. "And you think it's easy?"

"Easier for you than me."

He exhaled hard. "Look, I'm sorry about how things worked out. I just…I can't…" He paused, taking a deep breath. "We're always either going to have to walk on eggshells in our relationship for the sake of the band, or walk on eggshells in the band for the sake of our relationship. When do we get to decide what we want and what we need?" He sighed, rubbing the back of his neck with both hands. "It'll always be a competition between us and the band."

I narrowed my eyes. "Doesn't sound like much of a competition. Sounds like you've made your choice."

"Aaron, the band needs both of us, and—"

"And I need you."

Bastian dropped his gaze and swallowed hard. After a moment, he looked at me. "We can't have both. I'm sorry."

"Yeah, I'll just bet you are."

He met my eyes again, this time narrowing his with barely contained fury. "I'm *not* getting trapped in another goddamned relationship."

The words pushed the air out of my lungs. "Bastian, I'm not—"

"It doesn't matter who or what or how," he growled. "I just spent six years of my life being trapped with someone. I can't do that again."

"And you think I want to trap you?" I snapped. "I want you to be with me, but only if you want to be."

"Tell that to the rest of the band."

"Fuck the rest of the band."

He laughed bitterly. "Yeah, good idea. Listen, the pressure is there whether you want to be blind to it or not. First it was the Battle of the Bands. Then the Rock-out. We've been through this, Aaron, we're—"

"Do you love me?"

He jumped. Blinked. "What?"

I shrugged. "Simple question. Yes or no."

He set his jaw. "We can't do this, Aaron, we—"

"Yes. Or no."

He held my gaze. I wanted to believe his eyes were wet, but couldn't tell where reality ended and my wishful thinking began.

"I'm here again," I heard myself singing, *"but your eyes don't see me."*

I wet my lips. "Just a simple answer, Bastian. Yes or no."

Our eyes were locked for another long moment. Then he whispered, "It doesn't matter."

He brushed past me. I closed my eyes and exhaled, listening to the echo of his footsteps over the music and noise all around me.

"You fade from me. My unfading love can't bring you back."

I swallowed hard, forcing myself to believe it was anger rising in my throat, not all the other emotions that came from watching him leave *again*.

With the echoes of a string of growled curses hanging in the air, I walked out the same door. On my way to anywhere but here, as luck would have it, I passed Rob in the hallway.

He stopped me. "I assume things are settled?"

I glared at him. "Oh yeah, it's *much* better now. Thanks for your help." I didn't wait for a response before I started walking again.

CHAPTER TWENTY-SEVEN

I finally found some solitude in a far corner of one of the empty, sprawling parking lots. I leaned against the guardrail and stared out at the endless line of headlights whizzing by on the interstate. I couldn't stomach thinking about that conversation with Bastian, but that didn't matter. I couldn't concentrate on it either, not when my mind kept going back to this evening's show.

(Un)Fading moved me every time. No matter how many times we'd played it, whether in rehearsal or onstage, it moved me, but it had never rattled me straight to the core like it had tonight. I wondered how it had affected Bastian. There was no way I could believe it hadn't affected him on some level. I couldn't have imagined both the tears in his eyes *and* that unsteady, hesitant note, could I? Was it all wishful thinking?

Exhaling hard, I ran a hand through my hair. We needed to talk again. Preferably before we had to take to the stage together in less than twenty-four hours, but I just couldn't work up the nerve to be in his presence. Not yet. Soon, though, we had to talk things over and at least land somewhere close to civil ground. We couldn't keep doing this, or the band would collapse under our weight just like my last band had buckled under Jason's and my emotional shit and stupidity.

Shoes scuffed on pavement behind me. They were coming closer.

I stiffened, closing my eyes and swallowing. *Please be Bastian. No, not Bastian. Not now. God, please, I need to talk to him now. I can't face him now.*

The footsteps came closer, unhurried but determined. This wasn't someone happening past. They were coming toward me. Deliberately. Seeking me out.

Bastian. Please.

Anyone but Bastian.

Perhaps ten feet away from me, the footsteps stopped, but the presence was heavy in the air. Either I was getting terribly paranoid, or a scrutinizing set of eyes was burning holes into my back.

I waited. Couldn't turn around. Needed to know. Didn't want to know.

"You okay?" Todd's voice gave my lungs permission to release the breath I suddenly realized I'd been holding.

My shoulders slumped as I exhaled. "I'm fine."

"I doubt that."

I moistened my lips and turned around, folding my arms across my chest to keep him from seeing how badly I shivered. "Then why did you ask?"

He regarded me silently for a moment. "How did things go with Rob?"

"Beautifully," I muttered.

Todd cursed under his breath. "You two barely made it through the set, didn't you?"

"I can't speak for Bastian," I said coldly.

"But you can speak for yourself. And I doubt you'll disagree with me."

"Then I don't need to speak for myself, do I?"

He sighed. "Now do you see why we don't like people dating within the band?"

I rolled my eyes and shifted my weight. "Is that why you came out here? To lecture me for the hundredth time about something I already fucking know?" I swallowed, forcing my emotions back.

"Aaron, I don't give a shit if you don't like hearing about it." The anger in his voice startled me. "Personally I don't like watching my band falling apart because two of its members couldn't stay out of each other's pants."

"Jesus, Todd. Enough." I threw my hands up. "I fucked Bastian without thinking about how badly the band would suffer. I dared to have feelings for someone. I dared to live by your own philosophy that sometimes you just have to tell the rest of the world to go fuck themselves when you know something is right."

"When you know it's right?" He snorted. "Yeah, I can see that. The only thing that's right about the two of you now is that I think the cold air between you might be enough to counter global warming."

I looked away. "What do you want me to say, Todd? If you're just here to bitch me out, then save it. I don't imagine you hunted me down just to tell me everything I already know."

"You're right, I didn't. I came out here to tell you that while you're busy feeling sorry for yourself out here, my band—*our* band, Aaron—is falling the fuck apart." He stepped toward me, stabbing a finger in my direction. "You can't change the past, but you can cancel your damned pity party, get in there"—he pointed over his shoulder at the coliseum—"and *do* something about it."

I blinked. "What do you want me to do? Tell everyone to just ignore us?"

"Whatever you have to do. Starting with Bastian."

"I'm open to suggestions, Todd, because I'm certainly not enjoying this any more than you are."

"Talk to him, work this out, do something," he said. "But find a way to put up with each other enough that we can be onstage without fans in the fucking nosebleed section being able to feel the drama."

My shoulders went slack, and I stared at the pavement between us. "Fine. I'll talk to him. But I can't promise—"

Todd put his hand up and shook his head. "Do whatever you have to do. When we go onstage tomorrow, we need to go on as Schadenfreude. Not five people who can't even look at each other. That starts with the two of you."

With that, he turned to go.

I called after him, "I don't suppose you know where he is, do you?"

Over his shoulder, Todd said, "Last I saw him, he was talking to Rob. Looked like they were headed out to the crew parking lot."

I drew in a long breath and blew it out. Todd was absolutely right. Everything that had unraveled within Schadenfreude had started with my relationship with Bastian, so resolving it needed to start there too.

I headed back toward the coliseum and went looking for Bastian.

* * * * *

Just as Todd predicted, Bastian and Rob were in the parking lot. Rob paced, and Bastian sat with his legs hanging off the tailgate of his truck. They didn't seem to notice me; there were enough crew members, performers, and coliseum employees milling around, they had no reason to look if they'd heard me coming at all. I stopped behind another band's U-Haul, watching them from the shadows.

"Bastian, I have to know," Rob said. "What the *fuck* were you thinking?"

Bastian blew out a breath but didn't look at Rob. "Which part?"

"Sleeping with a band member? Come on."

I gritted my teeth.

"Listen, Rob, I think I've defended myself enough." Bastian glared at him. "I fucked him. I got involved with him. What more do you want me to say?"

My blood turned cold. Was that really all it was?

"I want to know why," the manager growled.

Bastian released a sharp breath. "Well, you see, Rob, when a couple of men love each other very much—"

"Cut the crap," Rob snapped. "I'm not fucking around here. Some very important people saw that catastrophe you idiots called a show."

Bastian rubbed his eyes, then ran his hand through his hair.

"Look," Rob said. "You're the brains behind Schadenfreude. I could understand Andre doing something like this. Maybe even Todd. But you?"

"And how many times and ways are you going to tell me it was a fucking mistake? Jesus, Rob, what can I say?" Bastian made a sharp, frustrated gesture. "Instead of lecturing me, just tell me what the fuck you want me to do about it."

"I want you to do whatever it takes to straighten all of this out. Get back on speaking terms with him. Get rid of all this fucking tension with the whole damned band."

"Easier said than done."

"Not my problem." Rob folded his arms across his chest. "My problem is when I'm watching Schadenfreude with executives who are considering signing us to a record label, and they ask me if what we're watching is really the same band. My problem is when I don't have an answer for them because I don't even recognize the cluster fuck of a performance that's going on in front of me."

"I get it, Rob," Bastian said through his teeth.

"No, I don't think you do. Do you realize we had an agent from Hurricane Records making noise about a possible record deal? Do you also realize that after tonight's performance, he wasn't nearly as enthusiastic about that deal?"

Bastian exhaled hard. His shoulders sagged under invisible weight.

Rob wasn't finished. "If they don't like what they see tomorrow night and the night after, you can kiss a Hurricane deal good-bye."

Bastian rubbed the bridge of his nose with his thumb and forefinger. I could barely hear him as he said through grinding teeth, "I'll talk to the rest of the band, but I'm not sure what to do about Aaron."

"Aaron *is* part of the rest of the band," Rob said.

"Yes, thank you, Captain Obvious." Bastian glared at his manager again. "Things with him are just more complicated."

"I'm sure they are, and quite frankly, it's not my problem. Just sort it."

"Thanks a lot."

"Your fucking mess," Rob said with a flippant shrug. "Don't expect any sympathy from me for getting yourself into it. Look, Bastian, the band needs both of you. Whatever petty bullshit is between you and Aaron—"

"It's *not* petty bullshit," Bastian growled.

Rob gestured dismissively. "Whatever. Listen, without both Bastian Koehler *and* Aaron McClure, Schadenfreude just *isn't*. Whatever the two of you need to do to sort this out, do it, because tomorrow night I need both of you onstage with your heads out of your asses."

Bastian sighed. "Fuck."

"Right. That's how you got into this crap."

"You're really helpful, you know that?"

"Whatever. Like I said, you got yourself into this mess. Honestly, Bastian, I couldn't care less about your personal life. Fuck a man, fuck a woman, fuck your neighbor's dog. I don't give a shit. When it starts affecting your—"

"I told you, I fucking get it," Bastian snapped.

"Good. Now fix it."

Bastian shook his head. "Goddammit. If I'd known how all of this would have panned out, I never would have fucked him in the first place."

The comment slammed into my chest and knocked the air out of my lungs. Before I could stop myself, I stepped out of the shadows.

"Is that right, Bastian?"

His head snapped up, and his lips parted when we made eye contact. He jumped off the tailgate and started toward me.

"Aaron, I didn't mean—"

I held up my hand. "Save it."

He stopped in his tracks. "Wait—"

"So, what? This was all just a casual fuck? You wouldn't have given me the time of day if you knew all of this would have happened?"

"No, no, it's not—"

"What, Bastian? Because that's exactly what you just said." I cursed the lump that tried to rise in my throat.

He paused, looking away for a moment. When he met my eyes again, his expression was tense. Angry. "I've been working my whole life for this," he said. "Now it might be going up in smoke because of us."

"Because of me, you mean?"

"You. Me. Us. Whatever you want to call it. Either way, this"—he gestured sharply at me and then himself—"could quite possibly destroy something I've worked far too long to let go of easily."

"You son of a bitch." My voice shook. "You said you loved me. If you want to end it, fine. If you want to walk away, fine. But I can't believe that's all it was to you."

"Aaron—"

"You're willing to call the whole thing a fucking *mistake*, boil it down to a fuck you wish you'd never had, because of what's happened with *the band*?"

He dropped his gaze, running his hand through his hair.

Before he could speak again, I snarled, "If you were feeling trapped, it had nothing to do with me. I never made you feel that way. I never would have asked you to choose, Bastian. I never would have asked you to walk away from your dream for me. You chose to be with me, and I thought we had something, but obviously we didn't if you can blow it off like that."

"Aaron, that's—"

"No. Enough. If you can walk away from me so easily, then I'll save you the trouble."

I turned on my heel and stormed into the coliseum.

I leaned against a wall, closing my eyes and willing my knees to stop shaking. I prayed that Bastian didn't follow me. I needed to collect my thoughts again.

Fuck. So much for talking to him. Well, at least we agreed on one thing: getting involved with each other had definitely been a mistake.

CHAPTER TWENTY-EIGHT

Backstage before the next show, I pulled Todd and Andre aside. "I want to make a change to the night's set."

"We're just about to go onstage," Todd said. "We can't change the set now."

"Please, I need to."

Andre raised an eyebrow. "Why?"

"We're not playing *(Un)Fading.*"

"The fuck we're not." Bastian's voice came from behind me.

I glared at him over my shoulder. "No, we're not." To Andre and Todd, I said, "I want it out of tonight's set."

"That's one of our signature songs." Andre shook his head. "The fans will shit if we don't play it."

"I can't. Not tonight." My eyes flicked toward Bastian. He flinched and looked away.

Todd looked at me. "I, we—"

"Please," I said. "Not tonight."

Andre sighed and grabbed the set list. "Fine. But I can't promise the fans won't demand it in an encore." He struck it off the list and glared at Bastian, then at me. "I would suggest the two of you get this sorted out. One way or another. We can kill *(Un)Fading* tonight. One time and one time *only.*"

Bastian cursed under his breath and walked away.

Elena touched my shoulder. "You okay?"

"I'm fine." I watched Bastian go. "I just can't deal with that song tonight."

Todd pursed his lips. "Are you sure you can handle the rest of the set?"

I forced a smile. He didn't need to know that just being in Bastian's presence was excruciating. "Of course. As long as the guitarist doesn't fuck the whole thing up."

His jaw dropped. "Hey!"

I laughed and elbowed him. "Just kidding."

"I should hope so."

"I know full well that you'll fuck it up." I smirked. "I've just learned to roll with it."

"He's got you there, Todd," Rochelle piped up.

"Little shit," Todd muttered. He laughed and shook his head before he walked away.

Onstage, I managed to ignore Bastian enough to get through most of the set. I pretended not to feel the bass reverberating through my every nerve. Pretended I didn't feel his presence behind me. Pretended Bastian didn't exist and had never existed.

Another song ended and I exhaled. *Just get through it. The fans don't need to know what's going on. Only three songs to go.* I listened for Andre's intro to *Terra Firma*, waited for—

An all too familiar bass line sent a chill up my spine.

My breath caught, and I looked over my shoulder. Bastian met my eyes, his expression blank. Neutral. Focused right on me, the bastard.

The fans recognized the bass line too, and they went wild.

Todd and Andre exchanged glances, then looked at me and shrugged apologetically. No turning back now. At the designated point, they joined Bastian.

Three bars until my entrance.

Bastian, you son of a bitch.

I took a deep breath, pretended the lyrics didn't hurt, and poured my heart into them.

"You lift me up, don't fade away." I sang like every line didn't tear me to pieces. "No one else, only you, I fade away, your unfading love brings me back…"

Somewhere in the back of my mind, I remembered that he'd written the song long before we'd started dating, and I wondered bitterly if it had ever resonated so deeply with the man or woman for whom it was written. I wondered if—

My voice cracked.

I recovered quickly. *Focus, McClure.* I gripped the mic like my life depended on it, because in that moment, it may very well have. If I let it go, my hands would shake, letting him see just how badly this hurt me, and I wasn't about to give him the satisfaction of seeing what he did to me.

"Fade away no more," I went on. "Our unfading love remains unfaded."

The final verse ended, and I went into the chorus, throwing everything I had into it, pretending I didn't feel every last stinging emotion in the song's lyrics. I didn't hold the last note as long as I usually did. It hurt too much to drag that song out a single beat longer than I had to.

The fans didn't mind. They roared their approval, and hopefully they didn't see the tears in my eyes or the way my hands shook.

The next song started, and like *(Un)Fading*, I poured myself into it. Being on the verge of tears gave me a little extra vibrato, but I was terrified my voice would break at any moment. Through nothing more than years of practice and sheer, stubborn willpower, I made it through the set without breaking down.

As soon as we left the stage, though, away from the scrutiny of fans and record agents, I didn't hold back anymore.

I threw the microphone across the room. "Bastian, you son of a bitch!"

"The fans want to hear it, Aaron." The calm in his voice made me wish I'd thrown the mic *at* him. He took his bass off and laid it in the case. "This is about the fans, not us."

"Oh, like hell it was," I snarled. "What happened out there had nothing to do with the fans and everything to do with us, and you fucking know it."

Bastian glared at me. "I'm not the one who can't separate my personal feelings from the goddamned music."

"Yeah, you've done a damned good job of that, haven't you?" My voice shook. "So good that apparently you don't give a fuck anymore if I *have* personal feelings, regardless of the goddamned music."

"I—"

"Go fuck yourself, Bastian." I stormed out of the room.

I needed air. And distance. As far from him as I could get. I was more than a little thankful we'd done the autograph signings, meet and greets, and all of that earlier in the day. I wasn't so sure I could keep a smiling, professional face when I just wanted to choke Bastian.

Outside, not far from where Bastian had dropped the "I wouldn't have fucked him" bomb last night, I leaned against a wall in the back parking lot. Closing my eyes, I rested my head against the wall and relived the show over and over again.

Not the show, the song. *That* song.

How could he do that to me? Did he not have a fucking clue what that song did to me? I sighed. Every time I thought he couldn't hurt me any more, he found a way to do it.

Footsteps approached. I listened to them for a moment, trying to decide if it was someone just passing by or someone coming to talk to me.

They stopped a few feet away. I guessed it was Todd or Elena coming to make sure I was okay. I really didn't want to see or talk to anyone, but I could deal with either of my siblings.

When I opened my eyes, fury tightened my chest. "What the fuck do you want?"

Bastian stopped, thumbs hooked in the pockets of his jeans. His voice calm, he said, "I just want to talk."

"About what?" I folded my arms across my chest. "What more do you want from me, Bastian?"

"I—"

"No." I put both hands up. "We've tried talking, and it gets worse every time we do."

"I know," he said quietly. "But we need—"

"No. I've heard more than enough. But you're going to listen to me." I stepped toward him, stabbing a finger at him. "Whatever happened between us in the past is over, but we're stuck together. We have to work together, whether we like it or not."

"I, I know, we—"

"Shut up," I snarled. "I'm not finished." I couldn't stop myself. If I stopped, I might let him talk, and I couldn't listen to him hurt me again. I had to stay angry long enough to get away, because that was the only thing keeping me from breaking down, something I refused to let him see. My voice shaking with rage, I said, "I will do whatever it takes for Schadenfreude to be a success. I care about this band as much as you do, and I'm not going to bail out. But if you *ever* pull a stunt like that again—"

"Look, I'm sorry, Aaron—"

"Oh, I doubt that."

"I—"

I balled my fists at my sides. "You knew I didn't want to play that song tonight, Bastian, and you knew damned well why." My voice cracked, and I quickly wiped a tear away, angry at myself for breaking. "You *knew*."

"You're right, I did." His voice wavered. "And I—"

"But you fucking did it anyway." I clenched my teeth. "You knew how bad it would hurt, but you made me sing the fucking thing anyway."

"Would you just listen to me?"

"No. I won't." *I love you too much to hear why I can't have you anymore.*

"Why not? Aaron, please, just—"

"I don't want to hear any more, Bastian," I said. "You've already made your decision about us. It hurts like hell every time I look at you, but these are the cards we've been dealt. The cards *you've* dealt." I paused, trying to keep myself together. "We're stuck together because of the band. You were so worried about us being trapped together, and now look at us. Is this what you wanted?"

He put his hands up. "No, this isn't what I wanted."

"It's what you have," I said with a shrug that didn't feel nearly as flippant as I tried to make it look. "And if you give a shit about Schadenfreude the way you say you do, if you care about anyone in this fucking band besides yourself, you'll let me walk away and deal with this on my own."

He flinched, looking away from me.

"It's over, Bastian. Let it go." I paused. Barely whispering, I added, "Let *me* go."

He pursed his lips, still avoiding my eyes.

"You've made your choice. I'm respecting it. I just need you to respect my choice to walk away just like you already have." With that, I brushed past him and went back inside.

* * * * *

Elena caught up with me backstage.

"Hey, kiddo," she said. "You doing okay?"

I hesitated, then nodded, but I had no doubt she saw through me.

In a gentle voice, she said, "You guys really are through?"

I nodded, releasing a long breath.

Elena came across the room and hugged me gently. "I'm sorry, Aaron. I really am."

"Thanks," was all I could say.

She let me go and pulled up a chair. "Have you guys talked? I mean, since..." She trailed off, lifting her eyebrows.

I shook my head. "A few times, yeah. And it just keeps getting worse. I tried to talk to him again last night and overheard him telling Rob that if he'd known this would happen, he never would have fucked me."

"Jesus," Elena whispered. "Look, Aaron, he probably just said it without thinking. He's under a lot of pressure—"

"So am I. We all are." I took a deep breath. "I mean, he'd already ended things. Fine. I was hurt, but...I guess it just hurt to hear him say he regretted sleeping with me, as if that's all we did. I thought it was something more."

Elena sighed. "Yeah, I hear you."

I ran a hand through my hair. "Anyway, it was a mistake as far as he's concerned. I just hope we can at least work together. For the band's sake."

She watched me silently for a moment. "You still love him, though, don't you?"

"I always will. But I doubt it's mutual."

"Aaron, he lost his head—"

"And he lost me. I can't be with someone who can tell me he loves me, then turn around and make it sound like a one-night stand he wishes he never had."

"I don't think it's like that, Aaron. I know him."

"I thought I did too."

"If anything, he's probably feeling like an ass for walking out on you and he's too damned stubborn to say anything."

"Well, if he thinks I'm going to chase him down and beg him to come back, he's got another thing coming."

"Fair enough." Elena shifted in her chair. "But maybe he'll get his head out of his ass and realize he was an idiot."

"So what am I supposed to do? Just pretend it never happened, forgive him, go on like everything is peachy?"

"Not necessarily. But I'd at least listen to him. Give him a chance."

"Look, Elena, I appreciate your concern," I said, fighting back emotion. "But it's over. I love him, but he made his choice. He chose the band. So did I. The more we keep trying to work things out, though, the worse it gets, but hopefully once things settle down a bit between us, we can at least work together. Otherwise I'm done with him."

"Aaron, give him a chance."

"I did. I have. He made his choice. I mean, what does he think? That he can regret it when the band is at stake, but once it's safe and intact, he can come back to me and pretend he never said what he did?" My voice cracked. "I love him, Elena. I do. But I can't be with him."

We were silent for a moment. Elena looked at me, her expression completely serious. "You want me to kick his ass?"

I blinked. Then I laughed and she smiled. "You might have some explaining to do to Rob if you do," I said.

She shrugged. "I'll make sure he can still play his bass."

"From a wheelchair, I'm sure."

Elena winked. She stood and hugged me again. "I'm really sorry things didn't work out between the two of you."

"Such is life."

"Yeah, no kidding. Come on, kid, let's go grab something to eat."

CHAPTER TWENTY-NINE

I struggled to keep my composure while I got dressed in my motel room. How I was going to make it through this show, I had no idea. Thank God I would have my back to Bastian for the majority of the show, or I thought I just might break down onstage. Either that or smack him.

That thought made me laugh a little, but the ache in my throat killed my humor. I took a few deep breaths, willing myself to keep my emotions in check.

Andre and Todd had assured me over and over again we wouldn't be playing *(Un)Fading* tonight. From the sound of it, they'd warned Bastian against even thinking about it.

My shoulders slumped as I thought about last night's performance. He had to have known what that song did to me. I snorted bitterly. Obviously he was over me if he could play that song so close on the heels of our relationship falling apart and not even flinch. Or it had never affected him at all. Or he just never gave a shit about me to begin with.

"Goddammit. If I'd known how all of this would have panned out, I never would have fucked him in the first place."

"Fucking bastard," I muttered.

Someone knocked. I glanced at my watch. We were forty-five minutes away from showtime, so either someone was coming to hustle me along or they needed something.

I went to the door, pulled it open, and nearly jumped out of my skin.

Bastian looked at me across the threshold, eyebrows up.

I clenched my teeth. "What do you want?"

"We need to talk." He looked exhausted.

I folded my arms across my chest. "Bastian, we can't do this now."

"No, we *need* to do this now." He shifted his weight. "It can't wait."

"So you want to have it out right here, right now? Before a show? Then pretend nothing ever happened and go onstage?"

He shrugged. "That's what we're going to have to do if we don't settle this now."

"What else is there to say, Bastian?" I swallowed. Ticking the points off on my fingers, I said, "Our relationship was a mistake. It almost cost you the thing that's most important to you in the whole fucking world. You have no qualms about playing a song that you know tears me up. Am I missing anything?"

He flinched. "Will you just listen to me? Please?"

I gritted my teeth and avoided his eyes. "Fine." I stepped aside and let him in, then shut the door and leaned against it for support.

Taking a breath, he said, "Aaron, I'm sorry."

I tensed, not willing to let my guard down.

He waited for me to say something, but when a long silence passed, he released a breath and went on. "I was wrong. About all of it."

I watched him quietly.

Closing his eyes, he sighed. "I resented you because I blamed you for everything falling apart. I never should have held any of this against you. None of it was your fault."

I looked away from him and focused on the floor. Bastian came closer. I wanted to step back but couldn't.

"If anyone was at fault, it was me."

I clenched my jaw.

"Look at me," he whispered, almost pleading. "Please."

Swallowing hard, I did.

He took a breath, dropping his own gaze for a moment, lips tightening as if he was struggling to keep himself together. Finally he met my eyes again. "But more than that." He took a ragged breath and touched my face, the gentle contact sucking the air out of my lungs. "Aaron, I was angry when I said what I did to Rob. Not at you, not at anything you've done—I was angry about everything that had happened. I felt like the band's weight was on my shoulders, and I felt guilty because our shot at a record deal was in jeopardy. Maybe none of this would have happened if we'd never gotten together, but—"

I jerked away from his hand. "Of course it wouldn't have. I get it."

"Let me finish." His voice was unsteady.

"Fine."

He exhaled. "Look, if you hadn't joined the band, a lot of things wouldn't have happened. Some of the most incredible shows we've ever done. The win at the Battle, these shows we're doing now, a possible record deal. Everything. None of that would have happened without you."

I sniffed sharply. "Pity you decided to fuck me and screw it all up, then."

"Just listen to me." He paused, taking a breath. "The most important thing is that if you'd never joined the band, I never would have fallen in love with you. I knew we were taking a chance because of the band, but I was willing to take that chance."

I glared at him. "And from the sound of it, that was a mistake."

"No. It wasn't. It wasn't a mistake. Letting everything fall apart was a mistake, but—"

"Right, then I guess you should've just kept your fucking hands off me." I clenched my teeth. "I'm sorry I made you choose between your music and me, Bastian, but—"

"No, you didn't make me choose."

"Maybe I should have. Would've saved myself a hell of a lot of trouble." I blinked back the threat of tears. *Come on, Aaron, get it together.* "I never would have made you choose me over the band, but I also never thought you'd regret choosing me along *with* the band."

"Aaron, it's not like that."

"Then tell me what it is like, Bastian, because I'm confused as hell."

He pursed his lips. "I thought our relationship would tear the band apart, but it was..." He sighed. "It was everything but you. It was about putting the band before us. I was so afraid of letting our relationship fuck up the band that—" He paused, his voice catching. "I didn't pay attention to what the band was doing to us. You never wanted me to choose between you and the music, but I realized if I *did* have to choose—" He barely whispered as he said, "I wouldn't have to think twice."

Tears stung, but I blinked them away before they dared show themselves to him.

"Aaron, I love you more than anything," he said, his voice trembling. "I thought I was going to lose the band, that I was losing everything I've ever worked for, but I didn't even realize how much it would hurt to lose you." He paused. "The band is important, but you're the world to me."

Biting back emotion, I forced myself to look at him.

Avoiding my eyes, he released a breath. "You were right about why I played *(Un)Fading* last night."

I blinked. "What?"

"I didn't play it for the fans." He ran an unsteady hand through his hair. "It had nothing to do with the fans."

My eyes narrowed. "Then why—"

"Because I needed *you* to hear it." The emotion in his expression and his voice nearly knocked my knees out from under me.

My heart pounded. "I don't understand."

He looked up, took a deep breath, then dropped his gaze to the floor. "Look, I speak two fucking languages. I write music about every goddamned emotion I can think of. But I couldn't..." Rubbing the back of his neck, he looked anywhere but at me. Finally he blew out a breath. "It was the only way I could think of to say what I needed you to hear." He met my eyes. "I made a huge mistake when I walked away from you. I didn't mean to hurt you when I went into the song last night. I didn't want to hurt you. I just..." He paused, the corner of his mouth twitching. "I needed you to hear it, and I didn't know how else to say it."

I watched him silently, searching his eyes for insincerity. For confirmation. For something. I could barely remember how to speak.

After a long silence, he reached across the distance between us and touched my face again, pausing as if waiting for me to recoil. "The last thing I ever wanted to do was hurt you. I've never loved anyone like I love you, and I was an idiot to even think of walking away from you." He stroked my cheek with his thumb. I realized then that his hand was shaking. Leaning forward, he tenderly kissed my forehead and whispered, "I am so sorry, Aaron."

Finally I raised my head and looked him in the eye, forcing myself to hold his gaze in spite of the pain and tears and emotion in his expression. I took a breath. Started to speak. Hesitated.

He pursed his lips and looked away, obviously trying—but failing—to keep his emotions in check.

"Bastian."

He raised his eyebrows in an unspoken question, his body stiffening as if steeling himself against whatever I had to say. The longer the silence lingered, the more he watched me, eyebrows raised, an unspoken *give me something here* in his eyes. I couldn't breathe, let alone speak. Whatever doubts I may have had, whatever walls of anger and resentment I'd put up between us, came crashing down around my feet, and in disbelief, I simply couldn't move.

Pursing his lips and dropping his gaze, he took a step back, and my paralysis was suddenly broken.

"No," I said.

"What?"

"Don't." I grabbed the front of his shirt, pulled him back to me, and kissed him.

We were still for a moment, both of us probably equally surprised and unsure just what to do. Then he put a hand on the back of my neck. I eased my grip on his shirt and slid up his chest to wrap my arms around his neck. When his tongue met mine, I couldn't remember a time when his kiss tasted so, so good.

His fingers ran through my hair as his kiss deepened, as his tongue gently parted my lips. The tongue stud sent a shiver up my spine, that subtle but emphatic *this is Bastian* jarring me. I was still angry and hurt, but I ignored my mind's command to push him away. Instead I drew him closer.

Even when we broke that kiss, we stayed close, his forehead touching mine. We held each other in silence for a long moment. He kissed me again, gently stroking my face. My shoulders relaxed as the furious tension between us disappeared, replaced only by familiar affection. It seemed like a lifetime had passed since I was in his arms, and just the touch of his lips to mine was enough to restart my heart.

He touched my face, running his thumb along my jaw. "Aaron—"

"Bastian, don't—"

"Please, I—"

"No—"

"Aaron—"

"Shut up."

Beat. "What?"

"Just...*shut up*." Before he could respond, I kissed him again.

He got the message, wrapping his arms around me and returning my kiss like never before. His hands were in my hair, under my shirt, on my hips, around the back of my neck, as if he couldn't touch me enough. Every brush of his fingertips across my skin, even through my clothes, made me tremble, and I needed him now more than ever.

His tongue stud brushed past my lip, and I shivered. Never had I been so relieved to have the warmth of his body against mine. His shirt bunched in my hands, and I pulled him closer, kissing him deeply.

Then I looked at him. Drawing an unsteady breath, I reached for his face. My voice trembled when I whispered, "Ich liebe dich."

His lips parted with a surprised breath. Then he smiled and pulled me close, embracing me tenderly and kissing me. "I love you, Aaron." His voice was thick with emotion. "I am so sorry I hurt you."

"I know." I kissed him again.

"God, I missed this," he whispered against my lips.

"Me too," I said. "In fact..." I let my hand drift down his shirt to his belt.

He tensed and caught my wrist. "We have to be onstage soon. We don't have time."

"I know we don't." I wet my lips and met his eyes. "We don't have a choice."

Bastian sucked in a breath and released my hand, letting me unbuckle his belt. Then I put my hands on his chest and gently pushed him back. His lips parted with confusion for just a split second, but when I pulled my shirt over my head, he did the same, quickly shedding his own shirt. He took me into his arms again. The heat of his skin against mine took my breath away, but it wasn't enough.

Our hands shook as we fumbled with belts and zippers.

Breathless desperation gave way to a kind of slow, sensual intensity I'd never before experienced. The urgency in his kiss and his touch was different this time, as if driven not by the insatiable need for my body, but a need for *me*. The feverish, frantic hunger was still palpable in his every movement, but the tenderness in his hands and the look in his eyes were almost reverent. Each time I shed an article of clothing, he looked at the newly bared flesh as if he'd never seen it before, watching his own hands trace my body.

Bastian pulled a couple of condoms and lube out of his jacket pocket. I raised an eyebrow.

"You just happened to be carrying them around?"

He looked somewhere between sheepish and mischievous when he shrugged. "Wishful thinking?"

I laughed and shook my head. "Come here, you."

Like the first time, like every time, we couldn't get the rest of our clothes off fast enough. Couldn't get into bed fast enough. Couldn't get close enough fast enough.

My back hit the bed before the last article of clothing hit the floor, and as soon as we made it that far, we slowed down again. Kissing, touching, holding on to each other. I was horny as hell and wanted him to fuck me right now, but first I needed to feel him. This needed to be real.

And my God, it was. His body heat. The softness of his hair and the coarseness of the shaved sides of his head. His deep, desperate kiss. This was real. He was here.

Solid again. My own voice echoed in my mind. *I'm here again.*

Bastian pushed himself up and looked down at me. His eyes were locked on mine, and I reached up to touch his face, tracing the familiar, warm roughness of his stubble.

WITH THE BAND

No one sees
You see right through me
I fade from sight
Your unfading love brings me back.

He lowered his head enough to kiss me lightly, and just before our lips touched, he murmured, "I want you so fucking bad right now."

I shivered. He'd said that in so many other times and places, and the effect was the same now. I just nodded, and he went for the condom and lube that *thank God* he'd thought to bring along.

As soon as they were on—*come on, come on, hurry up, Bastian*—he sat up and guided himself to me. We both held our breath as he pushed in, and I finally let my breath out in a low groan as he slid deeper. When he was all the way inside me, he stopped and leaned down to kiss me, and we were back where we were before all of this broke down. He'd never walked away. He'd always been here.

He held himself up on one arm and reached between us with the other. As soon as his hand was around my cock, my eyes rolled back. Jesus fucking Christ, he knew just how to touch me, just how to move inside me.

"Oh God..." My back arched. "Fuck, don't stop..." He didn't, and when I forced myself to open my eyes, granting myself one last look directly into his stunning blue eyes, I lost it.

As soon as I came, Bastian shuddered, throwing his head back and growling, forcing himself a little deeper. "Fuck, I can't...I can't get enough of..." He paused, moaning softly. "I can't get enough of you." He drove his cock deeper inside me with each violent thrust, and I could barely breathe as I watched him slowly come undone. With every stroke, every desperate, passionate stroke, he fell apart a little more, screwing his eyes shut and clenching his jaw until finally he threw his head back, released a throaty roar, and came.

When the aftershocks had come and gone, Bastian pulled out, but he didn't pull away. We were still for a long, silent moment, bodies shaking, breath coming in short, shallow gasps. He rested his head on my shoulder, and I stroked his hair, closing my eyes and just breathing him in. He'd come back. He was back. We were back.

Fade away no more
Our unfading love
Remains
Unfaded.

Finally he lifted his head and met my eyes again.

Your unfading love…

"I love you," I whispered.

…brings me back.

"I love you too." He paused, shifting onto one arm. Running his fingers through my hair, he said, "Aaron, I'm so sorry. About everything."

"I know." I traced his jawline with the backs of my fingers. "So am I. I think we both fucked this one up pretty good."

He managed a soft laugh. "Maybe, but I'm the one who really screwed it up."

"Well," I said, shrugging one shoulder, "we're here now. I guess we just try not to screw it up again."

His humor faded a little, and he avoided my eyes. "This is still going to be complicated. I mean, with the band and everything."

"Then we'll just have to work at it." I combed my fingers through the fringe of his hair. "Keep it separate from the band as much as we can."

He nodded. "And if things…don't work out?"

I swallowed. "We'll deal with that if and when it comes, but I would hope we can both still be professional and work together. Better than we did this time around."

"True." He came down and kissed me again, just gently this time. "Hopefully it won't come to that again, though."

I wrapped my arms around him. "I don't think that'll be a problem."

His lips curved into a smile against mine. "Guess we'll have to see, won't we?"

"I guess we will."

For a long moment, we just looked at each other. His fingers trailed down the side of my face. I brushed the fringe of his hair out of his eyes, my thumb grazing the ring in his eyebrow, and he turned his head just enough to kiss the heel of my hand. Then our eyes met again, and he came back down to kiss me.

After a long, gentle kiss, Bastian whispered, "We should get dressed and get out of here." He started to get up. "We're on soon."

I grabbed his arm. "Wait."

His eyebrows jumped. "Hmm?"

Grinning, I put my arms around him.

"Aaron, we—"

"Just one more kiss."

EPILOGUE

About a year later.
On the road somewhere in the Midwest.

Another town. Another show. Another ice pack after another minor mishap while crowd surfing. Such was the life of a rock star, I mused to myself, chuckling as I adjusted the ice pack and stack of cheap motel pillows under my knee.

I leaned back against the headboard and closed my eyes. I was exhausted, my knee ached, but I wouldn't have traded this for the world.

The last year had been insane. Schadenfreude's final performance at the End of Summer Rock-out—a show that I swore was a lifetime ago—had persuaded the agent from Hurricane Records to sign us. Within months we were on the road, touring as the opening act for a bigger band. In a few weeks, we'd be home again for three months, during which time we'd be back in the studio, working on our first record. We'd finished cutting three songs before we'd hit the road. The other nine wouldn't take long.

The *click* of a key card in the door turned my head, and I opened my eyes just as Bastian stepped into the room.

"Hey, you." He smiled.

"Hey." I returned the smile. "You brought food, I assume?"

He feigned offense and held up a paper bag. "Like you have to ask. Of course I brought food."

"Healthy, as always?"

"As healthy as it ever is on the road." He set the food down on the table between the beds. "How's the knee?"

I shrugged. "I think I'll be back in stage-diving condition by the next show."

He laughed. "Don't tell your sister."

"If she's not over it by now, she never will be."

"Good point." He dug into the bag and handed me my food, and then he sat cross-legged on the other bed to eat his own.

This had become pretty routine for us. The rest of the band sometimes stayed out or went to after-parties, things like that, but Bastian and I usually retreated to our room. It wasn't that we were becoming antisocial. Quite the contrary: we spent days on end around the rest of the band, and we always made sure to hang around for autographs for a while after a show. We'd both learned early on in this tour, though, that a little downtime was a luxury to be taken advantage of whenever possible.

The last year had had its ups and downs. Things were icy between Bastian and Andre for a while, but after a few long conversations between the two of them and the three of us, the tensions had eased. There had even been some good-humored jabs about Bastian and me horrifying the family by dancing together at Andre and Rochelle's wedding in December.

It was a rough patch for the band, but we'd come through it more solid than ever. Ditto with Bastian and me. We had our moments. We'd had a few arguments while we were on tour, once necessitating separate rooms for three nights in a row, but we'd learned to keep it offstage. Sometimes even the rest of the band didn't know when we were fighting, though Elena usually caught on if there was even the slightest hint of trouble in paradise.

Still, I wouldn't have traded this for the world. Our band was closing in on the level of success we'd all dreamed about. I had found the love of my life. With all its imperfections, this life was perfect.

Even if my sister *did* still disapprove of me stage diving.

(UN)FADING LYRICS
By Lia Wolff

Please don't fade from me.
No one else, only you,
I fade away,
Your unfading love brings me back

I fade away,
unfading love

No one sees
You see right through me
I fade from sight
Your unfading love brings me back

I fade away,
Unfading love.

Solid again,
I'm here again
But your eyes don't see me.
You fade from me,
My unfading love can't bring you back.

WITH THE BAND

We fade away,
fading love.

Love fades no more
Solid again
Gazes touch
They see only us
Our unfading love

Fade away no more
Our unfading love
Remains
Unfaded.

ABOUT THE AUTHOR

L.A. Witt is an abnormal M/M romance writer who has finally been released from the purgatorial corn maze of Omaha, Nebraska, and now spends her time on the southwestern coast of Spain. In between wondering how she didn't lose her mind in Omaha, she explores the country with her husband, several clairvoyant hamsters, and an ever-growing herd of rabid plot bunnies. She also has substantially more time on her hands these days, as she has recruited a small army of mercenaries to search South America for her nemesis, romance author Lauren Gallagher, but don't tell Lauren. And definitely don't tell Lori A. Witt or Ann Gallagher. Neither of those twits can keep their mouths shut...

> Website: http://www.gallagherwitt.com
> Twitter: @GallagherWitt
> E-mail: gallagherwitt@gmail.com
> Blog: http://gallagherwitt.blogspot.com